He Looked at Her Strangely.

"Why do I get the feeling that you always say something other than what you're thinking?" he asked.

She licked a drop of wine from her lips. "Maybe I can't say what I think because my thoughts aren't appropriate to our conversation."

"Try me."

The tightrope between truth and falsehood was thin and sharp. Cassie balanced on it precariously. She decided to give him a bit of herself that would keep him from suspecting her deception. "I think," she said haltingly, "you're a very . . . attractive man."

His gaze never wavered. "I don't see anything inappropriate about that."

NATALIE BISHOP

lives within a stone's throw of her sister, Lisa Jackson, who is also a Silhouette author. Natalie and Lisa spend many afternoons together developing new plots and reading their best lines to each other.

Dear Reader:

Romance readers have been enthusiastic about Silhouette Special Editions for years. And that's not by accident: Special Editions were the first of their kind and continue to feature realistic stories with heightened romantic tension.

The longer stories, sophisticated style, greater sensual detail and variety that made Special Editions popular are the same elements that will make you want to read book after book.

We hope that you enjoy this Special Edition today, and will enjoy many more.

The Editors at Silhouette Books

NATALIE BISHOP
Lover or Deceiver

Silhouette Special Edition

Published by Silhouette Books New York

America's Publisher of Contemporary Romance

Silhouette Books by Natalie Bishop

Saturday's Child (SE #178)
Lover or Deceiver (SE #198)

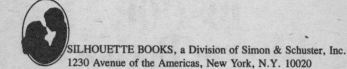

SILHOUETTE BOOKS, a Division of Simon & Schuster, Inc.
1230 Avenue of the Americas, New York, N.Y. 10020

Copyright © 1984 by Natalie Bishop
Cover artwork copyright © 1984 Howard Rogers

Distributed by Pocket Books

ISBN: 0-671-53698-2

First Silhouette Books printing October, 1984

10 9 8 7 6 5 4 3 2 1

Map by Ray Lundgren

America's Publisher of Contemporary Romance

Printed in the U.S.A.

BC91

Lover or Deceiver

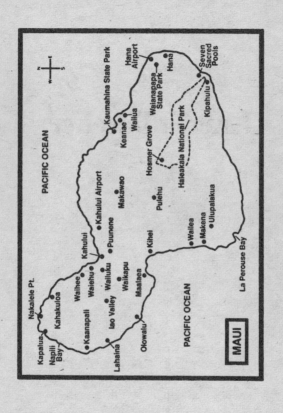

PACIFIC OCEAN

Nakalele Pt.
Kapalua
Napili Bay
Kahakuloa
Kaanapali
Iao Valley
Lahaina
Olowalu
Kapalua

Waihee
Waiehu
Wailuku
Waikapu
Maalaea
Kahului
Puunene
Kihel

Kahului Airport
Makawao
Puuehu
Wailea
Makena
Ulupalakua

Kaumahina State Park
Keanae
Wailua
Hosmer Grove
Haleakala National Park
Waianapapa State Park
Kipahulu

Hana Airport
Hana
Seven Sacred Pools

PACIFIC OCEAN

La Perouse Bay

MAUI

N
W E
S

Chapter One

If anything was designed to keep one humble, Cassie thought resignedly as she flung herself into one of the chairs scattered on the patio, it was the limits of the human flesh. Her legs ached, her chest heaved and her lungs burned for air. With a heavy arm she pulled the limp sweatband from around her head, releasing a riot of reddish blond curls.

Her stringent exercise campaign was more a way to assuage guilt than to ingratiate herself to a man she despised, although the latter was the accepted reason. Taking up running had been the last thing on Cassie's mind when she'd begun this assignment; athletics had never been her strong point.

But she had to have something in common with the man she hoped to interview—and expose—and running seemed to be her only choice. Three weeks of exercise had gained her a healthy respect for professional athletes.

Cassie looked around herself. No one else was up at five

this morning. The tourists and late night partiers were still snug in their beds, unaware of the beauty of a Hawaiian sunrise. Cassie herself had never had much of a chance to appreciate nature's beauty—her demanding schedule didn't allow her the time. It was ironic, she mused wryly as threads of sunlight pierced the gray horizon, that the man who'd stolen so much from her was giving her these treasured moments of solitude.

Joel Shepherd. Though Cassie was enough of a realist to admit that Joel Shepherd wasn't totally responsible for the accident that had taken her brother's life, it was his project—his company—that had been negligent in complying with state safety standards. The trouble was no one seemed to care! The whole thing had been hushed up. Three men perished in that accident, yet not a word of blame was leveled at Joel Shepherd. To Cassie, who had firsthand knowledge that Shepherd's company had made serious, unlawful cutbacks in safety, that smelled mighty suspicious.

It was this knowledge that had won her the job of exposing Joel Shepherd. Though she was an excellent staff reporter (she had a drawer full of journalistic awards she'd won while working for a small newspaper in Los Angeles), Cassie had never done investigative work before. Her expertise was not sleuthing but writing. Her personal connections to this story, and the conviction of her editor, Mike Casey, that she was up to the task, had given her this chance.

Mike had been stern. "Whatever you do, don't be foolish, Cassie. Just find out what you can and report it in your inimitable style. Try and keep your personal emotions out of it. You know I have no love for Joel Shepherd, but let's not embellish his reputation. He's done a good enough job destroying it on his own."

There was bitterness in Mike's words that Cassie only partly understood. Joel's ex-wife, Tali Paccaro-Shepherd, was somehow involved, and Cassie suspected that Mike had been romantically involved with her at one time. It was a fact that Mike had known Tali's prestigious family for years.

"How should I approach him?" Cassie had wondered.

Mike's smile was grim. "Don't tell him you're a reporter, for God's sake! He won't let you near him."

Now Cassie pondered that dilemma. How do you interview a man who detests reporters? The only way is to hide the fact that you're a reporter at all.

Cassie's fine brow puckered into a frown as she leaned down to untie her running shoe. She massaged her foot and considered. She couldn't lie about her profession, not even to Joel Shepherd. Professional ethics were involved. But she wasn't opposed to meeting the eminent Mr. Shepherd socially and telling him her intentions at a much later date. It was the only chance she had of finding out the truth.

She glanced at her watch. Five thirty. Another wasted effort. For three weeks she'd tried to catch him during his early morning run and failed. Maybe he's given up exercise, she thought darkly, swinging a glance toward the jut of land that was his private property.

Cassie closed her eyes. Thinking of Joel Shepherd invariably reminded her of Chris. Her brother had been warm in his praise of his employer.

"He's dynamite, Cassie! A real powerhouse. I swear, that man never rests!" Chris's eyes had glowed with admiration. "He's built an empire here, and this new development, the Polynesian Village, is his best deal yet."

. . . best deal yet . . . Those words echoed hollowly in Cassie's mind, setting spark to her smoldering anger. The Polynesian Village certainly had been Joel Shepherd's best deal. He'd shaved thousands off his budget where he shouldn't have, and the whole thing had ended in tragedy.

In the months prior to the accident, Chris's feelings toward his employer changed. He'd begun to suspect something was wrong and had stopped singing Joel Shepherd's praises. It was a credit to the man himself, Cassie supposed, that Chris had never actually blamed him for the cutbacks. Cassie, however, felt differently.

A movement in her peripheral vision caught her eye, and Cassie turned. Someone was coming.

Hurriedly she retied her shoe, her heart pounding. This was the moment she'd been waiting for. She'd planned this "accidental meeting" weeks ago, but now that it was finally upon her, she felt scared. Chiding herself for her inexperience, Cassie waited until the newcomer was close enough to recognize. It was Joel Shepherd.

"Here goes," she whispered, pulling on her sweatband and stepping from the patio. With an inner prayer she set her plan in motion. She hoped Joel Shepherd was in the mood for company.

Joel's morning was already a disaster. Some inner voice had warned him to check Scott's room, and when he found it empty, the bed stuffed with blankets to simulate the shape of a body, a cold rush of helpless anger left him shaken. It didn't take long to determine his fifteen-year-old son's mode of transportation. At the boathouse, his worst fears were confirmed. When had the boy gone? There was no lingering smell of exhaust. He'd probably left during the night.

Joel scanned the horizon anxiously, but the quiet waters mocked him. Scott had openly defied him once again, doing the one thing his father had warned him against. The grooves on either side of Joel's mouth deepened. Communication with Scott was nil. If he said black, Scott said white, and vice-versa. After all this time, Scott still blamed him for everything. He was the villain in his son's eyes.

He agonized for half an hour before deciding against calling the police—yet. If Scott wanted a joy ride, he'd at least chosen a time of day when other pleasure boaters were still asleep.

Joel's mouth twisted self-deprecatingly. He was just putting off the inevitable. Scott didn't have a license to drive the boat, and though he was certainly skilled enough, he chose to be reckless.

Joel swiftly donned a loose athletic shirt and a pair of cotton trunks, savagely lacing up his running shoes. He would give Scott one hour, and then he'd be forced to call the authorities. There was no other course of action.

Jerking open the door, Joel mentally shuddered at the scene that would take place between him and his son. This whole last year had been the same: one blistering argument after another. He'd been unable to get Scott to meet him even halfway. His determined son wouldn't even try. Scott wanted to live with his mother, Tali, and her new lover in Los Angeles, and he was bent on making life so miserable for his father that Joel would be forced to give up custody. What Scott didn't know was that Tali didn't want him, and Joel was unwilling to shatter his son's faith with that knowledge.

There was something else, too. Joel knew the man Tali was living with by reputation and had serious doubts about him. He was a full-time pleasure seeker. A Hollywood drifter. Joel wasn't eager to leave Scott in his charge; in fact, he was adamantly opposed to the idea. But explaining that to Scott had been a mistake.

"You're just jealous!" Scott had rifled back immediately. "Ian loves Mom. And she loves him. You just can't handle that!"

Joel had hung onto his temper with difficulty. "Your

mother's life is her own," he retorted evenly. "We're talking about yours and mine. You're living with *me*, not her, and not Ian Carstairs!"

He'd been rewarded with a baleful glare from Scott that spoke of trouble ahead. And there had been trouble. Scott had a talent for scheming up new ways to undermine his father. Resignedly, Joel had to admit that he was losing the battle. At this point he needed nothing short of divine intervention.

It was with extreme difficulty that Joel pushed his self-doubts to the back of his mind and concentrated on running. This was the only time he felt the grip of pressures loosen, his one part of the day solely for himself. Lately the turmoil of his life had been so great he hadn't had time to run, and the anxiety and frustration within him warned him that he needed this exercise. It was his only release.

The beach curved inward invitingly, and Joel struck out to the north, keeping just abreast of the waves. His normal route took him past Kaanapali Beach, a famed resort with high-rise condominiums and deluxe hotels, a tourist's paradise. Ahead, the beach stretched out endlessly, a ribbon of sand beginning to glow warmly in the growing light.

He hadn't run far when he realized he wasn't alone on the beach. A pair of tracks still visible at the edge of the sea warned him that he was trailing another early riser. They came from a small villa near his home that had been renovated and divided into apartments. Joel cast a swift glance in that direction as he passed. Someone must have just moved in, because he knew the other occupants to be wealthy, elderly couples who wintered in the sun.

He frowned. He hoped this new arrival didn't make a practice of sunrise jogging; Joel selfishly wanted to keep this his private domain.

A feeling of resignation passed over him as he caught his first sight of her. A mane of lustrous red gold hair bounced off her shoulders; a designer label for expensive running clothes blazened hot pink down one hip of her white shorts, and her matching top was trimmed in pink piping. The only wear her shoes had seen was recent; the white soles gleamed. A novice, Joel decided. Tan limbs peeked out from beneath her clothes, firm thighs, not too muscular . . .

With the unconscious superiority of an expert meeting a novice, Joel's mouth twisted derisively. She had a lot to learn. She was too perfect to be a serious runner.

Long strides brought him close behind her, and he debated whether to pass her; the gap between them was narrowing rapidly. He was just about to swerve around her when she sensed him. Tilting her head slightly, she looked his way and smiled.

Joel nodded curtly and passed her by, eager to be alone. But the splendor of the empty beach was superimposed by an image that burned onto his brain: a woman's smile. It seemed to spread slowly from one corner of her mouth to the other. The hint of a dimple appeared, no more, and white even teeth, perfect except for one slight attractive overlap, flashed in his direction.

He had the vague impression of blue green eyes fringed by gold-tipped lashes, a promise in their depths that he might have just imagined. He was conscious of one slim arm curving upward slowly to toss back an errant lock of tumbling hair. The movement was quick, seen in the half-second glance he allowed her. But Joel held that memory in his mind's eye the rest of his run.

Cassie's steps slowed, the pace she'd vainly set to try and match Joel Shepherd's longer stride finally taking its toll. She stopped and leaned down, resting her palms on her knees as she took deep gulps of air. Her shoulders slumped. Three weeks of waiting for one brief second of Joel Shepherd's attention hardly seemed worth the effort.

Cassie stood and wearily flexed her shoulders. Up ahead

she saw the thatched umbrellas occupying the patio of an all-night bistro. Until the early hours of the morning it served as a quiet outdoor bar, and when the late night partiers finally drifted to bed it changed its menu to include orange juice, breakfast rolls, and fresh fruit. Cassie walked toward it, her eyes unwillingly casting a lingering glance toward Joel Shepherd's disappearing masculine form.

She felt depressed. She had never been in the position of trying to capture a man's attention before; male interest had always come her way whether she wanted it or not. Once she'd even made the mistake of falling in love and marrying a man who'd openly professed his love for her. She had learned the hard way that words meant to be warm and sincere could be bitterly cold and empty.

But Cassie had never had to fight to be noticed, and Joel Shepherd's lack of interest was a disappointment. Just what did you expect? she asked herself honestly, carefully sipping a scalding cup of coffee. Passing strangers on a beach rarely gave one another more than a smile or nod of acknowledgment.

That was what rankled. Cassie had provided the opening, a warm smile and interested glance, but Joel Shepherd had barely noted her existence. His eyes flicked over her briefly, impatiently, then he passed by, never breaking stride. She'd been left to marvel at the strength in his thighs and calves, the firm tone of his skin, the hard muscles of his upper arms. Perversely, whereas he was completely unmoved by her, she'd been supremely conscious of him, of the muscles that worked so effortlessly beneath his taut skin.

Cassie burned her tongue and gasped softly, taking a deep drink of iced grapefruit juice to nurse the injured area. She wondered if she hadn't taken on an impossible task. Her natural reserve balked at playing the aggressor, yet was there any other way? Joel Shepherd didn't know she existed. He would hardly seek *her* out!

And, along with that, she couldn't afford to let him know who she was. Her brother, Chris, had known him well, but Cassie had never met him. She'd seen him once or twice from afar on rare occasions when she'd visited Chris at one of Shepherd Construction's work sites. But they were never introduced, and since Cassie's last name was now different from her brother's, there would be no way Joel Shepherd could make the connection.

At least, Cassie thought, superstitiously crossing her fingers, that's what she hoped for. Her whole plan was contingent upon Joel's ignorance of who she was.

Unfortunately, since she was unable to bring up Chris's name, it forced her to resort to feminine wiles to make Joel's acquaintance. And sadly, so far she'd failed.

"More coffee?"

Cassie looked at her handsome, dark-skinned waiter in his ubiquitous Hawaiian print shirt and shook her head. Chris had been a waiter when he first arrived in Maui, then, after several other jobs pandering to the tourists, he finally landed one as an apprentice to a local carpenter. His employment with Joel Shepherd's firm had been a natural progression. Shepherd Construction was one of the largest and most prestigious firms in the islands. They specialized in shopping centers, restaurants, and low-rise hotels. Chris had been jubilant when he'd gotten the job.

"Shepherd's jobs are expensively done," Chris had confided with pride. "They're not cheap. When he puts a building up it has everything. And you'd love it, Cass. He always sticks with the prevailing feel of the area. You're not going to see Plexiglas and chrome in Maui if Joel can help it!"

Cassie's lips tightened. Maybe not. But then, there were other places a wily contractor could cut back that wouldn't be quite so obvious to the public.

Recurring painful memories saddened her. Her brother

had meant a great deal to her. He'd always been there when she needed him. Chris had been the one to force her to pull herself up by her bootstraps when her marriage failed. She'd been buried in her work, accomplishing incredible tasks, making a name for herself in journalistic circles, working endless hours, not wanting to go home. Chris had gently helped her see that her work, though important, could not be the panacea to all her ills. He'd urged her to make a clean break with her newspaper and move to the islands with him.

Cassie had been reluctant at first. Her career was her lifeline. But with her brother's guidance and coaxing, plus a healthy salary offer from the *Island Breeze*, Mike Casey's newspaper, she began to see the advantages. Suddenly she couldn't wait to get away. Chris was ecstatic and so was Mike. The *Island Breeze* needed some fresh young blood; Cassie was as much a godsend to them as they were an antidote for her.

Now it was two years later. She'd been feeling restless for a new challenge when Mike dropped the Shepherd story in her lap. She'd almost refused—too many raw, unhealed memories. Then she quickly reconsidered; she could finally be at least partially vindicated for Chris's death. And Joel Shepherd would finally get what he deserved.

The waiter brought her check, and she signed it to her apartment. Over the last few weeks she'd become familiar with some of the perks allowed the cafe's regular customers, one of them being that they would bill you if you were staying nearby.

Feeling the tired ache in her muscles that warned she'd overexercised, Cassie trudged home. Tomorrow, she told herself bleakly. Tomorrow she would try again.

She was halfway to the villa when she heard someone coming up behind her, running. She stopped.

Joel stopped, too, facing her, his back to the sea.

Looking at him, a detached portion of Cassie's mind thought that he could never know how attractive he was against that backdrop. With dark hair ruffling in the breeze, surprisingly light brown eyes watching her intently, his chest heaving slightly and blue sea and sky behind him, Joel Shepherd made a startling picture.

But Cassie wasn't foolish enough to be swayed by mere good looks. She knew the ruthless kind of man he was. Realizing her chance had come, she hid her growing apprehension and looked him straight in the eye.

"Hullo," she said pleasantly, conscious of his bare chest and the thin trickle of sweat at the side of his neck. "You must have run quite a ways."

"About seven miles," he agreed. One corner of his mouth curved. "And you?"

"I'm lucky if I get through three." Cassie's nerves were jangling. It was an effort to sound casual.

"I'm impressed." Joel's eyebrow lifted, and she saw that he really was. "I'd pegged you as quitting at one, maybe two."

"Last week you would have been right."

Cassie was surprised to find herself responding to his charm. She hadn't known what to expect from their first meeting. She'd envisioned herself more than once coming at him with fists flailing, accusing and hateful. Instead, her poise had rescued her. She began to relax.

"Last week? Then you've been here awhile."

"About three weeks." Casually, she inserted, "I'm staying at the villa."

"I know."

Cassie's breath stopped. He knew? Her moment of ease vanished and alarm shot through her. How could he know? Unless her deception had been discovered before it ever began!

"You know?"

Joel's gaze was so penetrating that Cassie felt a flush of color spread across her face. Oh, Lord! she thought desperately. Nothing had prepared her for meeting Joel Shepherd in the flesh.

"I saw your tracks in the sand this morning. I didn't think the Gablers or Mandrakes were up to running, so I assumed there was a new guest."

"Oh." Of course. She was letting her fears make her paranoid. Cassie managed a small smile. Joel was referring to the two elderly couples who occupied the villa's other two apartments. Ordinarily she would have laughed out loud at the mental picture of Claudia Mandrake jogging along the beach, replete with chiffon gown and backbreaking heavy jewelry. But the situation didn't allow her the luxury of enjoying the conversation. She was too keyed up.

"Do you live around here?" Cassie inquired, anxious to prolong this small contact. It was almost embarrassing how inept she felt at holding his attention.

Joel inclined his head. "Over there."

Cassie knew perfectly well where his home was, but she pretended interest, shading her eyes from the growing brightness. The beach was broken by a wall of lava rock on the other side of Joel's house, insuring its privacy. The house itself was built on rock and, from what Cassie had discerned, was connected to the beach via a natural stairway of stone. The beach was only semiprivate. Trespassers could reach it if they dared. During these past few frustrating weeks she had actually considered stretching out on a towel in front of Joel's home. That would have gotten her noticed! But she just wasn't that brazen.

"Then we're neighbors," she said, smiling.

Joel watched her smile with fascination. In actuality he knew far more about her than he was letting on. Disturbed by the afterimage of her smile, he'd found himself unable to keep from glancing back to see what had become of her.

Normally nothing interrupted his run, but on realizing she'd stopped at the cafe, he'd had the absurd desire to stop and join her.

He'd been amazed at himself. *He* was the one who wanted complete privacy, wasn't he?

He couldn't prevent himself from slowing beside the cafe on his run back. Wondering what drove him to care, he'd walked slowly up the steps, pausing briefly before unobtrusively flipping over her check with his thumb. She'd signed it to her apartment, and her name was easy to decipher. Cassie Blakely. He was still figuring out why it sounded familiar.

"Are you just vacationing?" he inquired casually.

Cassie's lashes flickered. "Mmmhmm. I just needed to get away from it all for a while."

It was the kind of remark that dangled invitingly, and Joel chose to ask the obvious. "And what are you getting away from?"

Cassie lifted her shoulders dismissively. "Pressures. Problems. Routine. What do people normally get away from? All of the above apply to me."

Cassie had practiced this speech daily, hoping to speed the intimacy of friendship by breaking down the barriers of social convention and pouring out her soul as quickly as possible. She'd already determined just how much of her personal life she was going to tell Joel. She was eager to get the ball rolling.

But Joel was disinclined to probe. Instead he asked abruptly, "Do I know you?"

Alarmed, Cassie's heart leaped. "I don't think so."

Joel's eyes assessed her thoroughly, a thoughtful line deepening his brow. For Cassie, it was acute discomfort. Although knowing it was smarter to remain silent, she couldn't prevent herself from rushing into speech. "Maybe I remind you of someone. It's my face. I'm often mistaken as someone's . . . relative.'' She swallowed tightly. She'd almost said sister.

Cassie held her breath, hating herself for her ineptitude. Deception, she decided belatedly, was not one of her strong points. She'd bungled this interview from start to finish, and it showed. She was so sure of her transparency that she half-expected Joel to level an accusing finger at her at any moment. She couldn't hold his gaze.

Joel felt her tension and his eyes narrowed. He was used to women he could figure out in just a few minutes. He'd always found they fell into two categories: shallow and spoiled, or high-powered, defensive and a general pain in the neck. Admittedly, there were one or two exceptions, but overall his generalizations were correct.

However, this woman didn't fit. One moment she was forthright and direct, the next her cheeks were flushed with self-reproach. Now she looked uncomfortable, her face averted, her shoulders drooping dispiritedly. Her vulnerability touched him, and Joel had to restrain himself from reaching out and gathering her close, offering comfort for something he didn't understand.

Joel felt a stirring of emotions, an unanticipated lust developing as he looked at his slim companion. Tali had soured him on the female species as a whole, but suddenly, he wanted, needed, the feel of a woman.

Cassie didn't see the way Joel's expression stiffened. She didn't know how aware he was of her, of everything about her. She had no idea that he was intrigued by the curve of her throat, the humor that lurked around the corners of her mouth, her arms, the allure of her breasts and thighs. She read his sudden silence as suspicion and waited fatalistically for the axe to fall.

When nothing happened, Cassie chanced a glance back. Joel's lashes partially obscured his eyes, but she knew he was watching her keenly. What punishment would he mete out? she wondered fearfully. Just how betrayed would he feel if he knew she was out to learn his secrets?

Surprised, Cassie realized she actually cared. No matter what his faults were, she didn't relish the thought of being the object of his contempt.

You're softening already! she chided herself. Remember why you're here!

It would be easy to forget that Joel Shepherd was behind a fatal tragedy. He was an extremely attractive man, and under different circumstances Cassie realized she could be very susceptible. There was something about him that touched a chord in her heart, even though she was determined to hate him. She saw the pain etched around his mouth and wondered fleetingly if the accident had bothered him after all. How did it feel to know you were responsible for three men's deaths? Did it hurt? Or was Joel Shepherd too calloused to care?

The silence continued. Cassie felt breathless. Against her will, an acute awareness of how attractive this man she'd sworn to expose grew within her. She dragged her eyes away from him and concentrated on the sea.

The hum of a power boat broke the spell. Joel's head jerked around, his eyes hardening. Cassie looked at him, then at the boat, then back again. An angry, purposeful expression covered his face, masking all traces of vulnerability. Cassie's softening opinion of him did an abrupt reversal. Joel Shepherd was a man to be reckoned with. He was still the insensitive businessman who'd risked her brother's life for the sake of saving money. She wouldn't let herself forget again.

The boat passed by. Cassie watched curiously, conscious that for some reason Joel Shepherd was really angry.

He moved sharply. "I've gotta go."

"Are you going to run tomorrow?" Cassie asked desperately, lest he forget her entirely.

Joel's attention had switched to Scott, and the attraction of the woman beside him was set aside for the moment. But her anxious question arrested him. He turned and gave her a long, searching look, intrigued by the bloom of color traveling up her neck. Picking up strange men wasn't her hobby, that much was certain. She was obviously acutely uncomfortable. So, why did she keep trying?

"I might," Joel replied. "What about you, Cassie?"

He said her name deliberately, expecting surprise and maybe even pleasure to cross her smooth features when she realized he knew something about her. But he was totally unprepared for the look of shock that froze her mobile face. "You are Cassie Blakely, aren't you?" he asked quickly.

"Yes." Cassie heard a buzzing in her ears. She could barely speak. How could he know? "Yes," she repeated.

Joel didn't have time to figure her out now. "Then, maybe I'll see you tomorrow," he said lightly, leaving the intriguing mystery of Cassie Blakely unsolved. He had more important things to do.

Cassie stared after him. He had asked if he knew her, then had uttered her name. Panic swelled inside her. The only way he could know her name was to know who she was! And if he knew who she was, wouldn't it follow that he would also know her reason for making his acquaintance?

Just who was conning whom?

Chapter Two

*N*o, Mike. I'm not holding back. There is nothing, and I mean *nothing*, to report. I've only spoken to the man once, and since then he's barely given me the time of day. I guess I'm just not his type.''

Cassie's last words were said with a wry grimace that Mike Casey, on the other end of the line in Honolulu, couldn't appreciate. After that first disturbing encounter with Joel, Cassie had been on the verge of giving up and flying back to Oahu. She was convinced he saw through her deception.

As she thought about it, however, she grew certain that he hadn't made the connection. Cassie didn't know how he'd found her out, but she had been staying at the villa for over three weeks. The Mandrakes or the Gablers could innocently have given him her name. If Joel Shepherd had really known who she was, Cassie was sure he would have acted differently.

Still, he'd shocked her speechless. And since that time she'd been too off balance to make another attempt to meet him. Twice she'd stopped at the beachside cafe for breakfast after she'd completed her run and had been there when Joel went for his run. He'd nodded to her the first time. The second time he hadn't even seen her.

"You don't want to be his type," Mike disabused her quickly. "You just want to get to know him. Don't get too close, Cassie."

"Don't worry. I'm about as far away as I can be."

"No, no. He knows your name. It looks to me like you've captured his interest already." Cassie could hear Mike's pen scratching across paper and visualized him furiously writing notes to himself. Mike worked best under pressure and wasn't completely happy unless he had dozens of irons in the fire. Though distanced by a professional relationship, Cassie counted Mike one of her personal friends. They'd helped each other when they'd both badly needed assistance.

"Just give it some more time, Cass," he went on. "You've made the move. He knows where you are. Don't worry—he'll be there."

"What makes you so sure?"

Mike's harsh laugh made Cassie uneasy. "I know Joel Shepherd. He can't resist a beautiful woman."

Knowing it was foolish to argue, Cassie couldn't help raising a few doubts. "He's not exactly a womanizer, Mike. Since Tali there's been no record—"

"Trust me," Mike interrupted. "Just make yourself available and not too eager. He'll seek you out." The pen paused dramatically. "But be careful, Cass. I know that man."

Their conversation was more well-worn than an old shoe. Cassie was enough of her own woman to resent Mike's protective and, as she saw it, chauvinistic attitude.

"There's really no need to worry," she said tartly. "I'm not about to get involved with Joel Shepherd. I can't forget what he's done."

"Okay, okay. Enough said. Just find out what happened as quickly as you can."

Cassie hung up thoughtfully, her hand wrapped unusually tightly around the receiver. She didn't like the undercurrents in her conversation with Mike, and an uneasy suspicion grew in her mind that there were other reasons she'd been granted this story than her own personal involvement. True, she was a gifted writer with a concise yet descriptive style that was the envy of many of her contemporaries—she was honest enough to admit that to herself. But she was a fledgling at the investigative angle. Lynnette Cosgrove, one of the *Island Breeze*'s longtime employees, a clever journalist and a beautiful woman to boot, was far more experienced in this particular field. Yet she'd been passed over for Cassie.

Why?

Mike, for all his benevolence, was unlikely to take a chance—not with Lynnette as his backup. Though Cassie had helped upgrade the *Breeze*, turning a mediocre paper into one of the most well read in the islands, she was not—and never wanted to be—Lynnette.

So, if it wasn't chance, then it was a calculated risk.

From Mike's intimations Lynnette seemed the more likely candidate to appeal to Joel Shepherd's masculinity. Except for one thing: Lynnette looked and acted as if life held few mysteries for her.

Not too eager . . . Mike's words haunted Cassie and caused her to examine herself critically in the handsome oval teakwood mirror above her dresser. Sad blue green eyes looked back at her; vulnerability hovered in the curve of her lips. Her cheeks were tanned but hollow. She turned away instantly, horrified. It was as if she'd come face to face with a stranger. How long had she looked this way? Since the divorce? No . . . since her brother's death.

Frowning, she hardened the image in the mirror, blaming her impression in part to the soft, off-white, gauzy dress that exposed her upper arms and shoulders. Romantic, touchable—whatever had possessed her to buy it?

Mike was banking on her lost fawn look to get past Joel's defenses. She saw it now. For some reason that hurt, and Cassie left the mirror's reflection, wishing she hadn't seen the truth.

Just how skillful was she? she wondered, stepping outside, her bare foot making contact with the gritty, sand-covered surface of her patio. Could she ferret out the truth while keeping up her deception? Or was everyone in for a colossal disappointment?

Twilight brought relief from the intense tropical heat and dazzling sunshine, and Cassie breathed deeply, turning her face to the cool island breeze. Glimmers of fading light trailed across the restless sea as Cassie walked to the beach, her sandals dangling from one hand. Across the Auau Channel, still outlined dramatically against the gold and magenta sunset, lay the peaceful island of Lanai.

A wave circled her feet, engulfing her legs halfway to her knees. The hem of her dress darkened and clung to her skin, but Cassie barely noticed. She stared across the water silently, feeling loneliness creep in like an uninvited guest. She shuddered and wrapped her arms tightly beneath her breasts, squeezing to keep the emotion from spilling into tears.

She was not the ingenue Mike planned to present to Joel Shepherd. For five years she'd been married to a successful man who'd provided for her every need save one—he couldn't love her. Every ounce of love he possessed, which Cassie learned the hard way wasn't much, was poured into his business. There was nothing left for his wife.

Kurt Blakely's determination to achieve money, power and respect was all-consuming, and he'd spent every waking, breathing minute in their pursuit. Eventually he'd recognized his goal, becoming one of the most prominent divorce lawyers in southern California.

A divorce lawyer. Cassie had hated how he'd used his law degree, but Kurt was philosophical. "If that's what's paying, Cassie, why be a snob? It's a case of cutting off your nose to spite your face. You can't stop divorce."

There was some truth in that, but Cassie had never been able to accept the ways and means. She'd tried to come to terms with it, and maybe eventually could have, but then she'd found out Kurt was having an affair. Cassie was completely stunned. Kurt's passion had never been other women. When she'd realized he was just keeping some of his customers happy, she left him. That passionless exploitation of his clients was almost worse. She had no love left for her cold-blooded husband.

He'd tried to talk her out of it. Cassie, in one of the rare moments of humor the situation provided, had answered wryly, "You'd better get yourself a good divorce lawyer."

That had been the end.

Unable to completely forget her bitterness and disillusionment, she still carried the hurt inside her. Chris had been the one bright spot left in her world, and it was a cruel, senseless twist of fate to have him taken from her, too.

Up to now strolling rather aimlessly along the water's edge, Cassie stopped, realizing she'd been walking in the direction of Joel Shepherd's house. She could see his lights far above the beach and pictured him relaxing comfortably, oblivious and uncaring. Rage burned in her chest. She blamed him for everything—for stealing Chris and for being so much like Kurt. If that was unfair, she didn't care. He'd hurt her and she wanted to hurt him back.

Mike had told her to keep her personal emotions out of it,

but even he had to realize that was impossible. At some level her feelings would always be involved; the trick was to keep them inside. She had enough confidence in herself to believe she could, and apparently so did Mike.

Cassie walked to the edge of Shepherd's property. It would be simple enough to climb the rock stairway to his back deck and knock on his door. What would she say when he answered? What possible excuse could she have for dropping by? Did she have the courage to say, "I just wanted to see you again?"

The stone was smooth and worn beneath her bare feet as Cassie mounted the first few stairs. She slipped on her sandals and hesitated, glancing anxiously up to the deck. It was a long way, and she felt like a trespasser already, sneaking in the back door.

She decided it would be better to arrive by the front door and had just reached the bottom step again when she heard voices above her. Recognizing one was Shepherd's, she hurriedly moved a safe distance away, then stopped, her heart racing. Here was another opportunity to express her interest. Either he took the hint this time or she gave up. There was no point continuing this charade if she couldn't intrigue him.

She saw him first, his athletic form easily recognizable, then she noticed the boy behind him. She wondered if he was Shepherd's son, Scott. From what she knew of Shepherd, his son lived with him, not his ex-wife, and she wondered if he had fought her for custody. According to Mike, Tali Shepherd loved her son fiercely. Cassie could only surmise that his father had taken him from her.

They were both wearing running gear, and Cassie now understood why she missed Shepherd most mornings. He also ran at night. She watched as he reached the bottom step and then waited for his son.

Scott, for now Cassie was sure that's who he was,

brushed past his father, deliberately ignoring him. Belatedly Cassie realized she'd overheard the end of an argument.
Cursing her luck, she wished she could just disappear. Now
was not the time to meet her quarry.

But it was too late. At that moment he looked over and
saw her. Pasting on a smile she hoped wasn't too artificial,
Cassie raised her hand. "Hello again," she said. "I seem to
always catch you when you're about to go running, don't I,
Mr. Shepherd?"

Cassie had rehearsed this line already, drawling his name
familiarly. "I asked Claudia Mandrake who owned the
house on the cliff," she went on. "Now maybe you'll tell
me how you know me?"

Shepherd paused fractionally, staring at her through the
night air. Cassie held her breath. She sensed he was about to
answer when Scott interrupted.

"Why don't I go back up to the house and leave you two
alone," he said insolently. Without a glance at his father,
he turned away.

"Scott!"

Heedless of his father's call, Scott took the stairs two at a
time, showing off the lithe gracefulness of youth that was
otherwise disguised behind his gangly form.

Cassie watched him leave in dismay. "I'm sorry. I didn't
mean to interfere."

"It doesn't matter."

But it did matter. Cassie could tell. Shepherd's mouth
had tightened into a thin line, and his shoulders were stiff
with tension.

"I really am sorry," she repeated, meaning every word.
"Was that your son? I didn't intend to spoil your run."

"You didn't." The response was terse. "Scott wasn't
exactly eager in the first place." He sighed. "Were you
coming to see me?"

"Actually, I was just taking a walk and ended up near

your house. I did think about knocking on your door, though.''

"Then why don't you come on up?" he invited, gesturing to the stairs.

It all happened so quickly Cassie didn't have time to worry until she'd reached the top step. She was extremely conscious of him behind her, of the movements of his body. She wondered what he thought of her. Was he used to forward women?

Joel Shepherd's house was made of cedar beams extending from a shake roof. Bougainvillea and hibiscus perfumed the air. Cassie skirted the bushes, but Joel's shoulder brushed some of the petals, causing them to spill unheeded down his shirt. Jalousies were thrown open, lending a view to an inner solarium that ran along the east side of the house. It was tiled, with scattered straw mats in various designs dominating the space. Rattan furniture and big glazed pots with enormous tropical plants were set under a lazy paddle fan.

Shepherd opened the door for her, and Cassie stepped inside. Sheltered from the breeze, the room was warm but airy. Near the center was a rattan coffee table with a glass top barely visible under a flood of papers. Cassie passed a casual eye over them, wondering what Joel was working on, but he scooped them out of the way before she could tell.

"Would you like a drink?"

She followed him to the bookcase that cleverly concealed a full bar. "Sure." She searched the titles of the books but found nothing revealing except that someone in the household liked thrillers.

"I have Scotch, bourbon or vodka. Or beer," he added as an afterthought.

"Scotch," Cassie decided, though it was far from her favorite drink. Normally a glass of white wine was about as heavy as she chose to get, but tonight she needed something to occupy her hands and cover their betraying quiver. "You never answered my question," she reminded him as he handed her the drink and eased himself onto the couch beside her.

"About how I knew your name? I read it off your bill."

Cassie blinked. "My bill?"

"At the cafe." A smile hovered at the corners of his mouth. "I stopped to find out who you were."

Cassie brought the glass to her lips, taking a slow drink of the burning liquor. So he wasn't immune to her. The knowledge was curiously unsettling. "Well, then I guess we're past introductions, Mr. Shepherd."

"Then why don't you call me Joel, Cassie."

He hadn't asked if he could use her first name, and Cassie knew it was because she'd already presumed far too much for him to waste time with formality. Subtly, he was telling her what he thought he knew about her, and she didn't like the feeling one bit. But she'd asked for it, and there was nothing to do but continue playing the part.

"All right, Joel," she agreed, smiling. At least he still had no idea who she was and what her relationship was to Chris Tanner. "Have you always lived on Maui?"

"Most of my life. I was brought up in Seattle but moved here as soon as I was out of college. You?"

"A native Californian," Cassie answered instantly. "One of the few left in the world." She gave him a quick smile. "I'm just vacationing on Maui."

"And what do you do in California?"

The question was casual, but Cassie had to force herself not to react with noticeable nervousness. Gathering as much courage as she could muster, she looked him directly in the eye, "I used to work for a small newspaper," she said steadily. "I don't anymore."

Joel's face went rigid. "A reporter?"

"If you could call it that. I mainly took calls about local happenings, and someone else followed up." Stay with the truth as much as possible, Cassie resolved, trying to ignore Joel's change of attitude. If she'd had any doubt about her reception as a reporter, she didn't anymore.

"Why did you quit?"

Cassie took another swallow of her Scotch. "Because I was going through a very painful divorce."

As she knew they would, these words, too, had the effect of a douse of cold water. Her voice shook slightly, giving credence to what could only sound like a very well-used phrase. Joel's brows drew down. Unexpectedly he observed, "You're not over it yet, are you?"

The soft tone of his voice caught Cassie off guard. For a moment she forgot the role she was playing and turned to stare at him, blue green eyes wide and vulnerable. She hadn't expected empathy, least of all from him, and for the space of a heartbeat neither of them said a word.

His gaze dropped to her mouth, and Cassie's heart climbed to her throat, robbing her of breath. She was stunned by her reaction, surprised how physically she could respond to this man from his merest sign of interest. Her voice, when it came, was too husky. "No . . . no, I guess I'm not." She cleared her throat. The room seemed very warm and close. She was conscious of the man beside her, aware of his every movement. Her body began to respond to him, even though her mind desperately sought to remain cool. What was wrong with her? She felt her nipples tighten beneath the soft material of her dress.

"How long have you been divorced?"

The tip of Cassie's tongue licked her lips. "Over two years." He shifted slightly and a chill ran up Cassie's spine, breaking her arms out in goose bumps. She crossed her arms and rubbed her elbows. "It seems longer."

It was an impossible task, but she tried to keep reminding herself whom she was with. Her mind insisted on dissociating the man sitting next to her from the one responsible for so much of her pain. With almost no male provocation she'd responded, her breath quickening, her pulse racing madly. She could only conclude that she'd been out of the dating game too long, that her body was listening to a tune of its own, disregarding all the danger. Joel Shepherd was taboo, but physically Cassie found him very alluring.

"Scott is your son?" she asked again, her tone blessedly neutral.

Joel let out a slow breath. "Yes." His mouth quirked in self-derision. "But as you can see, we have a communication problem."

"I could leave—"

He cut her off with a gesture of his hand. "No. It won't make any difference. Scott's got to work out some things on his own. Your being here isn't really a factor."

"But you were going to go running."

"I was dragging him with me." Joel set down his glass, and it clinked against the glass table top with disturbing finality. He turned to her, the look in his eyes causing her to tremble inside. "You don't want to hear about my domestic problems."

"Yes, yes I do!" Cassie was more vehement than she intended to be. "I feel sort of responsible."

Joel's arm was around the back of the couch, and his fingers grazed her bare shoulders. Cassie reacted electrically, her whole body stiffening. She'd asked for this, now she didn't know what to do about it.

"Responsible?" Joel frowned. "Why?"

"I ruined your evening. Look, if I left right now, you would still have time to go running. Maybe we could see each other tomorrow?" she added hopefully.

"What's wrong with tonight?" Now Joel looked suspicious, and Cassie felt a flutter of fear. "I thought you wanted to see me."

"I did—I do. But I hadn't expected your son . . ." She trailed off, remembering her role. She cast a glance toward the back of the house, but Joel's tawny eyes never left her face.

"He won't bother us," he said softly, disturbingly. Cassie sensed he was carefully assessing her.

For Cassie it was a crossroads, a delicate dilemma she wasn't sure how to handle. Her every instinct warned her to leave lest she invite real trouble, but if she tore away like some kind of outraged Victorian heroine, she would never realize her objective.

Her shoulders were tight, her back stiff. It took supreme willpower to unwind those muscles and relax against Joel's arm. Inside she was a mass of nerves. She could hear his even breathing, feel the heat of his arm curved around her shoulders. Heart thudding, she knew that he intended to kiss her.

Joel's finger lifted her chin, turning her to meet his searching gaze. Cassie stared at him, seeing the rough texture of his skin, the thickness of his lashes and the lurking passion in his eyes. She imagined the feel of his lips against hers, hard and demanding, and the pleasure of his body molded to hers. Powerless, she watched as his mouth descended on hers.

He tasted like she'd expected—warm and male. His breath was sweet with Scotch and her lips grew hungry, seeking a pleasure too long denied.

The touch of his mouth against hers should have sent out a warning, like the unexpected shock of an icy shower. But no bell sounded. All she could feel was the warm, gentle texture of his lips, the restraint and patience in the cautious way they took hers. His flattened palms slid gently over her bare shoulders, gathering her to a terrifying closeness, caging her wildly beating heart between them. Briefly Cassie wondered how long this could go on before she ran into danger, then she felt his tongue explore the polish of her teeth, the softness of her inner lip. It was a quest she was helpless to deny, and her mouth parted to allow him the velvety secrets within.

It was a kiss that went on and on. The expression "Time stopped" had never seemed more true. The moment stretched endlessly. Cassie's mind ceased to function. She only knew she wanted it never to end.

She pressed even closer against him, her arms wound around his neck in a tight embrace. She let her senses go wild, reveling in his whip-lean hardness, the smooth muscles of his back that could suddenly ripple and shift beneath her fingers, the texture of his tongue stroking hers.

When he drew back it was to regard her with dark, somber eyes. Cassie looked back through glazed blue green pools, her focus softened, her mind rearranging the pieces of her charade and allowing her to see a different Joel Shepherd. He wasn't cold, he was warm; he wasn't hard, he was gentle; he wasn't her enemy; he was her lover . . .

She watched in a kind of fascinated trance as his fingers moved down one soft shoulder, hooking the elastic band of her bodice and pulling inexorably downward. She felt the fabric move against her breast, felt her nipples tighten and rise, saw the line where her tan ended and the pale, tender skin her bikini always covered began.

"Joel . . ." she tried to protest, but his name sounded like a husky invitation. Her hands were against his shoulders, palms spread in denial, but her eyes were filled with confusion.

His answer was to drop a feathery kiss on that line. Cassie trembled. He made no sudden demands, nothing she could readily fight. It was frightening and mesmerizing at the same time. Cassie's lips parted on a question that never got voiced—how could this be happening?

He shifted her gently, carefully, never hurrying or allowing her to feel she should object. But suddenly her bare shoulders were caressed by the ribbed, corduroy couch and she was lying on her back. Her heart was racing in rapid counterpoint to his shallow breathing. Then one breast fell free. Before Cassie could object, Joel's hand cupped it with a possessiveness that seemed somehow right.

In the far reaches of her mind she remembered something —something about Joel—something important. It was a lancing thought that warned her to beware, but it was gone before it registered fully. Cassie forgot all but the most primitive pleasures of taste and touch as Joel's mouth found her rigid nipple, the warm, velvet of his tongue breaking something free in her heart, something that had been swathed in layers of self-protection, armored from another man's deceit and lies. Cassie was too absorbed to appreciate the sweet irony of it all. The man she'd set out to hate had somehow opened her up for love.

She slid her hands beneath his shirt, tugging, begging, and Joel tore it from his back before he lay upon her, his chest hard and warm against hers. She counted his heartbeats, sixteen rapid pulses against her bare flesh, and felt a quiver of dazing anticipation.

His kisses followed one after the other. Cassie drifted between the powerful recognition of true desire and the disturbing reality that tomorrow would be filled with regrets.

"Cassie . . ." Joel's voice was soft and thick. His mouth moved thrillingly from her ear to the delicate curve of her neck. "We can't stay here . . ."

She turned vulnerable eyes to his, hearing the premonitory rumble of rejection in his low-timbred voice. But his dark gaze was burning with need, a dangerous warning that Cassie's self-protective instincts tried to heed.

"I didn't come here for this," she tried to explain, unable to verbalize the true reason for her visit. How could she say she was plotting a sweet revenge? Dear Lord! What would he think of her then? "Joel . . ." Her desperation made it impossible to speak.

"Shhhh. It's only important that you're here."

He lifted her with dizzying ease, the swift movement cooling her overheated flesh. It made her conscious of her half-nudity and fragments of sanity returned.

His mouth again descended slowly on hers, wiping the unhappy curve from her lips. Her mind was screaming at her—Fool! Move! But she was chained by perilous emotions. Cassie opened her eyes. Reality thundered down on her, making her feel embarrassment and horror, reminding her of her mission and drawing her awareness to a new, treacherous side of her nature she hadn't known existed. Overhead, the paddle fan spun slowly. The bright, bell-like lights at the base made her feel exposed.

"I can't," she whispered softly, alarmed at how far she'd let him take her.

Joel stared at her, the heavy desire in his eyes unmistakable. Though his gaze stayed on her face, Cassie knew he'd seen every vulnerable part of her. She couldn't blame him for his hesitation. She was sending out very conflicting signals.

"I can't," she repeated in a stronger voice, but his mouth descended swiftly, capturing hers. She responded instantly, her passion easily stoked. But her conscience wasn't far behind. It tapped gently and insistently inside her head.

"You taste like honey," he said against her mouth.

"Joel, please . . ."

She heard his deep sigh and knew she was getting

through, but then she pressed her face against his chest and let him carry her easily across the room, blotting out the future. Her eyes were squeezed shut. If only . . .

"Where are you taking me?" she asked suddenly as he took her inside, the door hissing softly behind them on an airlock.

"My bedroom."

"Joel, no!" She reached for another excuse. "What about Scott?"

Joel hesitated, frustrated and confused by the tender woman in his arms. In his own mind he had doubts about the sanity of making love to this woman with his son brooding upstairs. But he wanted her, and Scott would isolate himself in his room until morning no matter what his father did. There was a sadly rigid pattern to Scott's behavior. "He's in his bedroom," Joel said tersely. "He won't come out."

"How can you be sure?" Cassie's voice was strengthening by degrees. Her folly was growing more and more clear. She reached one hand downward, plucking at her bodice. Joel impatiently stopped its futile attempts, capturing it and trapping it beneath her under her own weight. She was exposed and vulnerable, the backswept arch of her throat and her trembling body testimony to her defenselessness.

"I know my son," he told her. "Too well, sometimes, I think."

Cassie twisted in his arms. "Joel?"

"What?" He was looking down at her, his gaze frankly sensual but observant, too.

Cassie didn't know he'd already given up the idea of making love to her. There was something about her that warned him off, told him she was too complex. Emotions ran like deep currents just below the surface, and he was at a loss to understand why.

Cassie's eyes were wide with a kind of desperation. How could she explain how she felt. She still wanted him—the signals her body was sending her were very explicit. But she couldn't have him, and she was horrified at herself for even entertaining the idea that she could.

"I can't," she said weakly. "Not now . . . not here."

There was a moment of heated silence. Cassie held her breath, wondering if she'd gone over the limit. For one shining moment she wished she had given in. Let him love me, she thought recklessly. The hell with tomorrow!

But Joel released her slowly, setting her firmly on her feet, wordlessly pulling the bodice of her dress over her breasts. Covered, Cassie felt a belated embarrassment, color washing up her neck and shaming her cheeks.

"What is it with you?" Joel muttered. The dimly lit hallway made his expression impossible to discern, but the query of his voice held suspicion and Cassie's raw nerves quivered. "One minute you come on like you know the game, the next you're quaking in my arms. I swear, you're not real."

"Of course I am!"

"Then you're afraid of me."

His words hit like stones. "Don't be ridiculous," Cassie replied airily, but her attempt at scorn fell short of its mark. She turned away, shivering, hating herself for her transparency.

His hand caught her upper arm. "What's your game, Cassie? Just what are you up to?"

"Nothing!" She managed a breathless laugh. "I think you're the one who's paranoid." She swallowed, then attacked. "Maybe you're the one with something to hide."

Joel muttered something under his breath then abruptly dropped her arm. "This isn't getting us anywhere. I'll walk you home."

Whatever intimacy had been between them was sorely

missing on the walk back. Cassie searched her mind for the right words to fill the gap, but nothing seemed adequate. She kept silently by Joel's side, the only noise the incessant rush of the waves and the muted sound of their footsteps in the sand. Eventually they reached her door.

Cassie thrust her key in the lock, a banal good-bye forming on her lips. She turned resignedly to Joel.

"I want to see you again," he said with quiet determination.

Cassie's heart lurched. "When?" she whispered, her question unconsciously seductive.

"Tomorrow." He looked past her through the now open door. The golden glow from her single living room lamp bathed a circle of the room, illuminating the sparse furniture and bare appointments of the apartment. It was cold and uninviting by day, for Cassie hadn't bothered to make it appear lived in.

What about tonight? The request hovered on Cassie's tongue, almost uttered. She pulled herself back from the precipice of impulsive commitment. "Tomorrow," she agreed, breathless. Part of her was scared witless, but part of her wanted him as a man.

"I'll call you," Joel said, stepping away. Cassie watched for a moment then closed the door, leaning back weakly against it. She felt elated and let down at the same time.

What must he think of her?

Joel was pensive during the walk back, his thoughts restless and disturbed. He had the strange sensation that he was missing something, something important, and it was all tied up with Cassie Blakely.

"You *are* getting paranoid," he muttered wryly to himself, thinking of her earlier accusation. It was incredible how her littlest comment could get under his skin. When had he become so sensitized?

Perhaps it was her timing. The letter he'd received from Tali that afternoon had made him apprehensive and tense. Who was he kidding? He was downright scared. Tali had hinted that she was considering marriage to Ian Carstairs, something Joel didn't approve of but had no control over. It was the hidden references to Scott, however, that had caught his attention and started him worrying. Was she interested in custody after all?

Joel's mouth tightened grimly. If that was the case, she was in for one hell of a fight! Tali was as irresponsible now as she'd been the day they'd gotten married, and she wasn't fit to take care of Scott any more now than when he was a baby. Besides, Joel was suspicious of her motives. Why? *Why?* She'd never wanted Scott. It defied his credulity to expect her to change at this late date.

A headache pulsed at the back of his brain. It reminded Joel only too clearly of the time during which he'd suffered both mentally and physically while trying to keep his marriage, and Tali, hanging together. He'd thought it was finally over. Now he wasn't so sure.

And Scott? Attempting to communicate with him as an adult had been pointless. Their last argument had deteriorated to the point where Joel had ordered him to come out of his room and join him on the beach. Since the episode with the boat, Joel had kept his son firmly reined in, and Scott had responded by sulking day and night. So much for handling the situation, Joel thought with disgust.

Cassie Blakely's inopportune appearance was almost a relief. For a moment Joel allowed himself the luxury of thinking of her in a purely lustful way, recalling the sway of her body, the astounding velvety softness of her skin and her mouth, the hint of wickedness in her eyes. He'd never noticed that in a woman before, an almost unconscious beckoning that was like quicksilver, seen one moment, imagined the next. Was it real, or did he just imagine it?

Whatever the case, Cassie Blakely's eyes had seemed to promise him his wildest fantasies.

Joel rubbed his hand around the back of his neck. He felt the tightness in his shoulders and forced the muscles to relax. The trouble with Cassie Blakely was that he just didn't have time for her. She was a mystery he wasn't willing to unravel. He wanted her for an hour, maybe an afternoon or a day. But that was it.

But she hung in his thoughts, unshakable and tantalizing. Wryly Joel decided he much preferred thinking of her than his other pressing problems.

Tomorrow. He had a feeling she would be worth whatever price he had to pay. There had to be a price, he reasoned. There was too much about her that didn't ring true. What would it cost him for an afternoon with her, a chance to drown in the scent, taste and feel of her?

Right now, he couldn't think of anything he wanted more.

Chapter Three

Cassie lifted a pen from Mike Casey's desk, and her brow furrowed as she began writing copious notes on their conversation. She ignored the expectant tension in the air, refusing to look at either Mike, Lynnette or even Bryan Kerr, the *Island Breeze*'s most talented photographer. Cassie had seen the sympathetic glance he'd thrown in her direction but couldn't respond. Mike was doing nothing short of interrogating her, and though Bryan's alliance was welcome, she couldn't afford to draw him into the battle.

"You're avoiding the question, Cassie," Mike reminded her as a warning.

She stalled. "What question was that?"

"About Joel Shepherd." Mike's tone was sharp. His patience had worn paper thin. "I get the distinct impression you're losing your journalistic edge. Do you want to keep up this assignment or not? If you can't handle it—"

"It's not a matter of handling it," Cassie interrupted.

She'd been through enough of Mike's questions and innuendos this afternoon. Never before had she been called on the carpet, and she resented it now. "I just don't like the way we're going about it."

"What do you mean?" Mike demanded.

Lynnette crossed her legs, looking intensely interested, and Bryan shifted his weight from one foot to the other. Cassie felt her temper rise and the back of her neck grow hot. She was furious with Mike for dressing her down in front of an audience. Couldn't they have had this conversation alone, in the privacy of his office? Why was Lynnette here? To put more pressure on? Mike was making it seem that Lynnette was the competition, ready to pounce on Joel Shepherd's story. "I mean," Cassie said evenly, "that I think we should play fair with Joel Shepherd. I don't like this deception. It's underhanded."

Mike was incredulous. "Play fair? Underhanded? Do you hear yourself, Cass?" He sucked in a long breath and let it out slowly. "This isn't some kind of game, damn it! Your goal, your objective, is to interview Joel Shepherd, the man responsible for Chris Tanner's death! Does that sound like a game to you? We're playing for keeps here, sweetheart. Now either you're up to it, or you're not. Which is it?"

Cassie's knuckles shone white in their grip around the pen. Bringing up her brother's name wasn't necessary; she knew the stakes.

Her emotions were in turmoil. Mike had homed in on the problem too accurately. Cassie was finding it harder and harder to believe that Joel Shepherd was responsible for the accident at the Polynesian Village. Evidence pointed to his involvement, but her heart had become a traitor. It was incredible, foolhardy maybe, but after last night she'd found herself unable to blame him anymore. He couldn't be the cold-blooded, ruthless businessman that she'd imagined and be such an apparently sensitive man.

Or was he just a consummate actor?

Looking across Mike's desk into his angry eyes, Cassie wondered about Joel. The truth was, she hadn't had the courage to find out any concrete information. She'd spent a restless night after Joel left, alternately being horrified by her reaction to him and fantasizing about him the next day, her mind spinning out romantic dreams. She frightened herself; she was playing a dangerous game and the stakes were high.

Daylight had made everything clear. She knew that if she stayed on Maui she'd end up going to bed with Joel regardless of his guilt or innocence. That alone was a worrisome dilemma. How could she disregard the whole reason for her investigation?

It seemed that the sane thing to do would be to take a break for a few days and try to put her attraction for the man in perspective. So thinking, she'd telephoned the offices of Shepherd Construction and left a message, pleading a family emergency to his secretary, hanging up before Joel could be found. She'd boarded the next available flight to Oahu.

Unfortunately, Mike Casey hadn't been pleased to see her. Worse, he seemed to feel her sudden appearance in Honolulu was some kind of defection. He'd been criticizing her decision all afternoon, and Cassie felt tired and frazzled.

"I'm up to it, Mike," she assured him, unaware of how youthful she looked. Maui's sunshine had given her skin a healthy sheen, and her freshness was alluring. She was the only one in the office who didn't notice. "I just needed a break. It was very difficult meeting him in person."

Mike nodded knowingly. "I'll bet."

"I want to know what happened as much as you do, Mike," Cassie insisted. "Maybe more so. But I'm not so sure this is the way, or that it'll even work. I get the feeling he's not a man to open up to a total stranger.''

"You're not supposed to be a stranger. That's the whole point."

"Exactly!" Cassie's eyes flashed.

"Do you mind if I say something here?"

Bryan's quiet intervention forced Cassie to hold back her objections and explanations. She angrily pressed her lips together.

"Go ahead," Mike said laconically.

Tall, tan and well-muscled, Bryan was a commanding presence even when he said nothing. Cassie had dated him once or twice, but neither of them had been interested in anything romantic. They were, however, close friends. Bryan was one of the very few people Cassie trusted completely.

"Maybe you're expecting too much from Cassie," Bryan suggested to Mike.

"Bryan!" Cassie's chest filled with pain.

He raised a placating hand and looked at her. "Look, Cass, what you're really objecting to is the part you're playing, not the story. We're not talking about journalistic skills here. We're talking about honesty. Isn't that right?"

Cassie nodded. She flashed a glance toward Mike and saw his dark expression. For a second she wondered why he was so upset, then Bryan drove the thought from her mind.

"The trouble is, how else are you going to interview him?" Bryan was still addressing her. "Is there any chance he might simply consent to an interview?"

"No." Cassie was sure on that point. All she had to do was remember the look on Joel's face when he found out she'd been a reporter.

"Then there's your dilemma. How else are you going to find out?"

Cassie felt them all watching her. "I could interview

some of the other employees, the ones who were at the scene of the accident.''

''Yeah.'' Bryan was thoughtful.

''What's the problem with Shepherd?'' Mike cut in. ''You weren't so adamant before.''

''I hadn't met him before,'' Cassie responded honestly. ''He was a lot easier to hate when I didn't know him, okay?''

Cassie's defensiveness caused Mike to raise his eyebrows. Knowing the conclusions he was drawing, a flush spread up Cassie's neck. Her cheeks colored and she couldn't meet Mike's eyes.

Lynnette broke the tension. ''You want some advice, Cassie? Try one more time. Get to know him a little better. Right now he sees you as an attractive female he's trying to impress. He's on his best behavior. But give it a little more time.'' A smug smile crossed her rose-colored lips. ''He'll slip up. They always do.''

Cassie was silent. Lynnette saw Joel Shepherd as the quarry, not the man. How could she explain that she felt something deeper?

''If you're that hung up on scruples,'' Lynnette went on. ''Don't make a decision yet. Just get closer to him. When the time comes, you'll know.''

''What do you mean?'' Cassie felt out of her depth once more. Lynnette was the pro; Cassie was the novice, and it had never been more obvious.

''Mike'll give you a tape.'' As Lynnette spoke, Cassie's eyes turned to her editor. He pulled a small cassette recorder from his desk and pushed it across to her. ''It's six hours long. When he starts talking, start taping. He doesn't need to know you have it. It'll fit in your purse.''

Cassie felt helpless. What had started out as an intriguing assignment had turned into a monumental deception. She felt guilty, as if everything were her fault.

But what if Joel Shepherd was guilty? a voice inside her mind nagged. What if Lynnette was right? Wouldn't there be some justification for her journalistic methods?

Mike saw the indecision in her face and pressed his advantage. "This'll prove his innocence, too, Cassie," he said softly, "if, as you seem to think, he is innocent."

Cassie unclasped her purse. "I didn't say that." Her voice was taut, controlled. What was the matter with her? She was at a loss to explain her ambivalent feelings. Chris had been the most important person in her life. She needed to know the truth.

She picked up the cassette player and dropped it in her purse. Mike was right about one thing. Joel's innocence could be proven by the tape as well as his guilt.

"Good girl," Mike said, smiling.

"Don't expect miracles," Cassie warned. "But I'll do the best I can."

"That's all anyone ever expects." Mike rose from his chair, and Cassie followed suit, anxious to get out of the room. She felt stifled and weary.

Bryan caught her at the revolving door that led to famed Kalakaua Avenue. He followed her outside, then, with his hand on her elbow, guided her through a throng of tourists.

"Need a drink?" he suggested.

"At least one," Cassie concurred. She was hot and tired, and the back of her plum-colored silk blouse was sticking to her. She let Bryan lead her to a small bar in one of the nearby hotels, passing unseeingly through the richly carpeted lobby, ignoring the burgeoning displays of blood red anthuriums and huge webbed palms. They passed through French doors paned in bamboo and glass and sat at a small table in the corner near an open window that faced the hotel's inner courtyard. Cassie absently watched tiny black birds with yellow bills peck at the crumbs tossed to them by a young couple at an outdoor table.

"Pretty rough," Bryan commented when their drinks arrived. "Mike's not usually so unfeeling."

"I know." Cassie was pensive. "What's going on, Bryan?"

He shrugged. "Your guess is as good as mine."

"It's almost as though he's determined to get Joel Shepherd, no matter what."

"They're not the best of friends," Bryan remarked cryptically.

"Because of Tali? Joel's ex-wife?"

"Mike knew the family. Maybe he blames Joel for divorcing her."

"Well, if that's the case, why did he put me on this assignment? I'm totally new at this!"

Bryan's blue eyes looked meaningfully into hers. "But you've got an axe to grind, too, Cassie. You've made it no secret how you've felt about Joel Shepherd, either. Or, how you *used* to feel, anyway."

Cassie ran her finger around the base of her wineglass. She was having trouble confronting her emotions. They were so diametrically opposed to everything she should be feeling.

Her attraction to Joel bemused her. It had been electric, charged. It seemed to supersede everything else. Why did she feel that way?

Bryan's hand dropped over hers. "Don't look so gloomy. Everything'll work out."

Cassie smiled, looking into his eyes. Part of her problem, she thought, noticing his clean, chiseled face, was that she had neglected her need for male attention far too long. Bryan was certainly everything she admired in a man. Why hadn't she seen that before?

"Are you busy tonight, Bryan? For dinner?" Cassie asked impulsively. "I could use some company."

"Are you cooking?" He looked amused.

"If you'll accept my invitation."

For a moment his eyes stared searchingly into hers, then he said quietly, "I'd love to."

Two hours later Cassie wiped her hands on her apron and cracked the oven door to check the roast. She'd been in a frenzy of activity ever since getting home, trying to prepare an exotic meal at the last minute. She'd fallen back on an old favorite from when she was married: prime rib roast in burgundy wine, with parsleyed potatoes, honey-drizzled carrots and a mixed avocado and asparagus salad.

Assured that the roast was right on schedule, Cassie checked her clothes, wrinkling her nose at the stain on her sleeve. She hadn't planned to change, but now the idea appealed to her.

It was with a new realization of herself that Cassie bypassed anything soft and romantic in her closet. When I get through this assignment, she vowed, I'm going to go on a shopping binge that'll send shock waves all the way to the mainland!

Her mind was on Joel as she dressed. Remembering how quickly she'd fallen into his arms, under his spell, she felt a growing incredulity. She'd been interested in attractive men before but had never been so weak. Why now? Why him? The way she felt was insane! Totally self-destructive.

How in the world could she forget Chris?

Thoughts of her brother were sobering. Cassie could never forget, nor forgive, his death. Revenge was a poor motive at best, but it had been her driving force until—

She stopped in the act of furiously brushing her hair. Until what? Until she'd let her emotions cloud the issue! Mike was right. What kind of reporter was she that she couldn't keep her sights on her objective? She was better than that! Too intelligent to be veered off course from finding out what had really happened at Shepherd Construction.

The doorbell chimed, and Cassie hastened to answer its call. She felt she'd slipped for a moment, but now she was back on track.

"You know, Bryan, I've been thinking about this afternoon," Cassie started in after she'd murmured a perfunctory greeting and closed the door behind him. "Mike's right. I haven't been thinking straight about Joel. I've been nervous and worried, and so afraid I'll give myself away that I've been acting crazy."

Bryan was noticeably quiet, and Cassie raised her delicate eyebrows in question, wondering what she'd said. His shrewd eyes slid over her appraisingly, his expression telling her he was pleased with the new Cassie. He gestured curiously. "Is that for me?"

Cassie glanced down at herself, seeing only a taupe, slitted skirt and an ivory silk blouse. A gold bracelet was her only jewelry, a hint of musk cologne the only seductive invitation she could possibly present.

"I don't know what you mean," she said tartly.

"Oh, come on." Bryan wagged his head in disbelief. "You're so gorgeous and elegant and fragile. Did you think I wouldn't notice?"

Cassie blinked, her lips parting in shock. Unequipped to deal with Bryan's unbridled interest, she turned away. It was true she'd invited him over because she felt she needed his company, but to have him confront her with it, staring at her with frank male admiration, was something else again.

With jerky movements she yanked open a drawer and grabbed the corkscrew, reaching for the bottle of wine Bryan had deposited on her counter. She suddenly felt very prosaically feminine and absurdly useless. Bryan sighed impatiently, stealing the bottle from her hands and deftly removing the cork. He poured them each a long-stemmed glassful, then leaned back against the counter. "By the way, you look terrific," he told her.

"Thank you."

Never having been uncomfortable with Bryan before, Cassie resented the sensation now. She had the feeling things were changing all around her while she was powerless to make them stop.

Bryan took a deep gulp of wine, eyeing her. "You know," he said at length, recognizing her unease, "I thought for a minute you'd dressed for me. Now I'm not so sure."

"You're making too big a deal of this."

"Nope. You're using me as a stand-in, Cass. And I don't like it."

Her eyes flew open in affront. "Oh, Bryan. Don't be ridiculous!"

"I'm not." Pushing the cork back into the bottle with a vicious thump he shook his head. "How in the world did he get you to change your mind so fast? That's the question. And don't ask *who*, Cass. Don't insult my intelligence."

She wasn't about to give in so easily, though. "I wonder who's insulting whom," she murmured, setting her glass down on the counter. She didn't want Bryan interrogating her, too; she wanted—needed—his friendship.

"There was a time when I would have given anything for you to invite me over," he said, his mouth grim. Cassie felt her arms grow cold as she sensed a forthcoming confession. Bryan's eyes, serious and half angry, met hers. "I've wanted our friendship to develop into something more. I've wanted you to desire me, too."

"Bryan—"

"Shhh. Don't say it. I already know." His gaze roamed over her once more, and he made a frustrated move. "But I refuse to be a stand-in for another man."

"You're not. You couldn't be." Cassie drew a nervous breath. "Bryan, look, you don't understand."

"Then explain it to me. Who were you dressing for tonight? Me?" His voice lowered. "Or Shepherd?"

"I dressed for myself," Cassie snapped, her temper coming to her rescue. "I don't know why you act like I've planned a seduction! I asked you here because you're my friend and I need a friend."

"But not a lover? Don't kid yourself, Cass. Maybe you're not interested in me, but you are in Shepherd. No"—he raised a cautionary hand—"don't argue. I know you, Cassie, and you're right—you have been acting crazy. But you've got your motives all screwed up. It's Shepherd—your interest in him—that's doing it."

Cassie was so angry she didn't know how to begin. It wasn't that he wasn't right; she'd already admitted as much to herself. But his forwardness, his manner of delivery, was unfair. Her silence grew more unfriendly, and she wished he would leave her alone.

But Bryan was like a needle in a groove. Once started, he couldn't be turned off. "Try to tell me I'm wrong," he challenged. "Hell, you practically begged Mike to pull you from the story this afternoon! If I hadn't intervened he probably would have. Is that what you want?"

"No! Of course not. I was trying to tell you when you walked in but you started—" Cassie didn't finish her thought. This was not the time to criticize Bryan's behavior, especially when she was the cause.

Bryan, however, picked up where she left off. "I responded to a very sexy woman in a beautiful outfit."

Cassie had no response. Everything she said just got her into trouble, aggravating an already explosive issue. "You're making too much of this."

"Really?"

Frustrated and tossed into battle in a war that couldn't be

won, Cassie sucked in a slow breath. Bryan was attacking her from all sides and she didn't need it. Instead of being the sounding board she'd wanted, he'd turned to some very infuriating, very male tactics.

"You're jumping to conclusions about me, Bryan," she said levelly. "I'll admit Joel Shepherd's at the root of it, but only because he wasn't what I expected. There's a lot more to him than I gave him credit for."

"That doesn't mean he's innocent, Cass."

Cassie laughed harshly. "You don't have to tell me! Believe me, I know."

"I don't think you do. Not really." Bryan wagged his head negatively. "He's got to be involved. He has to be responsible for what happened to Chris and the others. There's no other explanation."

Cassie's eyes narrowed into a blue glare. "Now you sound like Mike."

"Then you tell me how his company could make those cutbacks without his knowledge."

Cassie held out her glass for another refill. At least the conversation had been turned away from her personally. "We don't know for certain those cutbacks exist," she reminded him.

"Chris Tanner, your brother. Remember him?" Bryan's cruel words made Cassie's blue green eyes flash fire. "He's the one who told us about the cutbacks. They exist all right. And there's been one hell of a cover-up ever since."

Cassie couldn't reply. Bryan's blunt words were effective; they killed any hope of Joel's innocence.

"He's really gotten under your skin, hasn't he?" Bryan said with resignation.

Cassie opened her mouth, then closed it again. Arguing with Bryan was getting her nowhere. Besides, he'd made some very valid points, and it was time for a little honesty in return. "I don't know how I feel," she admitted carefully. "I've spent so much time hating him that I just don't know how to let go." She shot Bryan a look full of self-mockery. "He's a very attractive man."

"Cassie . . ."

"Don't worry, Bryan. I can handle myself."

"Really? Lots of women who thought they could have gotten hurt in the process."

Cassie took a deep breath. It seemed that the men in her life were continually treating her like some kind of starry-eyed adolescent. She wasn't some fragile flower that needed to be protected. Yet Mike, and now Bryan, couldn't seem to stop giving advice. "All right, I'll bite. Who?"

"Tali Paccaro-Shepherd, for one," Bryan responded without hesitation. "She made the mistake of actually marrying him. Look what happened to her."

Cassie became introspective, remembering what she'd read and learned about Joel's ex-wife. It wasn't entirely fair of Bryan to bring Tali up; lots of marriages went sour with ill feelings on all sides. Her own was no exception. But Cassie couldn't deny that Tali had gotten a raw deal.

Tali was a native Hawaiian, the exquisite daughter of one of the wealthiest and oldest families in the islands, the Paccaros. She'd married Joel when she was very young, and they'd had a son, Scott, soon afterward. It was rumored that she'd suffered during the marriage, turning to alcohol and other artificial stimulants as a substitute for her husband's attention. Mike was very familiar with the problems of that marriage, and Cassie suspected that Tali had cried on his shoulder more than once.

Joel was suspected of marrying Tali for her connections in the islands, some of which turned other mainland investors, who weren't accepted by the Hawaiian community, green with envy. In the end, Tali had been the one forced out. While Joel stayed on Maui, Tali fled to Los Angeles.

Thinking of her, Cassie asked, "What ever happened to Tali?"

"That," Bryan said pointedly, "you'll have to find out from Joel Shepherd."

It was as if his words were a signal that the conversation was closed. Cassie was relieved that she didn't have to discuss Joel anymore with Bryan. Rationally, she knew it was self-defeating to worry so much about her feelings anyway; they couldn't be helped. What did matter was that she had a job to do, one that required tact, intelligence and a certain amount of wiles.

"Be careful, Cass," Bryan warned as she put the finishing touches on the meal. "I don't want to see you get hurt."

The smile Cassie sent him was somewhat frayed. "You and Mike worry too much," she said, then ignored his dubious look and started planning for the next day.

Joel slammed the phone down, furious with himself for losing his temper, furious with Tali for being the cause. He couldn't smell the alcohol on her breath across a telephone wire that stretched the length of the Pacific, but her slurred, vicious words reminded him of her so strongly that the stench seemed to fill the room. Giving into impulse, he strode across the room and flung the window open wide, breathing the tangy sea air deep into his lungs. So she wanted Scott after all. His shoulders sagged. How could he possibly win? Tali was marrying Ian, she wanted her son to live with her and, damn it all, Scott wanted to live with her as well! What judge wouldn't reverse the decision and award her custody?

Joel raked his hands through his hair. All the scenes he'd had with Tali came rushing back, breathing down his neck like some inescapable monster. He'd consciously blotted out that period in his life, when Tali's self-destructive course nearly took her life and his and Scott's along with it. But now remembered images flooded his mind: Tali draped unconscious across the bed, an empty bottle of pills turned over on the nightstand; Tali pale and scared at Scott's hospital bed, filled with remorse and grief that she was the cause of the automobile crash; Tali in bed with a lover, a man who worked for Shepherd Construction . . .

He felt a headache building, another reminder. He'd never suffered from headaches until that time, had always viewed others with contempt when they complained of similar symptoms. It was an overused excuse to escape problems.

But his headaches were real, and the doctor's words had altered his opinion, humbling him.

"Migraine," the doctor said bluntly. "People get them for different reasons. I'd say yours is stress."

Remembering, Joel rubbed his temples, hoping he could overcome this one before it drove him mad. He loathed this weakness in himself but was powerless to change it. The only redeeming factor was that they'd disappeared after his split with Tali.

Tali. Even now he couldn't feel any real anger toward her. She wasn't bad or mean, just weak. He'd blamed himself a long time for her weakness, sticking with her through some very rough moments, but eventually he'd come to realize that he was only making things worse for her, giving her a pair of broad shoulders to lean on over and over again. When he'd stopped blaming himself and started to deal with Tali's problems through other methods, namely professional help, she was outraged. When she'd asked for a divorce, it had almost been a relief. He'd counted it a blessing that she'd left him Scott.

The lines of pain deepened alongside Joel's mouth. By the sound of it, things hadn't changed much in Tali's life. Why then, why, did she want the burden of a teenager now?

His secretary's crisp voice sounded through the inter-com. "There's a Mrs. Blakely on line one. Do you want to speak to her?"

Joel's demeanor changed instantly. Did he want to speak to Cassie Blakely? he asked himself. He could think of a hundred reasons why he shouldn't.

"I'll take it," he responded, walking back to his desk. His fingers hesitated, circling the receiver. He had half a mind to tell her to stop bothering him. The last thing he needed right now was to dance around with her. The way she'd cancelled the last time had convinced him that she was purposely playing some kind of hide and seek game.

"Joel Shepherd," he answered in a carefully neutral voice. Let her make the first move. Then if he didn't like it, he could simply hang up.

Her voice was sunny, but Joel's sensitive ears heard self-doubt lurking there, too. She talked a little too quickly. "Hello, Joel. Sorry I had to leave at the last minute, but some things came up." She hesitated, her anxiety evident. "I don't suppose I could make it up to you."

Joel was at a loss to understand her. She seemed genuinely distraught and uneasy. He decided to sit back and see what she'd do. "You might," he agreed easily, letting her hear the strength behind his words. "But only if you come over to my house around eight tonight. Scott won't be there."

"Eight o'clock sharp," Cassie accepted instantly. "I'll see you then."

Joel stared at the receiver for several seconds before he hung up. She couldn't have missed the implication in his words; she'd shown herself to be too intelligent. Then, she had to know what he meant, what he expected. What the hell was it with her? Could she possibly actually have had a family emergency? He'd been sure that was a ruse.

All the way home he thought about her, about the taste

and smell of her, the silky feel of her skin. If she showed tonight, he wasn't going to let her go through her disappearing act again until they had a few things settled.

He shook his head. "You don't have time for this nonsense," he said aloud, the wind from his sports car throwing the words back in his throat. Moments later, as he rounded the first curve of the long driveway to his house, he noticed that his headache was gone.

Chapter Four

Cassie set her purse on the passenger seat of her rented Toyota sedan, conscious of the tiny cassette recorder inside. Her lips were dry, her throat so taut that no amount of swallowing relaxed it.

She backed the car out of her driveway then turned south, rolling down her window for a breath of sea air. It was silly really; Joel's house was within walking distance, but Cassie wanted to arrive at the front door in her own vehicle. It gave her the illusion of freedom, if nothing else—something she found she desperately needed.

Joel's pointed invitation on the phone had set her reeling. She'd had the strongest urge to flee, but determination won out. Cassie pulled an invisible shield of professionalism around herself. Nothing would happen that she didn't want to happen. She knew enough about herself, and Joel, to guarantee that.

But what did that mean?

Realistically, Cassie couldn't forget her last meeting with Joel. Whatever was going on between them hadn't magically disappeared overnight. She was walking a tightwire, playing a dangerous game that left no winners. Trying to minimize her susceptibility, she'd dressed conservatively in a pair of slacks and blouse. There was enough of a charge between herself and Joel; she needn't amplify it.

Her hair was wound into a braid and wrapped across her crown in a coronet. Strands of vermilion and gold mingled together, glowing like jewels, bringing out the secret depths of blue in her eyes. Cassie had striven for austerity; she'd unconsciously achieved a regal softness, a distant and provocative allure.

Her emotional state wasn't aided by the questions that plagued her. Would Joel reveal anything to her tonight? How close could she get with her queries? What if she brushed a nerve? Was it possible he would make the connection?

She almost missed the turnoff to his property. Driving down the curving lane, she tried to minimize the importance of this evening in her mind. Instead, she concentrated on what this piece of journalism would mean to her career. If she handled it right, she could become a top-flight reporter, the *crème de la crème*, able to pick and choose her stories, a staff of underlings at her beck and call.

That's what you want, isn't it? she asked herself as she parked beneath a latticed cedar carport.

The whir of cicadas greeted her as she stepped from the car, wiping her moist palms on her slacks. She looked less than seductive, she thought, congratulating herself. Last night she might subconsciously have been dressing for Joel; tonight her attire was infinitely saner.

The front door had three insets of glass panes, and Cassie peeked through, surprised that she could see all the way through the house and solarium to the splendor of the sunset on the ocean. A unique home, she thought, wondering if Joel had built it. Had he lived here with Tali?

The doorbell rang solemnly, and Cassie held her breath, tension rising. Calm down, she chided herself. There's nothing to worry about . . .

Joel heard the bell and looked up from the architectural blueprints spread across the broad desk in his office. He glanced at his watch, noting with some surprise that she was early. He sat up, letting the edges of the blueprint roll together. His mind hadn't been on the new project anyway; his concentration kept getting interrupted by the image of a pair of blue green eyes.

It occurred to Joel that he hadn't been this distracted since the Polynesian Village was under construction. It was amazing that the project had ever been completed, especially since he'd been so mired in his personal problems with Tali at the time. It was a grim irony that the fire and subsequent deaths of several of his men had shaken him out of his private hell. He still felt entirely responsible.

He crossed the parquet teak floor in long, even strides. He caught a glimpse of fiery hair through the window as he opened the door.

Cassie's smile was crisp. "Hello there. I know I'm early but decided it was better to risk interrupting you than spend another half hour pacing around my apartment. I have a habit of being unfashionably early."

Joel opened the door a little wider. This woman continually took him by surprise. "You're not interrupting anything. As a matter of fact, I was having trouble keeping my mind on business anyway."

"Business? At this late hour?"

Cassie walked ahead of him, pleased with herself for appearing so poised. No matter that she was melting inside, as long as Joel was unaware of it.

The semblance of a smile crossed his lips as he guided her toward the solarium. The sky was turning a deep indigo as Cassie watched the waves breaking on the shore. Joel held the inner door. "Some jobs require more than nine-to-five hours," he said. "Mine's one of them."

Cassie linked her fingers together as Joel made his way to the bar. Her opening had come far sooner than she'd expected. "What is it you do for a living, Mr. Shepherd?" she inquired as he poured her a drink.

"Joel." As he placed the glass of Scotch in her hand, Cassie got a whiff of his clean scent, totally male and uninhibited by heavy cologne. He smelled good and looked disturbingly attractive in a light gray shirt open at the throat, his sleeves rolled up to expose strong forearms. "I'm a contractor," he explained. "I'm surprised you didn't know."

"Should I have?" Cassie's eyes were all innocence.

He shrugged lightly. "You live in the same building as the Gablers and Mandrakes. They talk a lot. And you did ask them about me."

Cassie looked thoughtful. "Now that you mention it, Claudia did say something about construction . . ." Inside her stomach was churning. She should have seen that one coming. "Do you build homes?"

Joel's keen gaze raked her face. "Shopping centers mostly. One or two hotels in Honolulu. We're currently putting up a hotel on some property near Wailea. It's a good project, but it's been snagged in negotiations time and time again."

Cassie knew all about that property. Tali's parents, the Paccaros, had given it to their willful daughter, who apparently had retained title even though she'd married Joel. Mike had filled her in on the intimate details of that transaction.

The cassette recorder was burning a hole through Cassie's purse. If ever she should have it on, it should be now, but she'd set her purse on the coffee table when Joel handed her the drink, and for the life of her, she couldn't think of a reason to pull it closer. Joel was watching her too closely. For the first time in her life she wished she smoked. Fishing for a pack of cigarettes would be perfect.

"Have you been in the construction business long?" Cassie asked, her eyes falling before his bold gaze. She focused on his chest, aware of its even rise and fall. He was provocatively male and Cassie could not forget it.

"Most of my life. I worked for my father, building homes when I was a teenager. I never really considered doing anything else."

"Is your son interested in your work?"

Cassie swept her gaze back to his face when he didn't immediately answer. She saw lines of worry deepening his forehead and a look of intense weariness around his eyes. She'd inadvertently hit on a very tender subject and her heart turned over at the pain she sensed.

"No," he said simply.

After a moment he walked to the bar, his back toward her. Cassie was uncertain how to proceed. She found herself growing curious about Joel's relationship with his son. There was something dramatically wrong between them that she wished she knew more about. "Where is Scott?" she asked at length.

"He's staying with his grandparents for a few days," Joel responded, still facing the bar. He picked up a crystal glass decanter and began to pour himself another drink. "My ex-wife's family lives on the Big Island . . . Hawaii," he explained, unaware of how well versed on the islands she was already.

Cassie's eyes were on his back. Half of her admired his strong, fit body; the other half contemplated the job she had to do. In the hesitation of his voice, she heard something of the deep personal problems he had with his son, and she felt a stab of contrition at prying into his affairs. Cassie's nature was forgiving, and it went against her grain to deceive a man she wasn't convinced was guilty. But what if he was?

She needed to know the truth; coming straight out and asking him was not the way to find it. Consoling her conscience by reminding herself that the ends justified the means, Cassie reached for her purse. It took less than ten seconds for her to toss back the flap, locate the recorder and switch it on. With an ease that belied her inexperience, she set the cassette in motion and reclosed her purse, conscious of the strategically placed microphone aimed to pick up their conversation.

She was standing in front of the window that faced the sea when Joel returned, trying to slow her madly racing pulse, hoping he didn't see the tremors that twisted her insides. She wasn't enjoying her revenge.

"My ex-wife's family is Hawaiian, and they've lived on the Big Island for years." Joel walked back to her with the easy stride she was coming to know. "Scott visits them several times a year. This is one of those times."

Cassie was hot and nervous; a trickle of sweat ran between her breasts. The overhead paddle fan was too slow; its light breeze barely ruffled Joel's hair. She had the urge to go out on the deck, but the thought of the revolving cassette kept her inside. "Do you see them much? Your in-laws?"

Joel's steady gaze unnerved her. "Once in a while," he admitted. "I have a lot of respect for them."

Oh, do you? Cassie wondered if she wasn't hearing a well-rehearsed line. She couldn't see how Joel and the Paccaros could have parted on friendly terms; he and Tali had had such a bitter divorce.

"You don't have any children?" Joel asked.

"No. Kurt didn't want any."

"But you did."

Cassie didn't like the way the conversation was progressing. The last thing she intended to do was talk about herself. "At first I did, but after a while I changed my mind. Our marriage wasn't surviving as it was. Hardly a healthy environment for a child," she added grimly. What she didn't say was how many times she'd wished she were pregnant. She had lain awake at nights all alone, wanting someone she could love. She'd longed for the uncomplicated love of a child; she still did.

Feeling raw, Cassie determinedly pushed those thoughts aside. "What made you decide to come to Hawaii?" she inquired. "There must have been lots of business opportunities in Seattle."

Joel shrugged. "I was interested in hotels, and when I came here, Hawaii was booming. I latched onto one of the major construction firms of the day and learned as much as I could." He smiled reminiscently. "I couldn't have had a more exacting, irascible teacher than my boss. It was the best education I could have had. He didn't have much respect for college boys who came to the islands for a suntan and a few hours of work."

Cassie wondered who this interesting character was. "I take it he made you work for a living."

Joel's face softened. "He kicked me hard," he admitted. "And I didn't like it one bit. It became a battle of wills. The harder he worked me, the more work I asked for." The look on his face was full of self-mockery. "I was never in such good shape!"

It was easy for Cassie to picture Joel slaving long hours to drive a point home; he struck her as that type of man. She could also visualize Joel's employer, a no-nonsense man who insisted on excellence above and beyond the call of duty. "This employer—do you still see him?"

"Nearly every day." Joel lifted his shoulders in a gesture that was meant to lessen the importance of his words. "He works for me now. In fact, he's the man in charge of operations of Shepherd Construction. Roger's my foreman."

And a whole lot more, Cassie surmised. The fondness and respect Joel had for Roger was evident. She doubted speaking to Roger about Joel would get her anywhere; she was sure the affection between them was mutual.

"Do you actually work at the construction site?" Cassie inquired.

Joel's mouth quirked. "You know something, lady? It's easy to see that you're a reporter. You ask too many questions."

Cassie's heart somersaulted then lodged somewhere in her throat. It took several moments before she realized he wasn't accusing her. "You don't have to answer," she replied offhandedly.

"No, I don't." His light eyes assessed her thoughtfully. "You might as well know, I don't usually have much love for reporters. I've had my fill of them."

"Really? Are you that newsworthy?"

"There have been times in my life when I've been hounded by the press, yes. My divorce was very public," he explained, his mouth tight. "Tali's family is very well known."

Cassie felt like a spy. "That must have been difficult," she murmured. In reality, she could sympathize from personal experience. A prominent divorce lawyer's divorce was news, and she'd been on the front page herself once.

Joel made a derisive sound. "Difficult?" He started to say something, then cut himself off. After a moment, he added, "There were other circumstances as well that made it even worse. A fatal accident at the construction site took the lives of three men, and the press had a field day. They tried to make more of a story out of it than there was, but it was just a terrible accident. I was sick, and I don't think

Roger's gotten over it yet, but the reporters . . . I wanted to strangle them.''

Cassie let out a pent-up breath. This was so close to the bone that she couldn't think. Joel's face was taut, the memory drawing white lines of outrage around his lips. She couldn't detect the least sign of guilt or remorse, but then, neither did she see sorrow. She had no idea what he thought about the tragedy other than a distinct distaste for the way it was presented by the press.

She got her voice working, though it sounded thin and frail. ''The accident?''

Her distress caught his attention. He frowned, as if he noticed how she overreacted. ''There was a fire, a problem with the wiring. They perished from smoke inhalation.''

Cassie was abruptly yanked back in time. She heard the carefully neutral report delivered by the officer in charge echo in her mind. ''I'm terribly sorry, Mrs. Blakely . . . a fire at the construction site . . . your brother . . . all purely accidental. . . .''

She hadn't believed it then—wouldn't let herself. Now she felt helpless, lost. It was as if someone had pulled the support from beneath her feet. For so long she'd concentrated on blaming someone for Chris's death that she was unable to believe it could have been just a cruel twist of fate. Yet, it was seeming more and more unlikely that Joel could be so complacent if he were truly involved. The man she was beginning to know didn't fit the cold, ruthless businessman mold.

''Are you all right?''

Cassie felt the hard strength of Joel's arm slip around her waist and heard the puzzled concern in his voice. She was certain she'd paled; the abrupt remembrance of Chris's death could still affect her. ''I'm fine,'' she assured him, upset that her voice shook slightly.

"Are you sure? You've lost your color."

Cassie couldn't look him in the eye. She felt like a fraud. "I'm sure," she said more steadily. "I just haven't eaten much today, and I think it's caught up with me," she fibbed.

"Then let's go to dinner."

"No, no!" Joel had already turned to get his coat, and Cassie reached out and grabbed his arm. "No, really. I'm in no hurry."

His look told her that he didn't believe her, and ignoring her protests, he hustled her out the door. Cassie barely had time to snatch her purse as Joel decisively steered her toward his sleek bronze Mazda RX7. Practical, Cassie thought. Japanese cars were the easiest to purchase and service in Hawaii.

They drove south through Lahaina, an old whaling village and now a thriving tourist town. They drove through the outskirts, bypassing several renowned restaurants. Cassie wondered where Joel was taking her.

The top was down on the car, and the wind tugged at Cassie's hair, loosening strands from her braid. The sunset was glorious, and she kept her eyes toward the sea, needing time to think. Sugar cane fields covered the land to the east, and ahead, a two-lane road wound its way along the coast. Maui could appear so untouched, yet mixed with stretches of empty beaches and rolling fields were condominium towers, strings of tourist shops, golf and tennis resorts and shopping centers. Cassie, for all the time she'd spent in Honolulu, on Oahu, had seen very little of the other islands. Now she felt and admired the peace of a slower-paced life. She knew why Joel had chosen to live on Maui, though Oahu was far more metropolitan.

He took her to a tiny restaurant in Kihei, its only outstanding feature being the size of the crowd waiting to be seated. One look at Joel, however, and the harried waitress at the desk ushered them to a small table in the rear. Bare wooden floors and walls surrounded tiny tables with nautical blue tablecloths, the color nearly disguised by numerous items scattered across the top. Cassie watched as a newly vacated table was whisked clean and reset in record time. Joel pulled back her chair and she sat down, carefully positioning her purse. The last thing she needed was to have someone jar it and spill her cassette onto the floor; in the close surroundings of this restaurant, anything was possible.

Wooden shutters that hinged at the top were propped open by brass rods. The whole place was open air, and birds hovered nearby, the braver of them waddling along the sill. Cassie began to appreciate the relaxed atmosphere, and she crushed a breadstick, spreading the crumbs on the sill between herself and Joel.

"You're going to hate yourself for doing that."

Cassie looked up, surprised. "Why?" she asked, seeing Joel's amusement.

"Because these birds never learned etiquette, and they'll probably dance all over that stuff."

Cassie laughed, the unaffected sound entrancing Joel. This woman had the knack of charming him with hardly any effort on her part at all. Instinctively he knew that he was becoming involved with her. Telling himself that there was no room for her in his life was just hot air unless he stopped seeing her altogether. But when it came to that, he was powerless; he wanted her too much.

"Good," Cassie said devilishly, her eyes daring his. "That'll make for good conversation." As if hearing her remark, a small brown bird lit near Joel, cocked its head, then turned a quick pirouette before flying away, sprinkling crumbs across the table in its wake. Cassie sensed Joel's indulgence even though nothing in his face save a small "I told you so" smile gave him away.

She began to feel warm; nothing had to be said for her to know what he was thinking. It was in the air between them.

The thought of her cassette brought Cassie back to the present. Letting out a pent-up breath, she tried to ignore the sexual message running like a current across their table. But that was next to impossible.

"How long have you been divorced?" she asked, wondering why that topic, normally a touchy one that people tended to skirt, was one she felt safe with. Her deception broke all the rules. Joel's divorce was like talking about the weather.

"Two years, give or take a few months." Joel's gaze dropped to the menu, and Cassie recognized her error. To him, it was still a festering wound.

"You were married a long time, then," she murmured. She desperately sought for some way to change the conversation.

"What makes you say that?" he asked curiously.

"Scott."

"Mmmm. It wouldn't have had to be that way," he said, watching her.

Cassie wondered if he was trying to trip her up. "No," she agreed, "but from what I know about you, I'd say that you wouldn't have had Scott without marriage, too."

"You know me that well, do you?"

Cassie's throat constricted. Was it her own paranoia, or was he digging? "I'm learning more about you all the time," she replied lightly, and pretended absorption in her menu.

"I was married thirteen years," Joel said after a moment. "An unlucky number, indicative of my marriage," he added with a grimace. "Tali and I were as opposite as two people can be. She was from a wealthy, old money family, and I was someone who'd come up the hard way. I was poor and ambitious; she was affluent and lazy.''

Cassie's professional intuition told her that Joel had, for reasons of his own, decided to drop some barriers. Forgetting her other motives, she found herself interested in his personal life. ''Why did you get married?'' she asked when he paused.

He shot her a look she couldn't fathom. ''Tali was beautiful. That's the worst reason I know of to get married, but it's all I can give you. If you'd known me then you wouldn't be that surprised, and if you could have seen Tali . . .'' He shook his head in self-derision. ''Anyway, it had to end sooner or later. I chose later because of Scott.''

''You asked for the divorce?''

''No, Tali did. She'd finally found someone else. Someone strong enough to make her file. She moved to Los Angeles after it was final.''

The waiter interrupted their conversation and asked for their orders. His timing was inopportune, and Cassie chafed at the delay. She wanted to question Joel while he was in an equable mood; she was afraid now he wouldn't want to continue.

Forced to wait until the waiter, and the meal, disappeared, Cassie studied Joel surreptitiously—or so she thought. She was intrigued by many things—too many things—and her eye found the smallest details fascinating. There was the faintest trace of a dimple on his left cheek, a tiny flaw that could be a charming pucker one moment, a rigid groove the next. His face was strong and angular, with a deep tan that spoke of working outdoors.

Once or twice she caught his eyes upon her and instantly dropped her eyes to her plate. What was the matter with her? She was on assignment; Joel was her assignment.

Romantic fantasies were self-defeating. And Cassie knew from experience that the move from fantasy to reality could be even more destructive.

"What are you thinking about?" Joel asked.

"You. Your life." Cassie's gaze slid away from the disturbing messages in his eyes. She reached for the bottle of wine, bumped it and felt the warm pressure of his palm as it closed over her hand and the bottle at the same time. Her breath caught.

He lifted the bottle and poured them each another glass. "My life," he repeated reflectively. "Not one of my favorite topics."

"Why is that?"

His eyebrows raised in silent query. "Is it one of yours?"

Cassie's heart lurched. She raised her glass to her lips, meeting his gaze over the rim. "Mine or yours?"

"Yours." His smile flashed. "How could it be mine?"

If you only knew . . . Cassie found it difficult to keep her smile natural. In his innocence, Joel had a way of putting her on the spot that made her palms break out in a sweat.

"I like hearing about your life," she assured him. "It's a prerequisite for getting to know someone."

He looked at her so strangely that Cassie replayed the words she'd just uttered in her mind. She couldn't see anything wrong with them, but his unwavering stare unnerved her so much she took refuge in her wineglass once more.

"Why do I get the feeling you always say something other than what you're thinking?" he asked.

She watched him pour her another glass while he waited for her answer. His astuteness left her speechless. As the silence continued between them, she found it more and more difficult to evade the question.

She licked a drop of wine from her lips. Joel watched as she struggled. "Maybe I can't say what I think because my thoughts aren't appropriate to our conversation."

"Try me."

The tightrope between truth and fallacy was thin and sharp. Cassie balanced on it precariously. She decided to give him a bit of herself that would keep him from suspecting her deception. "I think," she said haltingly, "you're a very . . . attractive man."

His gaze never wavered. A surge of heat spread inside Cassie's chest as she imagined what he was making of her boldness. Then his mouth quirked. "I don't see anything inappropriate about that."

The wine softened the edges of Cassie's world. Her breath came out on a long sigh that could have been relief or satisfaction. She felt a little of both. Later she realized that somewhere during the evening she'd accepted Joel's innocence in her brother's death. I would know, she thought. If he was responsible, I would know . . .

Her world, one that had stretched between two opposing feelings, righted itself. Everything was on course once more. Chris's death was just an unfortunate accident that had made her want to blame someone . . . anyone . . . Joel . . . Her heart had seen his innocence from the beginning, but her conscience had been hard to convince.

Her interest in him shifted. Now she wanted to know about him for herself. "Tell me about Scott," she suggested boldly.

Joel hesitated, not really eager to broach that heavy topic. His every instinct was trained on Cassie. He wanted to forget the world for a little while and concentrate solely on her. "What about Scott?" His voice was heavy with reluctance.

Cassie, understanding his difficulty, treaded carefully but

firmly. She wanted to know all of him, every facet that shaped his character. And she wanted to know Scott. "You have custody?" At his brief nod, she asked, "Was that a problem?"

"You do ask a lot of questions," he drawled. "If I didn't already know you'd been a reporter, I'd have my suspicions."

"It goes with the job," Cassie answered, the smile tight on her lips. She'd pretty much decided to wash her hands of the whole Shepherd story and let Mike scream at her over the waste of time and money. Someone else could delve into the accident. For her the question of guilt had been answered; the fire was just a terrible mistake, not a cover-up.

With her belief in Joel's innocence came something else. Sexually, her thoughts of him had been pushed to the farthest recesses of her mind. He was forbidden and therefore unacceptable. But now all that had changed, and those secret desires tumbled outward. What would it be like to make love to him? She'd been devastated by his kiss, his touch; she yearned to feel that again. She wanted supple strength and gentle hands, hard bodies and soft kisses, longing groans and tender sighs. She wanted everything she'd been denied. And she wanted it from Joel.

Only hours before she would have shocked herself. Now a dormant desire woke and stretched. Cassie looked at Joel as a woman looks at a man who interests and excites her—with straightforward admiration.

Joel saw the darkening blue of her eyes and recognized that sinful promise he thought he'd once imagined. The answer to her question was already formed in his mind or he would have forgotten it. "No. It wasn't a problem. Tali never wanted Scott in the first place. She never could handle him.'' Cassie's supple skin moved in the candle-light, breeding quicksilver flashes of desire within him. Joel's voice trailed off almost absently. ''Scott's dynamic. He could always play Tali. She was too weak . . .''

Weakness was an epidemic, he thought, feeling a hunger that had never been so real or devastating.

He dragged his eyes away from the sight of her throat, the skin disappearing into the demure neckline of her blouse. It didn't matter. His imagination ran rampant, and his memory saw her as she'd been once in his arms: quivering, excitingly wanton and eager.

He tried to recall their conversation. Scott. Tali. He had a feeling he was saying too much, but it was infinitely safer than letting his mind stray and embarrassing himself. Forcing himself to think of his last conversation with his ex-wife, he added, ''At least that's the way it used to be. Now I think Tali wants Scott.''

''To live with her?'' Cassie took the rigid set of Joel's face to be anger. ''Is that what you want?''

''No. But it's what Scott wants. Or at least what he thinks he wants. Cassie . . .''

''Yes?'' Cassie felt her nerves tighten at the urgency in Joel's tone. She wasn't completely sure of the emotion, but she felt its force. Bound by an irrevocable tie, her eyes searched his, the silent, smoldering message between them making his desire clear.

''Let's leave.''

The words were soft and innocuous, but what they represented made Cassie's lips part. She tried to feign indifference and couldn't. She managed to nod.

The way back was more tense than the drive to the restaurant had been. Cassie felt weak and pliable, and her breath seemed short. The recklessness of it appealed to her, adding a dimension that had never existed between herself and Kurt. She'd never felt such breathless anticipation, and her cautious self warned her that she was setting herself up for a colossal disappointment.

But it didn't matter. She was dizzy from the fast car and the warm wind. She thought about Joel and cast a surreptitious glance at him, seeing his strong hands clasped on the wheel, measuring the width of his shoulders, imagining the press of his mouth on hers. Kurt had accused her of being restrained in their lovemaking, but with new insight Cassie saw it had been the other way around. She'd never felt so deliciously wanton as she did at that moment and, incredibly, she and Joel weren't even touching.

At the house Joel opened her car door for her. Cassie clasped his hand and let him help her, but when they were both standing they were closer than either of them had expected.

"I . . ." Cassie felt the need to rush her speech, an automatic denial forming that he would know was a lie.

"What?" He didn't move, but the force of his stillness was intense.

She shook her head, amazed that her learned feminine role made her refute the fact that she wanted him. Still, she was unable to make the first move.

She didn't have to. Joel's arm folded around her shoulders, and he led her to the front door. Cassie was rigid, her right arm clamped around her purse. The heat of the moment kept her mind off the tape, but even so, some self-preserving need sent a message to her brain: Switch it off, switch it off. It took Cassie a while to understand what that message actually meant.

His bedroom was decorated earth brown and sky blue. Cassie was several feet inside the door before she consciously remembered the recorder. Joel's hands were on her shoulders, and he turned her toward him, his face shadowy in the half-darkness. Cassie couldn't move, though inside it felt as though her whole body were in motion.

He kissed her lightly on her temple, his arms sliding possessively but gently around her shoulders. It was a comfortable, companionable embrace more than one of passion, but even so Cassie stood paralyzed, weak-kneed and trembling.

When Joel slipped the purse from her shoulder she watched fatalistically, but he just set it on his dresser. Cassie was helpless, wanting him but unable to make any advance while her mind's eye watched the cassette turn round and round, recording their every breath. Rationally, she knew she could destroy the tape, but she wasn't *avant-garde* enough to be uninhibited and loving with that wheel spinning.

"Joel," she whispered, overcome by the need to confess.

"Shhh." His finger closed her lips. "You reporters talk too much," he teased, and Cassie nearly whimpered at the outrageous irony of it.

"I've wanted you from the moment I saw you," he said softly. "From that moment on the beach."

Cassie's bottom lip trembled. Her predicament made her want to scream. "Joel . . . Joel . . . there are things . . . between us."

His mouth found the sensitive area beneath her ear, and Cassie caught her breath. Her body responded, even with her deception; her breasts began to heave, her thighs quivered. She felt a moment of self-hatred and shame.

"What things?" he murmured, one hand stealing down her rib cage to rest tantalizingly beneath one breast.

"There are so many things left unsaid, unexplained." Cassie felt desperate.

He drew back to look at her, his expression telling her that he found her confusing. "You're a contradiction, Cassie Blakely," he said, his brows drawing together. "Sometimes I get the feeling you don't want to talk about yourself; other times you're like a repentant sinner, starved for the need to confess. But lady," he added softly, "you pick the most inopportune times." His eyes narrowed as he noted her distress. "Just what is it you want from me?"

Cassie squeezed her eyes shut then opened them. "Everything," she said shakily, aware that only she could understand what that entailed.

Joel was grappling to figure her out; she could see his confusion. "That sounds . . . important. Care to be more specific?"

Cassie nodded, then shook her head. She fought the urge to glance toward her purse, swallowed convulsively, then her shoulders drooped. Joel opened his mouth to say something, but at that moment the telephone on his nightstand rang. Cassie nearly jumped out of her skin.

"I'll take it in the other room," Joel said, casting a last puzzled look in her direction before closing the door firmly behind him. Cassie stood motionless, ravaged, as if she'd just played out some acutely emotional scene.

With an economy of movement she flicked off the recorder, tossing it to the bottom of her purse as if it were some poisonous reptile. One thing this experience had taught her was that she was completely inept at deception, for whatever cause. Her deceit had been a shackle, not an advantage.

When Joel returned she was again standing by the door, the furious flutter of her heart visible in the pulse at her throat. She sensed a purpose in him that hadn't been there before. "I'm getting conflicting signals," he told her, stopping about a foot in front of her. This time he didn't touch her. "I keep getting this crazy feeling that we've met before, or that we've known one another. Okay, maybe that's not true, but then what is? Did you really accidentally meet me on the beach? Or was that planned?"

"What d'you mean?"

Joel watched Cassie's hand restlessly rub her throat. "I don't know. But I get this feeling that you know me. There's something about the way you look at me. You're nervous. I'd go so far as to say scared, even. Just what do you mean when you say you want everything from me?"

Cassie had been holding her breath so long her lungs were screaming for air. She hadn't expected this direct attack. She'd just begun to feel safe when Joel abruptly turned the tables.

"What is it, Cassie?" he demanded when the silence had lengthened between them. "Don't tell me there isn't something going on here, because I just won't believe it!"

Cassie's hands were linked together in a painful embrace. Seeing them, she slowly pulled them apart, her fingers curling up protectively. It was incredible really that he'd put up with her erratic behavior this long. Inwardly wincing, she thought of all the nervousness she'd betrayed, all the times she'd colored then paled. She owed him some kind of explanation.

"All right. I'll tell you. I did know who you were."

"How?" His voice was clipped, terse. He was the interrogator now; she was his victim.

"You're not unknown in the islands, Joel," Cassie responded with a trace of her old spunk. "I've lived in Honolulu the last couple of years. I know of you."

Whatever Joel had expected, it wasn't this. The sharp movement of surprise he made gave him away. "Why didn't you tell me?" he demanded.

Cassie lifted a trembling palm. She found her stab at honesty cutting her lies to shreds. There was too much to lose to bring all the truth out now. "I wanted to meet you and I'm a reporter. I'm still a reporter. I knew enough about you to know you wouldn't let me near you if you knew my occupation."

Joel looked as if she'd punched him in the gut. "Why did

you want to meet me?'' he asked, half angry, half puzzled. Cassie sensed that even now she had a chance to make things right.

"Purely personal reasons,'' she said softly.

The truth of that statement touched him, even though he couldn't understand its double meaning. He stared at her so long she felt he'd seen inside her soul. She expected him to revile her with angry, hurtful words, but his silence was somehow worse. She didn't flinch under his intense scrutiny; she stayed perfectly still.

"Who do you work for?'' he asked, his accusing gaze never wavering.

Cassie sighed, feeling she was burning her last bridge. *"The Island Breeze.''*

Abruptly, Joel's restraint shattered. *"The Island Breeze!''* he hurled back at her. "Mike Casey's paper? Good God, Cassie! You're after blood, aren't you!''

"I don't know what you mean,'' she answered truthfully. Were there really that many hard feelings between Joel and Mike?

"Of course you do!'' he shot back, his face grim. "Just what are you after really? More dirt for that poor excuse of a newspaper?''

Cassie raised her head haughtily. "Now wait just a minute—''

"No!'' Joel lowered an accusing finger at her. "No. Mike Casey's a scandalmonger from way back, and don't even bother making excuses for him. What did he want you to find out? More intimate reasons why Tali divorced me? I ought to—'' He cut himself off abruptly, and Cassie knew he was remembering what he'd told her at the restaurant. "You print a word of that, and I'll break your newspaper,'' he said tautly. "I'm not kidding.''

"It won't be printed.''

Joel stopped in mid-tirade. In the face of his explosive

anger she'd become incredibly calm. His fears were groundless, and she meant to let him know it. "It won't be printed," she repeated. "I never even knew you and Mike shared such animosity. Believe me, Joel, I didn't come here to pry into your personal life."

Joel made a derisive sound. "Really?"

The ingenuousness that Mike had counted on to spark Joel's interest was her salvation now, although Cassie was not aware of that. Her eyes were an honest blue, her mouth full of resolve and touched with vulnerability. "Really," she answered, and because it was true she added, "I'm not after a story."

His brain railed at him to beware, but despite his every instinct, Joel found himself falling under a silken spell. He'd played the fool for a woman once before, but that was a long, long time ago, and he'd not been bewitched by another since. Cassie had something, some indefinable feminine attraction, that wound itself deep inside him and pulled at his heart. He didn't understand it; he certainly didn't like it, but he couldn't deny its existence. Perversely, though he'd wanted her before, his lust and need of her was now ten times worse.

"I don't like feeling that I can't trust a woman," he said softly. "And that's how I feel about you."

"I haven't betrayed you." Cassie weighed her words carefully. "You were someone I needed to know. Now that I do, I would never do anything that would hurt you . . . or Scott."

"You mean there was a time you would?" he asked quickly.

Cassie raised her chin. "I might have, unintentionally. If that's too honest for you, I could leave right now."

Joel rubbed his hand across the back of his neck. He couldn't believe he'd let himself be duped. Yet had he been, really? Her honesty now was almost painful to behold.

"Oh, Cass," he groaned, unconsciously endearing her name, "what am I going to do with you?"

Her eyes shimmered a brilliant aquamarine. "Love me, Joel."

"Cassie . . ." He weighed her name on his tongue, feeling the strongest primal pull he'd ever known. Indecision wasn't part of Joel's nature, especially when confronted with such a lovely offering. And Cassie's intrinsic beauty and soul-giving honesty were impossible to resist. He wondered if he dare trespass into her woman's world. He felt as if there were an unseen trap.

Still deciding, he brought his hand to her face. She stayed perfectly still, barely breathing. When he didn't move, she placed her palm over his hand, drawing it down along the contours of her cheek and lips.

It was Joel's past association with his ex-wife that created his dilemma. His marriage was a lifetime ago, yet it still intruded, making him doubt any other woman, causing him to prejudge and condemn. The phone call he'd just received was from Tali. She'd wanted to speak with Scott, and Joel's reply that he was at her parents had made her sound thoughtful and, he feared, scheming.

Now, looking into Cassie's clear eyes, he tried to equate Tali's treachery with her. There were too many similarities to deny. But there were differences, too.

Cassie only understood part of what he was going through. She just needed time for him to trust her. Deliberately, she parted her lips against his palm, kissing him gently. She sensed his muscles shift in surprise, and then she was yanked against him.

His chest was hard against her breasts, unyielding and masculine, a flame to the passion inside her. Her boldness was new and bemusing. Cassie felt the same glorious light-headedness she got from drinking champagne.

Joel's mouth pressed against her forehead, restraint still

there but desire quivering beneath. His kisses melded one into the other. Her eyes fluttered closed as his lips touched her lashes. Cassie's heart beat in rapid counterpoint to his shallow breathing.

Joel's other hand was wound in the fabric of her silk blouse, the emerald fabric crushed beneath his strong fingers. A shudder passed through him. "I want you," he murmured. "You know I want you."

She heard the sound of an imminent rejection. "Shhh." She turned her mouth to his, their lips nearly touching. "Don't turn me away. Let me stay."

"Cassie . . ."

He kissed the corners of her mouth, and she opened to him, her body pressing against him, her hands sliding up his shoulders to find the silky vitality of his hair. He shifted her in order to feel all of her, his kisses deepening, his hands strong and holding her tightly. Cassie's breath came in gasps. Although they were suffocatingly close, she felt somehow free, raging with fire.

His restraint vanished. His hands found her heated cheeks and trapped her face. He kissed her with an abandonment that left Cassie weak. His touch reminded her of how long she'd been without a man. The quivering inside made her realize it had never been like this.

Buttons came free under his deft fingers, and Cassie watched in wonder. He felt her weakness but did nothing to alleviate it, burying his face in the luminous softness of her shoulder, spreading her blouse to expose an ever-widening triangle of warmly tanned skin. Cassie was helpless beneath his dominant male touch. It was a feeling that was new yet utterly acceptable with Joel.

Her bra was sheer and tempting. He unsnapped it, spilling her breasts into his hands. He'd already seen their beauty, but in the luminescent half-light her firm, silken contours made him suck in a deep breath.

"God," he murmured, aware of a tightening web. But restraint was gone. His finger traced the line of her tan.

A nameless ache throbbed deep within her. Cassie's loneliness and desire were intermingled, inseparable; she wanted Joel to assuage her pain.

Her blouse slid from her shoulders, gliding to her feet. A cool wisp of ocean air wafted through the window, lifting loose tendrils of hair, its unseen hand brushing her skin. Cassie trembled as her clothes came free while Joel's hand gently cupped the underside of one breast.

This was all new. This passion, this desire. Cassie had felt glimmers but nothing this real. She gripped his shoulders tightly as he finished undressing her and lay her carefully on the bed, the warm weight of his body following hers.

She made a disappointed sound when he levered himself away from her, leaning over her but supporting himself with one hand. "I want to look at you," he said in response to her troubled expression, slowly unwinding the braid around her crown.

"My hair will be crimped and dented," Cassie said. But she forgot her protestations under his inspection. His eyes raked over her bare and firm breasts, lowered to her stomach to see the gentle swell of hip and thigh, memorized all of her, then returned slowly to her face.

Her breathing quickened but she felt no embarrassment. Her hair came free and he said simply, "You're beautiful."

She'd been told that before but never with such sincere simplicity. She felt beautiful. Silently she watched as he threaded his fingers through the fiery strands, his expression meditative.

His tawny eyes looked into hers. "I don't want any lies between us."

Cassie's heart missed a beat. "There won't be."

He looked down at her shadowed skin, his quiet gaze

fanning Cassie's smoldering desire. She couldn't wait; he was forcing her to wait. She'd never wanted like this, had never known this aching, driving force. As a woman with a failed marriage behind her, she knew about sexual desire, but she'd never known this wild frustration, this blind need. The word *love* suddenly popped into her consciousness, but she furiously crushed it. She was too wise to equate love with sex.

She wanted to say more, to tell him that she cared too much ever to hurt him with lies, but his mouth had gently closed over her breast. The feel of the velvet roughness of his tongue against her nipple raced like a lightning bolt through her body. Sensations radiated through her veins. Savoring the feeling, she moaned and her hands tightened around him, pulling him downward, needing to feel his hard muscles against her yielding ones.

With the barest touch of his tongue Cassie felt waves of pleasure. His mouth roamed between her breasts, teasing and rubbing and biting gently until she twisted against him.

"You're so eager," he muttered. "Your body responds instantly."

Belatedly she wondered what he thought of her. She knew his initial conclusion about her and felt slightly sick. She couldn't bear the idea he had of her. Not now.

Her sudden stiffening alerted Joel to her mood change, and he looked up, his eyes dark with passion. His soft laugh nearly undid her, but then his lips curved sensuously. "Oh, Cassie, you're too much. Can't decide whether to be an angel or a vixen, can you?"

His warm indulgence erased her fears. He cares, she thought. That's enough.

Intrigued by the contours of his mouth, she ran her finger over his bottom lip, rubbing, tantalizing. "Which would you prefer?" she asked huskily.

"Now?" His expression became more intense at her slow nod. "Vixen."

Without a word, holding his tawny gaze, Cassie deliberately released each button of his shirt. One by one, she worked her way downward, pausing briefly at his pants. Then she tugged his shirt free and ran her hands over the supple strength of his back, moving slowly over the ridges and swells and finally coming round to his chest, her fingers sliding through the whorls of hair and stopping over his thudding heart.

A detached part of Cassie's mind marveled at her calm. She'd never felt so comfortable and uninhibited with a man. Never had she played the pursuer. But now she wanted to be everything for Joel: lover, vixen, pursuer, surrenderer . . .

Her mouth moved over his chest, following the path of her hands. When she touched his male nipple he couldn't disguise the tremor that ripped through him.

He groaned and pulled her face up to his. "Do you know what you're doing to me?"

"No more than what you're doing to me."

He freed himself of the rest of his clothes with swift motions and lay down beside her, his warmth penetrating and deep. When he touched her it was light, a caress that took her completely by surprise. Cassie had never experienced such slow-building lovemaking and at first was baffled by his languid exploration of her body. She'd always thought that, once nude, the act was always quick and explosive, and she had difficulty matching Joel's slower pace. She was alive with long-buried feelings, awash in new and electric sensations. His hands savored the satin curve of hip and thigh, turning them to molten gold. Cassie was warm and flowing; the soft sighs of pleasure that escaped her lips gave evidence of the slowly mounting ecstasy she could feel within.

His mouth was everywhere, ranging her nakedness, pulling hard at her breasts, nibbling at her earlobes, gently rubbing against her inner thighs. She arched beneath him, asking silently. He answered with a swift movement that trapped her trembling beneath him.

He moved slowly, his hips angled over hers, his heart pulsing to the same rapid beat as hers. Cassie felt all of him against her and wanted even more. He denied the ultimate end to her agony, still exploring, still coaxing. She was weak and willing, but his denial turned her weakness to wantonness. She pulled his head down to hers, capturing his wayward mouth, plundering its heated depths with her tongue. She remembered telling him she wanted everything from him, now she wondered if it would be enough.

"Cass," Joel groaned, drowning in the scent and feel of her. His weight pinned her down, but she was a moving wave of exquisite torment under him.

She opened her eyes, dazed by the sensations shivering through her. "Joel," she whispered wonderingly. This was the man she'd sworn to hate!

He made a hoarse sound and pulled her to him, unable to hold back any longer, her sweetness enveloping him, pleasure expanding with every movement.

"Love me," she whispered, knowing he was, dazedly aware that she was asking for something more. Her senses were at a fever's pitch, every nerve stretched fine and tight. Her passionate nature eagerly followed his dominating thrusts, aware of a building release that came ever closer until explosions dazzled like fire inside. At the moment of joy she cried out, a glorious sound that tore the loneliness from her soul. He felt her come apart in his arms and shared that moment of ecstasy, release shuddering through both of them.

In the afterglow of satisfaction Cassie knew this was more than lovemaking—much, much more. She couldn't feel this way, couldn't give and take as much as she had without there being something deeper than physical attraction.

But what? Not love. Surely not love.

Joel swept a strand of sweat-dampened hair from her forehead, his eyes heavy-lidded with satisfaction. He kissed her mouth and cheeks, tasting her salty skin. "You are beautiful," he said softly. "So beautiful."

Wrapping his arms around her, he pulled her into the shelter of his strength, her back curved against the warmth of his chest and abdomen, his breath lightly rustling her hair. The intimacy of their position was exactly what she wanted. She brushed her cheek against his muscular arm.

"Don't leave," he murmured sleepily. "I want to see you in the morning."

So it wasn't just for an evening. His words reassured her more than he knew. Cassie couldn't help wondering just exactly what he thought of her, what kind of woman he imagined her to be.

"I'm not going anywhere," she assured him, and his grip around her tightened for a moment.

However, her senses were too keyed up for her to fall asleep. Long after Joel's even breathing told her he'd slipped into untroubled sleep, Cassie lay awake, her mind and body attuned to every nuance of sound and movement.

To be in bed with a man was unusual enough to destroy any chance she had of falling asleep, but the questions and feelings that kept probing her consciousness only added to her insomnia. What was happening here? These feelings for Joel were hard to analyze; she was afraid to analyze them.

She curled deep into his security, squeezing out all thought. But there was no wall to keep her feelings at bay. She was deeply involved . . . maybe too deeply involved. *What if he found out about her assignment?*

Her deception still followed her like some dark, evil

monster, ready to pounce on her unawares. Even though she had no intention of writing the story on Joel, she was in a potentially dangerous situation. She had to square things with Mike and wash her hands of the whole affair once and for all.

Plans solidified, her conscience eased enough to admit sleep. Drowsily she turned toward Joel's warm body, thinking that no matter what the future brought, she would treasure these hours in the safety of his arms.

Chapter Five

In the cool light of dawn Cassie awakened to the sensual caress of Joel's hand on the bare curve of her hip. She turned toward him, drowsy and relaxed. The lids of her eyes opened heavily to find him watching her. It is love, she thought, returning his stare.

"Why so sober this morning?" he asked.

His hand strayed and Cassie curved her body to meet his, smiling. "Mornings are a sober time. It's time to reflect about the day before and plan for the future."

"Not this morning."

"Every morning. I—" Cassie broke off and sucked in her breath as Joel's intimate probing brought back sensations and memories of the night before. Briefly, she struggled against the tide of desire that threatened to swallow her, then with a soft sigh of submission moved to allow him more freedom. "Joel . . ." she whispered, slightly dazed. It seemed impossible this was the same man she'd sworn she'd ruin.

Her body melted into his, and Cassie shut out the clouding thoughts of reality. But afterward, when she realized he'd fallen asleep once again, the thought of her incriminating tape brought with it a cold wave of fear.

Carefully disengaging herself from the strong, dark arm tossed over her waist, Cassie slipped out of bed. She pulled on her dress, throwing anxious glances toward the bed, then carefully lifted her purse and tiptoed from the room.

In the kitchen she let out a pent-up breath. So far so good. All she had to do was destroy the tape and get rid of it and Joel need never be the wiser. There was nothing on it that could harm him, but its very existence was a glaring red flag to Cassie's deception. After last night she felt sick that she'd tried to fool him at all.

Cassie sat down on one of the caned barstools at the kitchen counter. She yanked the cassette from her purse then stared at it, thinking of its implications. She would have to call Mike as soon as she could and tell him of her decision. Grimacing, she imagined how he would rant and rave, but so what? It wasn't her fault there was no story to be had, and of that last fact she was infinitely relieved.

With a swift movement she pulled the ribbon from the cassette, looping it out as far as her arm allowed. Let Mike find a story somewhere else. She, and Joel, were finished with this one.

"Aha. Trying to get away already." Joel's strong arms suddenly circling her waist stiffened Cassie's spine. She tried to quell a frightened gasp while at the same instant dropping the cassette into her purse.

"What's wrong?" Joel swiveled her chair around to face him, concern blunting his brow.

"Nothing," Cassie answered breathlessly, dropping her purse to the floor. Before he could say anything more she placed his arms around her waist again. "I just thought I'd let you sleep in."

The scrutiny of his eyes made her nervous. "An early riser, huh? For a minute I thought you'd disappeared again."

"Again?"

He nodded. "Like when you left me a message that you'd had a family emergency. That was a lie, wasn't it?"

Cassie's gaze fell before his. What had they said last night about no more lies between them? Already there were far too many. "You know it was. But you know why, too."

"No. I don't." He saw her uncertain expression and added, "There're a lot of things I don't know . . . or understand. Last night you surprised me, really surprised me. Today I want to know why."

Cassie found her pulse hammering again. Would she ever be able to feel secure? If he knew what she'd really been after . . .

"You're right. There was no family emergency. I went to Honolulu. Things between us were getting hard to control. I needed to get away for a while and put things in perspective."

Joel shook his head slowly, pulling her from her perch on the stool. "Why bother with me in the first place? You were after a story, weren't you? Don't lie." His fingers stilled the automatic protest on her lips. "Believe me, Cassie. That's the worst mistake you could make."

Cassie let him guide her onto the deck, wishing she had adequate answers to his questions. She'd made him suspicious by stealing out of bed. Or had he seen her stuffing the cassette into her purse?

She took a deep breath of moist sea air. It was all so difficult. One wrong move, one evaded question, and she knew Joel would never forgive her. *Deception*. The word had so many ugly facets. Just how much was safe to tell?

She knew she had to tell him everything: about her brother, herself, Mike Casey and the *Island Breeze* . . . All of it. But everything in time. Right now was too soon.

"Look, Joel . . . I know you can't understand me. You said last night you couldn't trust me."

"Can I?"

"Yes! Yes. Believe me, I don't have ulterior motives." Cassie turned her blue green eyes to his, their depths filled with honesty. She wouldn't hurt him.

A line formed between Joel's brows. "Why did you look me up, Cassie? Tell me that."

She was walking a narrow line of trust. "I just wanted to meet you. That's all." She lifted a casual shoulder. "I'd heard a lot about you."

It was a half answer at best, and the finality of her tone went unheeded. "From Mike Casey? You probably got an earful."

"Not really. Mike was a very small part of it. You're a man who attracts public attention whether you want it or not. And I'll admit, it's true that the idea of a story was circling my brain when we first met. But believe me . . . *trust me*—" Cassie broke off, knowing she was asking the impossible. She wanted him to believe in her blindly while there were too many bewildering half-truths standing between them. "Joel," she added earnestly, "you must know I'm not interested in that now."

Joel turned his gaze out to sea, squinting against the dazzling sunlight. Waves crashed against lava rock far below, spewing spray in all directions, capturing prisms of light.

"You know, yesterday I told myself you were too much trouble."

Cassie felt a terrible pressure in her chest. "And today?"

"Today I just don't know." Joel sucked in a long breath

and let it out slowly, flicking her an assessing glance. "You ask a lot, Cassie. Maybe more than I'm prepared to give."

Tension thrummed along her nerves. She had the sense of something important and beautiful slipping away. Her deceit was undermining her after all. "Joel . . ."

"I don't have room for an affair or relationship in my life," he said abruptly. "I just don't have the time or patience to give a hundred percent. Do you know what I'm saying?"

Cassie mutely shook her head. In reality she knew exactly what he was saying, but she didn't believe him. His instincts were telling him she was trouble, and he was trying to bow out now, before he discovered the worst in her. Only Cassie knew that there was nothing to fear.

Now was not the time to hide her own feelings. "Last night was beautiful, Joel."

He made an impatient movement. "You're not listening."

"Oh, yes I am. You're the one not being honest with yourself. Last night was beautiful, for *both* of us. Can't you just accept that?"

Joel turned abruptly, his fingers closed tensely on her shoulders. "No. And neither can you. I want you. I admit it. But I hope to God I'm too smart to fall in love with you. And that's what you expect."

Did he read her so well? Maybe. But he was wrong if he thought her an incurable romantic. Life had taught her its treacheries too well. "No, Joel. I don't need that much. All I want is you, just you. Now. And the chance that you'll trust me."

"Damn you," he whispered, pinning her against him. For Joel, her vulnerability was a torment. He saw through to the pain she held inside and was unable to remain immune. She touched him. And though common sense warned that there were too many unanswered motives, he was powerless to let her go. Her honesty was real, and that was enough to make him give in.

Time stopped. Cassie could feel the pressure of Joel's body against hers, his hands hard on the small of her back, his chin tense at her temple. She sensed his inner battle and knew with a growing, dizzy awareness that she was winning.

Her heart pounded unevenly. There was a chance . . . a chance . . .

"Okay," he said heavily against her hair. "Okay."

There was a wealth of meaning in that one simple word.

But as he led her back inside his house Joel added softly, "Don't disappoint me, Cassie," and the ominous undertones followed Cassie throughout the morning.

"Catamaran sailing?" Cassie asked dubiously.

"Ever tried it?"

She shook her head, trying to catch her breath. Running beside Joel had been an impossible task even though he'd tried to shorten his strides to match hers. She was embarrassingly short of breath, her limbs quaking from exertion. The last thing she wished to consider was another sport.

Cassie dropped into one of Joel's canvas deck chairs, attempting to control her heaving lungs. It gave her an inordinate amount of pleasure to see his rapidly rising and falling chest. Thank God he'd at least gotten a workout!

"It's easy," he assured her. He grabbed her hands and pulled her groaning from the chair. "I'll teach you."

"Now?"

"No time like the present."

Cassie considered her dilemma. She still had to call Mike and take herself off the assignment, but she hadn't been able to dissociate herself from Joel—not that she'd made any valiant efforts in that direction. But her own guilt was starting to make her nervous.

"Do you own a catamaran?"

"A small one. A two-man. Are you really too tired?"

No, but I'm scared. Cassie drew in a calming breath, a thin smile crossing her face. Let him just think she was tired yet determined. "Lead on," she murmured.

Joel's answering smile was warm. "You won't have to do a thing." After a tiny pause, "Trust me . . ."

Sailboats were something Cassie had long admired but always enjoyed from afar. To her it seemed the rigors and energy required to man the craft stole from its winged beauty. Standing beside Joel, surveying the lovely catamaran close up, Cassie's face reflected her skepticism.

The lean muscles in Joel's back worked effortlessly as he raised the main sail. It billowed out in a blaze of orange and magenta, and Joel lashed it down with strong, expert knots.

He gestured toward the canvas stretched between the cat's twin hulls. "Get on. Just lay back and relax."

"Picture postcards weren't meant to be stepped into," Cassie murmured. She flashed a smile to Joel, however, as she tentatively lay down, propping herself on her elbows. The one-piece swimsuit she'd hastily snatched from her villa hugged her smooth skin, its shimmery blue color darkening from a spray of water tossed up by the wind.

The boat tilted under Joel's weight, then steadied as Cassie dug her nails around the canvas. Before she could voice another misgiving they were running with the wind, their direction decided by Joel's hand on the tiller.

The wind was brisk and blew in gusts, slapping water over the bow and drenching Cassie. At first she sucked in her breath from the cold, but the exhilarating ride soon made her forget the water.

"How're you doing?" Joel shouted.

"Wonderful!" Cassie shouted back.

It took less than twenty minutes to convince her she'd been wrong about sailing. Picture postcards or no, there was something incredibly pleasing about skimming across the water powered only by the wind.

"Wanna go to Lanai?" Joel asked, gesturing to the island across from Maui. Cassie nodded, mentally calculating the distance. She realized instantly that she would never get back in time to call Mike before the office closed. Uneasily, she wondered if it could possibly make a difference. She didn't see how. One day couldn't matter one way or the other.

The water was so bright it hurt to look toward the island, so Cassie glanced back to Maui's shore. Kaanapali Beach was such a far cry from Waikiki, its hotels interrupted by stretches of palms and beach. Her memories surrounded her again. Chris's words: "You're not going to see Plexiglas and chrome on Maui if Joel Shepherd can help it. . . ."

Admiration swelled within her. How, upon meeting him, could she ever have imagined Joel to be less than what he was? She'd been so hell-bent to heap on the blame that she'd refused to listen to her instincts. Luckily, she'd finally heeded the truth before making a grave error.

When Joel splashed into the water to bring the boat ashore, Cassie jumped in, too, attempting to aid in the docking. She pulled on the rope with all her strength, taking up the slack behind Joel, then stumbling when it suddenly went limp.

Laughing, Joel sank down on the sand beside her as soon as the boat was secure. "Thanks," he managed, and Cassie glanced at him sharply to see if he was making fun of her.

But before she could decide, he pulled her to him, covering them both with sand. Cassie couldn't believe he could feel romantic, considering the circumstances, and was about to tell him so when his mouth descended on hers.

"We're covered with sand," she protested when the urgent pressure of his kiss abated.

His lips traveled down her neck. "Where's your sense of adventure?"

"It was used up during the sail."

"Ahhh . . ." His hand gently brushed the sand from her back, drawing lazy circles against her skin until, to her surprise, Cassie felt a heat begin to smolder within. "I don't believe that for a minute. It just takes you longer to get started."

Her lashes curved downward, hiding her eyes. "What makes you so sure?"

"You, darlin'," Joel drawled. "I'm beginning to know you. Whether you want me to or not," he added softly.

"Who says I don't want you to know me?" Cassie murmured, responding to the lazy, seductive pressure. She lay back, closing her eyes to the hot sun, letting herself be drawn into the romantic atmosphere of a deserted beach.

"You do. All the time. By what you don't say."

Joel's mouth found hers again, tracing its curves with the restraint of a plunderer who knows his victim cannot and is unwilling to escape. Cassie half smiled, liking the analogy. A burning primitive desire longed to be set free.

"What are you smiling about?" Joel asked, exploring the smooth hollow of her throat. Touching her, holding her, his doubts about their relationship seemed silly and insignificant. Never being the kind of man who worried about tomorrow, Joel was incapable of believing half the things he'd proposed. With a possessiveness totally foreign to him, he had the urge to hold her to him and never let go.

"You. This." Cassie's arm flung out in an encompassing arc. "Everything. It's funny. I've always been one to question the beauty of Hawaii, but now . . . the word *paradise* isn't strong enough.''

Joel kissed the slender bones at her shoulder, tasting her, his face close to the rise and fall of her breasts. The smell of coconut from her sunscreen and the flavor of salt water mingled with her own special scent. A powerful seduction. But a hidden message in her words imbedded itself in his consciousness. "What's wrong with Hawaii?" he questioned, raising his head, searching the feminine planes of her face.

Cassie's eyes flew open. With difficulty, her eyelids fluttered closed again, hopefully before he noticed the jump in her pulse. She couldn't seem to stop herself from hinting at the problems in her past, from making obscure references to Chris. She tested her inner feelings and decided she wasn't ready yet. Soon, but not quite yet.

"Memories follow you anywhere," she murmured, blaming her mood on her ex-husband. "Mine followed me here."

There was something unsatisfactory in her answer that Joel couldn't quite place. He wanted to press her, learn all there was to know about her, cut through the mystery once and for all. But cool logic couldn't fight the sultry beckoning of Cassie's eyes. He shook his head.

"What is it with you, lady," he growled, then captured her face between his palms and kissed her hand. Cassie laughed, made an abortive attempt to escape, then succumbed to the feel of his strong limbs entangled with hers. They were breathless for each other, more like desperate teenagers than adults who'd just spent the night making love to one another. Eager hands touched and explored, mouths searched and plundered, bodies strained to each other. It was the abrupt cutting of a boat's engine that told them they weren't alone.

Joel rolled away from her with a muttered curse. Cassie

drew in a shaky breath, then started to laugh. The small cruiser was pulling up to the beach about a hundred yards from them.

Cassie leaned over him, brushing sand from his back. "Too much sand here anyway," she said, grinning.

"Hell with the sand." He pulled her down beside him, his mouth descending on hers, his frustration obvious. But when Cassie's mouth curved into another smile so did his. "Oh hell!"

"We have the rest of the day," she promised softly.

"And night."

And what might come after that was a question neither was willing to ask.

Cassie watched the newcomers trudge down the beach in the other direction, slowly disappearing from sight. Even so, the illusion of solitude had been broken.

"Sometimes you look so unhappy," Joel said, watching Cassie's pensive features.

"Do I? I don't mean to."

"What is this terrible burden you're carrying? It can't be just your divorce. It's deeper than that."

There were dangerous undercurrents here. For a moment Cassie paused, hovering on the threshold of a confession. What was the point in waiting? Joel would forgive her for trying to ruin him. At least he would forgive her motives.

"Joel?"

"Right here, love."

Her throat was hot and dry. "Sometimes people do things for all the wrong reasons. Sometimes self-righteousness interferes with true feelings."

Joel felt tension like a tightwire stretched between them. "Have you been self-righteous?"

"Hasn't everyone at least once?" Guilt brought an edge of bitterness to Cassie's words. "Haven't you?"

"Of course. There were many times in my marriage

when I blamed Tali for things beyond her control. I was self-righteous." His hand was gentle as it cupped Cassie's chin. "But it's not something I carry around like a weight on my back. What is it, Cass?"

"I was wrong about you," she whispered. "I used to think terrible thoughts."

Joel's brows blunted quizzically. "About what? Tali?"

Unknowingly Joel had tossed her a lifeline. She wasn't ready to discuss Chris yet. Even if Joel could take it, it was too soon for her. She recognized that losing Joel was something she couldn't handle, and she knew that for him to forgive her he'd have to know her far better than he did now. She seized on the discussion of Tali like a drowning woman.

"Yes. Tali. I was convinced you used her, used her prestigious connections. I'd already judged you before I met you," Cassie confessed bitterly.

Joel shrugged uncaringly. "Forget it, Cass. Lots of people believe that. Still do. But most don't care as much as you do," he added softly. "God, what an incredible amount of guilt you carry. You're too hard on yourself."

No, I'm not. Cassie swallowed. She'd thought him little better than a murderer. She wasn't half hard enough on herself. As penance, she only hoped she could bring him something of the joy she felt.

"You wanna know about Tali?" Joel asked. "Would it help?"

Cassie's insides twisted. His thoughtfulness made her feel like a yellow traitor. Courage. She sorely lacked it. Inwardly she promised, someday I'll make it right.

"Yes. Tell me about Tali."

Joel nodded. "I already told you why I married her and why I stayed married to her. I didn't tell you why she married me." Cassie's brows lifted. "To be outrageous. To marry the type of man her family could only object to. To marry someone beneath her.''

Cassie's lips parted. ''Surely you don't believe that!''

''Of course I do. It's the truth. If you asked Tali, she'd tell you the same thing.'' Joel's mouth slanted dryly. ''We used one another. Maybe your first opinion of me isn't so far off base.''

''You don't believe that!''

''Maybe not. But neither of us was ever happy. The ironic part was that Tali's parents accepted me completely once they got over the shock. Anyway, it was a pretty rocky marriage, but after Scott was born we both decided to make it work.'' He shrugged, trying to diminish the importance of his words. ''It didn't. And you know the rest. I admit that my association with the Paccaro family didn't hurt me businesswise, and I took advantage of it.

''But none of that's really important now. It's past.'' Joel entwined his fingers in her hair, watching the coppery strands fall from his hand. ''Nothing to lose sleep over, Cass. Tali's perfectly happy with her new life, as I am with mine.''

His voice was steady, assured, but Cassie remembered something he'd said before. ''What about Scott?''

Joel's mouth tightened, then he shot her a rueful look. ''There's the rub. Tali's been making noise lately like she's changed her mind. She wants Scott.''

''Oh no.''

''Oh yes.'' Joel stared meditatively at Cassie's fiery hair. He hadn't wanted to bring up his son. Not yet, not until he'd laid all his uneasiness about Cassie to rest. But he had to admit it seemed crazy to refuse to talk about his personal life.

That she cared was obvious, but still . . . something didn't quite mesh. All her talk about guilt and self-righteousness was fine, but what if it was just a clever way to turn the topic? What had he really learned about her?

Her eyes, wide and solemn, seemed to melt from blue to green. "What are you going to do?" she asked quietly.

Joel tore his gaze from hers. He searched the sun-brightened water for an answer to the thousand questions that raged inside. Why was he being so cautious? Because she'd admitted to being a reporter? That alone wasn't enough to explain this feeling of being set up.

Her empathy and concern caught him in its spell. There was no denying that she cared. "I don't know," Joel admitted heavily, aware of the double meaning he alone could appreciate.

"Is there a reason she wants Scott?" Cassie questioned. "I mean, why now? Did something happen?"

She was awfully quick to interrogate. Perhaps it was just her training as a reporter. Feeling as if he were giving out far too much, he said, "Tali's getting married. She says she wants Scott to be part of a real family—their family."

Cassie read the reluctance in Joel's tense body and misunderstood. "And you don't believe that for a minute," she guessed.

Joel shook his head. Thinking he'd withdrawn from her because the discussion of his son hurt, Cassie kneeled beside him, winding her arms around his shoulders, laying her cheek against the taut muscles of his back. Scott was a touchy subject. She wished it was easier for him.

Joel didn't relax. "I don't trust Tali. She never does anything without an ulterior motive, one that benefits her. Scott's too much trouble for her. She doesn't know how to deal with real human need like the kind he represents. And Scott's not easy."

"So what's her motive?"

So suddenly that she almost lost her balance, Joel twisted around, capturing her upper arms, his tawny eyes boring into hers. Cassie's heart somersaulted in fear. She felt suddenly, abysmally trapped.

"What is it?" she whispered.

"It's you. Your questions. God, sometimes I feel like I'm under fire!"

"If you don't want to talk about it . . ."

Joel made an impatient sound. "That's not it and you know it. It's this whole reporter thing. I'm gun shy. This morning you said you're not after a story. I need to hear that again."

Her pulse was racing. Joel's instincts were too sharp. She had no hope of fooling him for long. Funny, she'd known that from the start but had gone right on tempting fate. Very firmly, she said, "I'm not after a story. I care about you. Too much maybe. If I wasn't so afraid of what you might think I'd even admit that I'm falling in love with you." Cassie's voice lowered, unconsciously dramatic. "But that would be suicide. You have trouble believing me already."

Joel took in a ragged breath. "Cassie"—his hands tightened on her shoulders, biting into her flesh—"you're unreal. You're either an incredible actress or the best thing I've ever known. Do you see why it's so hard for me?"

Oh, yes. More than he did. "I understand completely. It's not exactly easy for me either, Joel."

"I know." As if she were an inscrutable puzzle he was slowly deciphering, he nodded slowly. "That I know. Whatever's standing between us is hard for you. It's not something you want. But it's there, and you're the one putting it there."

Cassie clasped her hands together and stared down at her fingers. "Maybe it's just that I haven't forgiven myself for my preconceptions about you."

"Not good enough." Joel's gaze was deliberate.

Cassie wetted her lips. "Maybe I'm afraid of losing you before I get a chance to prove myself."

Her face told him she'd touched the heart of the matter. The uncertainty etched on her smooth features hurt him inside. "Oh, Cass . . ."

"Can't we just love each other? For now?"

Her plea claimed his soul. Knowing he'd been fighting a losing battle from the moment he'd seen her, Joel sank under her spell. Rationally, he knew he was wrestling with his own inner fears, fears Tali had created about the honesty of the opposite sex. And, damn it all, he wanted her! Cassie, illusion or flesh and blood, was a balm to his other pains.

All she was asking for was a modicum of trust.

Joel rose to his feet, pulling Cassie up beside him, looking into her anxious eyes. A little trust would go a long way toward bridging the gap.

Cassie waited, memorizing the angles and planes of his face, unconsciously implanting them in her inner vision in case sight of them was taken from her.

Joel looked thoughtful. He glanced at her, then toward the lowering sun, its golden light bathing the water. As if their conversation had never been interrupted, he continued. "Tali asked for and got an enormous divorce settlement. Wealthy isn't strong enough to describe her financial state. But she threw it away, along with extra support from her parents. She still has assets, probably enough for most people to live on comfortably for more than a lifetime. But Tali's not most people. I've thought about it a lot and decided she was born too beautiful. She's never had to use her brain; her face unlocked every door. It's too late now."

Cassie was so stunned by Joel's quiet speech that she wasn't certain at first why he said it. But in the space of a heartbeat the answer loomed clear: It was a token, an olive branch, and a way of saying, "I do trust you." He was allowing her to see inside him. He was convinced her motives were what she said they were.

She captured his arm as he heaved the boat off the beach. "Thank you."

He turned. Her eyes said much, much more. His hand cupped her nape and brought her mouth to his. Cassie clung to that moment, glad the worst was over. Time was now her benefactor. She had hours and hours to reveal her darkest motivations and convince him of her love.

They headed back to Maui before twilight could turn the golden water to lavender. Cassie, carefully clasping her fragile happiness around her, slowly realized something else. Joel's speech had another significance. Originally when they'd been discussing Tali Cassie had asked what Tali's motives were for wanting Scott back, Joel's answer had been about money. He hadn't said it, but Cassie suddenly knew he felt the two were interrelated.

It was a stunning thought. Was Tali's interest in Scott merely a way to apply financial pressure on Joel?

Chapter Six

"Come on, Mike," Cassie whispered through clenched teeth, counting the empty rings at the other end of the line. Ten, eleven, twelve . . .

Cradling the receiver on her shoulder, hoping some poor soul was still working late at the *Island Breeze*, Cassie reached for her purse, searching out Mike's home number. It seemed imperative that she get hold of him tonight. For some crazy reason she had a burning need to cut her ties to Mike's story on Joel. Symbolic purification, she thought wryly.

"Damn," she muttered softly, listening to the rings on Mike's home line echo just as hollowly. She waited, picturing him just arriving home, fumbling with his key in the lock. Eventually she had to admit defeat and reluctantly dropped the receiver in its holder.

What now?

Involuntarily her eyes strayed to her purse. The recorder

and cassette tape were safely hidden at the bottom under a mountain of what Cassie considered personal necessities. There was no danger of them being discovered. For reasons she hadn't fully explored, she hadn't erased the tape. Vaguely she pictured herself having to prove that Joel hadn't told her anything, and yet letting Mike or anyone connected with the *Breeze* listen to it was totally out of the question.

Cassie drummed her fingers on the villa's faded counter top and considered. Anxiety settled upon her like the ominous darkening of low clouds, and she had to shake herself to rid herself of the feeling. Still, the peace she'd felt that afternoon with Joel couldn't be recaptured and, thinking of the evening ahead, Cassie's misgivings grew.

Joel was letting her go at her own pace, allowing her time and trust. In a quiet unspoken way he'd assured her that he would ask no more questions, that she could come to him when she was ready. Tonight they were going to dinner in Wailea, near the site of his new hotel. Cassie's thoughts wandered back to what Mike had said about Joel using his wife's land, stealing what was rightfully hers.

With a sound of frustration directed solely at herself, she got up, grabbing her purse. She stared at it for several seconds, then took it into the bedroom and thrust it to the back of her closet. There was no sense in tempting fate. Prudently, she transferred her wallet to a slim black evening bag.

With a last look in the mirror to check the hang of her black slacks and plum, strapless blouse, Cassie firmly drove her uneasy thoughts away.

Tomorrow. Tomorrow she would get through to Mike.

If Cassie's introspective mood disturbed Joel he chose not to show it. She understood his patience and liked him immensely for it. Instead of pressing her, he kept up a quiet, comfortable conversation.

The restaurant was deluxe. Polished, square-topped tables with dusty rose napkins and pale lavender crystal were strategically arranged to offer the illusion of privacy. Their meal, lightly broiled fish with lemon and tarragon followed by a dessert of papaya halves filled with vanilla ice cream floated by Cassie like a memory. Later what she remembered most was the liquid warmth of the wine and the intimate touch of Joel's leg pressed against hers.

Logically, there was no reason to feel so anxious, but Cassie couldn't detach herself from her fears. Happiness was staring her in the face, but it was edged with despair.

"Want any more wine?" Joel inquired, examining the amount left in the bottle.

"No, thanks. You know what they say—alcohol's a depressant."

Joel was not immune to her mood. "Now, what does that mean?" he asked, studying her. Ignoring her words he filled both their glasses, a subtle challenge in the gesture.

Candlelight flickered on her bare shoulder as she lightly shrugged. "I don't want to fall asleep on you. And I don't want to be depressed."

"I think you're afraid to be happy."

Startled, Cassie's eyes widened. "What do you mean?"

"Oh, I think it's pretty obvious. Something's bothering you. One guess is that you let down your hair this afternoon and now you're regretting it."

"That's not true!"

Joel's mouth curved in an ironic smile. "I won't even bother asking what is, then."

A tiny silence ensued. Knowing she was responsible for the sober turn to their mood, Cassie reached out a hand and touched his. "I'm sorry. Really."

Joel matched her penitent look with a sober look of his

own. He nodded briefly, letting the moment slide. "Well, you should be. It's time to lighten up."

Cassie made a silent vow not to let her ridiculous fears upset her anymore. By mutual consent they left the restaurant and walked outside, an inky backdrop of surf and sky their companion as they strolled along the restaurant's boardwalk to their car.

Cassie had no shawl, but Joel's arm draped casually around her shoulders provided enough warmth. Tiny pearlescent buttons ran down the front of her blouse from the valley between her breasts to the waistband of her pants. Joel studied them with the concentration of a surgeon. Cassie smiled inwardly, but her pulse fluttered when his fingers traced the outline of her top, the featherlight caress a silent message of his thoughts.

"What," he drawled slowly, "should we do now?"

Cassie ran her arm around his back, beneath his sport coat, enjoying the touch of strong muscles. "Did you have something specific in mind?"

"I might. How about you?"

Cassie slid him a look. Flirting was something she'd never been good at, but this was somehow different. "I might," she agreed.

But once in the car Cassie thought of something else, and she placed her hand on Joel's arm. "We're so close. Take me to the site of your new hotel. I want to see it."

"Now?" The chagrin in his voice forced a dimple to appear.

"I promise I'll make it up to you."

"That," Joel said firmly, "I'm going to hold you to."

Cassie didn't know what prompted her request, as her thoughts more honestly paralleled Joel's. Maybe it was being near Wailea, so close to the construction site, or maybe it was just her wanting to draw out the evening. Whatever the case, Cassie peered ahead expectantly as

Joel's car hugged the narrow road and rounded the last bend.

It was nothing like what she expected—a collection of buildings at the crest of a cliff, a long walkway surrounded by palms and banyan trees. Cassie stepped from the car and into the wind. Her shoulders instantly chilled; her pants whipped against her thighs.

Joel dropped his sport coat over her shoulders, and she shot him a grateful smile. She didn't want to seem unimpressed, but the hotel was far less commanding than the Polynesian Village, which she hadn't counted on. Where was the famous Shepherd "first class"?

Her footsteps were muffled along the frond- and leaf-scattered stone path that led to the main foyer. She was halfway there when she saw the rest.

Letting out a small "oh!" Cassie turned and went around the buildings to her left to stand near the edge of the cliff. She craned her neck. She was at least ten stories above the beach and surf and stood back a good five feet from the rim. Cliff divers had probably risked greater distances, but Cassie showed it a healthy respect.

Still, she was interested in seeing if what she suspected was real.

It was. Twin towers rose majestically from a rock ledge far below; the north tower was connected to the buildings above. Cassie stared at the staggering architectural feat, overwhelmed that the man beside her had engineered it.

"How do you ever start one of those?" Cassie waved an arm outward expansively, the gesture full of disbelief. It was totally beyond her, like understanding television or what kept a 747 airborne.

From where she stood there was nothing spectacular about the cluster of buildings beside her. But sweeping her eyes downward, Cassie viewed the towers with open respect. From the sea it would look magnificent.

"Where do you begin, Joel?"

He laughed softly, enjoying her appreciation. "With an idea. A hope, really. Then you pose it to an architect, test the feasibility. If everything works, you build."

"So simple?" Cassie chanced one step closer to the edge.

"Hardly simple." Joel's dark hair was tousled by the wind, and he wiped it away from his eyes, concentrating on Cassie. He came up behind her, gently making her aware of his presence so she wouldn't be startled. "I think the hardest part was the red tape involved with this piece of property," he mused, admiring the shape of the woman in front of him. There was so much to Cassie. So much. Even as he told himself he had no time for her, that she was trouble he couldn't afford, he knew it was a lie. He needed her in a way he didn't fully understand.

"What red tape?" Cassie half turned, her face in profile.

Joel saw the pride and beauty stamped so clearly on her nose and cheekbones. Not a man to fantasize about the future, he found himself doing just that. "You name it," he answered, slightly angry with himself for being so caught up. What was he allowing her to do to him? Focusing on their conversation, he explained, "Everything about this project took time. Problems came from all directions. Even Tali."

The reporter in her couldn't let such a golden opportunity slide by. "Tali?"

"She was the owner of the property. For the first time ever—and I mean ever—she was against my developing her land. Always before she'd started counting dollars before I'd even finalized a deal."

A warning flashed along Cassie's nerves. Traitorously, the thought coalesced. How did you change her mind?

Cassie moved sharply. She hated herself for the leftover uneasiness Mike's suppositions had lodged in her brain.

"Take me inside," she urged, needing to get out of the wind.

The foyer was bare but beautifully done. Cassie had a glimpse of oak floors inlaid with teak and cherry. Then Joel flicked on the lights and an overhead chandelier glistened to life. Suspended from a silver wire fastened to the three-story vaulted ceiling, it was a myriad of bulbs and crystal. Patterns of light warmed even the farthest corners of the room.

"The lobby and reception rooms haven't been furnished yet," Joel explained, his footsteps echoing in the wide room. "The towers are completed, and the restaurant and ballroom. But the kitchen, maintenance rooms and second-floor offices have some work left to be done."

A molded oak circular stairway led to upper offices and Cassie walked toward it. The carpet had yet to be laid, but other elaborate details—an indoor fountain with a Polynesian scene done in brilliant, gilt-edged tile, for one—were stunningly finished.

Cassie stood silently, dazzled by the lavishness. The Polynesian Village had been first class—clever, but modest in its glamor. Joel's hotel here was not so humble.

"What's it called?" Cassie asked, the answer titillating her memory. She'd heard once but forgotten.

Without a pause Joel said, "The Maui Paccaro. Come on, I'll take you downstairs."

For Tali? The stab of jealousy that ripped through her was followed by a cold dash of sanity. No, not for Tali. Cassie suddenly knew Joel had named the hotel for his in-laws, Tali's parents.

They walked down a hallway that led to the north tower. Joel stopped at a pair of double doors, searched through a startling array of keys, then unlocked them. He ushered Cassie in ahead of him, then stopped.

"That's funny," he muttered.

"What?" They were inside the top story of the tower, the ceiling was a bubble of glass panes, the only barrier between the opulent restaurant and the star-studded sky. Broad-leafed tropical plants and the perfume of plumeria completed the illusion of being outdoors. Cassie's innate cautiousness searched out the girders and support beams before she stepped into the imaginative room.

"The lights were left on. Roger always checks things before he leaves. It's not like him to overlook something like that." Joel touched the switch, and the lights dimmed, bringing the dark sky even closer.

Cassie walked to one of the circular booths positioned in multi-leveled nooks and ran her hand along the surrounding brass rail. "Elegant," she murmured, looking at the plush velvety cushions and glass-topped tables. "I'm impressed."

Joel flashed her a smile. "Good." With a final thoughtful look he turned out the lights and clasped Cassie's hand, leading her back to the hallway, then preceding her to a bank of elevators. He pushed the down button, and a quiet hum assured them one was ascending from the bottom floor to meet them.

"Are you worried about Roger?" Cassie questioned, watching Joel's face.

"No. Just perplexed. Ah, here we are."

The rest of the tour showed off the suites. From small studios to deluxe three-bedroom apartments with conference tables, the unmistakable opulence and attention paid to detail held steadfast. Cassie followed behind, growing quieter in her awe and admiration. She couldn't begin to contemplate the cost. Her brother's observation held true: Joel did everything first class.

"Well?"

They were at beach level in the wide ballroom where the two towers met and became one. Above was a mezzanine that housed suites and conference rooms. The room was built in tiers that rose inward, an arched skyway connecting one wall of the mezzanine to the other. It was the last bridge between the towers, the south tower rising alone from that point. Cassie stood under its graceful span and threw her arms wide, turning in a circle.

"Stupendous!" she pronounced seeing the question on Joel's face. "And you know it. When I asked to see it, I had no idea . . ." She trailed off, rapt, knowing she was gushing. "It's incredible," she said simply. "My God, Joel! The workmanship, the luxury!"

"I've been told it won't work in Maui," Joel said.

Cassie reacted like a mother bear defending her cub. "By whom? The locals? Your competition? That's envy, Joel. You know it isn't true."

His smile flashed. "You're awfully good at telling me what I know," he observed.

"It's a bad older sister habit I've acquired over the years."

Joel glanced her way, amused. "You have a brother or sister? And here I thought you were alone in the world."

Cassie fell into stunned silence. Her careless remark had contained a hidden trap. "Why would you think that?" she managed when she had control of her voice.

"Your attitude. The way you talk." He came toward her, wondering at the white uncertainty on her face. Lifting one finger, he smoothed the pucker that had formed between her brows. "This," he said. "You seem so lonely."

It was impossible to disguise the least little thing. Her face was a window to her feelings; it betrayed her over and over again. "Joel . . ." She hesitated, wondering why life was fraught with impossible complications. *All of your own making,* she reminded herself.

"Shhh. Not now." Joel's finger found her lips. "When you're ready, Cassie."

To emphasize his point Joel turned, purposely pulling away from her and the mire of her emotions. He cast a critical eye slowly around the room, his gaze pausing on the skyway, his attention focused on the arc of concrete and steel elegantly wrapped in a casing of mahogany.

"The grand opening's only a little over a week away."

Cassie struggled with herself. The urge to confess slipped away; balance was restored. "So soon?"

"It's been years, Cass."

"Since you completed the Polynesian Village?"

He paused. "You do know a lot about me, don't you?"

Cassie felt her heart quiver. "Yes."

For a long moment nothing was said. Cassie waited, feeling how hard it was for Joel to hold himself back. It would be difficult for any man to place so much trust in her with so little to go on; it was nearly impossible for Joel.

At last he said, "I won't ask. Anything. But it can't go on long, Cass."

Cassie understood the hundreds of unspoken messages. "I just want you to know me. A little longer. Please."

"How can I know you at all?" he demanded. "You don't give a thing!"

Seeing the anger and bewilderment on his face, Cassie hurt inside. She didn't want to do this!

Before she could think, Joel clasped his hands around the slender bones of her shoulders, intending, or so she thought, to shake her. But he only forced her to stay still. Her chin snapped up fearfully.

"Nothing," he said severely. *"Nothing* can be as bad as what you've made up in your mind. Whatever it is, it can't be that bad. You haven't hurt me, Cassie," he added abruptly. "And everything about you says that you couldn't. Stop being so hard on yourself."

"I've thought you were capable of terrible things, Joel. Horrible things."

Urgency poured from her words. "What things," Joel asked tentatively, because he knew it was like treading in a mine field.

Cassie opened and closed her palm. "The accident. At the Polynesian Village."

"Yes?" She had his full attention now.

"I blamed you. For everything. I knew it was your company, your construction. I believed you were responsible."

Once out, Cassie expected the truth to be an incredible relief. But fear kept her body frozen. She had so much to lose—too much.

Joel's tawny eyes never left hers. She imagined his anger, his resentment, the disgust he would surely feel at knowing how she'd felt. Given these circumstances in a different case, she would side with him entirely. She'd been guilty of far more than preconception; she'd judged him without benefit of a trial.

"So why should you be different from anyone else?" he asked in a world weary voice.

"I am different, Joel! I am!" Cassie grasped a faint hope. "As soon as I met you I knew it wasn't true." Her breasts rose and fell anxiously. "I was wrong. God, I was wrong."

"You were trying to find a story there, weren't you?"

There was nothing outwardly threatening about his question; it sounded merely curious. Cassie inhaled and nodded miserably.

"And this is what's been eating you?"

"Yes," she admitted faintly.

Joel slowly shook his head. "For God's sake, Cassie. You certainly know how to blow things out of proportion!"

He sounded so relieved that Cassie's lips parted on a hopeful smile. "I thought you'd hate me."

"Hate you? For believing what you read in the *Island*

Breeze? All I can accuse you of is poor judgment. One of these days you'll learn about Mike Casey.''

"What do you mean?"

Joel tugged at her hand and led her to the south tower's elevator. "Later." He laughed softly. "You don't know what hell your silence put me through. Lady, you're too much."

Cassie felt a little out of her depth. How could she have been so wrong about his reaction? Given his feelings about reporters, especially ones trying to dredge up an unsavory story, how could he be so blasé? "Then you're not angry?"

He tucked a finger under her chin. "You didn't actually print it. That would have been grounds for divorce."

The elevator ride was swift. A slight dizziness made Cassie lean against Joel for support. Whether it was from the off-balance feeling over Joel or the breath-stopping ascent in the elevator's glass tube Cassie couldn't say. She closed her eyes and relaxed, Joel's warm arms surrounding her.

That would have been grounds for divorce.

So she'd misinterpreted the rules. Being after the story but rejecting it hadn't been a crime; printing it would have been. At last she began to feel the joy of relief. The worst had passed.

"Where are we going?" Cassie asked as they stepped off on the top floor. Her mind had wandered far from the hotel tour. Now looking around herself, Cassie saw a short corridor of doors that obviously led to suites. Her curiosity piqued, she followed Joel to the end, where a majestic pair of double doors terminated the hallway. Once again he pulled out his keys.

"What? . . ." Cassie let the question hover but got no response.

Joel pushed lightly and the door swung inward. He gestured invitingly and Cassie shot him a perplexed look, knowing they'd already seen the suites. His face gave nothing away—an ability she envied—but she sensed mischief in his bland expression. She stepped inside.

A smile broke across her face. "Aha," she laughed. "The honeymoon suite."

"Call it what you like—it's our most expensive room." Joel walked ahead of her and Cassie followed, smiling broadly. If she'd thought the rest of the hotel lavish, this took the cake. Everything was rose and antique gold. The bed—the room's most commanding piece of furniture—had a flat canopy made of carved cherry and a satin spread of pink and gold that shone like a beacon. A matching dresser and nightstands completed the set, and a desk with a rose needlepoint cushion on its accompanying chair stood majestically before a wide bay window. Cassie knelt to touch the dusky magenta carpet, its plush pile like deep velvet. A band of contrasting gold cut through the center, drawing a path toward the other rooms.

Cassie followed its course, stepping into a lavish sitting room with a cream-tiled fireplace and an elegantly carved mantle adorning the far wall. She ran her hand over the mantle, feeling the gritty texture of wallboard dust.

"As I said, it's not quite ready," Joel said, examining the streak her finger had left.

"It's extraordinary. But in Hawaii?" She cocked her head toward the extravagance of the fireplace.

"The Maui Pacarro lacks nothing."

Cassie weighed those words, hearing self-mockery and something more. Anger? "Did you design this?" she asked, lifting a palm to encompass all of the rooms.

"Hardly. Roger hired an interior decorator from Beverly Hills."

"Which you disapproved of."

Joel made a sharp movement. "It was his decision. I'd

put him in charge.'' Then he added dismissively, ''And she did design a lovely room.''

Cassie's training picked up the thread of a story, and she couldn't let go. ''That's not the point, Joel. You disapproved. Why?''

Without warning Joel suddenly swooped her up, planting kisses on her face and neck until she squirmed and writhed, her laughter muffled beneath his mouth.

''Joel,'' she panted, pleading.

''Hmmm?'' His mouth ranged down her throat, feeling her silent laughter as she sought to push him away. But when his lips journeyed to the soft hollow of one shoulder, she abruptly stopped moving.

Eyes closed, she accused, ''You're avoiding the question.''

''What question?''

''The one about Roger.'' Tiny nerve endings she hadn't known existed were buzzing with life. Damn the man! No matter how seductive the diversion, she wanted to know more. And she was determined to find out. ''Talk to me, Joel. Put me down and talk to me.''

He obeyed her second command, letting her slide like silk through his hands. His palms stopped at her waist, fitting neatly at her narrowest point, nearly spanning her small figure. A breath of cool air fanned her back, and she watched as Joel slowly lifted her blouse from her slacks.

''What are you doing?'' she murmured, the inconsequence of her remark making Joel smile.

''I told you before, you ask too many questions.'' Once more he examined the buttons of her blouse, placing a firm fingertip on the top one, pushing it between the swell of her breasts. ''I've been working out a plan to stop you.''

''Joel . . . listen.''

''I'm listening.''

But he wasn't, and she was fast losing track of the conversation. For some reason she felt its importance, as if something barely out of reach could be in her grasp if she just tried a little harder. However, Joel's warm hands against her skin, inching their way up her back, were driving it farther away.

"You're a dangerous man, Joel Shepherd."

"Not that dangerous."

"Yes . . . that dangerous."

His fingers found her ribcage, and Cassie felt their tender examination. Her pulse coursed heavily, anticipation built even though she fought it.

She had on no bra, and one of his hands gently cupped her breast, rubbing the tightened nipple between thumb and forefinger. Powerless, helpless, Cassie felt passion burn between them. She lifted her hand and traced the lines beside Joel's mouth, lines that could denote humor or pain, lines she wanted to soften for him.

"I think that conversation will have to wait," she whispered, feeling the texture of his skin. His eyes, a potent amber, burned into hers.

His grin was that of a conqueror. "There are other forms of communication."

Her hands found the hard muscles of his neck, muscles strong and enduring, flowing into powerful shoulders and arms. She didn't have to ask what he meant; her fingers told her all about him. The trembling of her body said even more to him.

Her blouse came free, and with shaking fingers she helped unbutton his shirt. She reached for him, but he twisted away, leaving her bereft until she understood his intention. Suddenly the room was dark, only moonlight illuminating the shapes and shadows of the room.

Cassie's figure was silhouetted against the window when Joel returned to her. He pulled her against the warmth of his chest and she wrapped her arms around him. The crest of her cheek lay against the reassuring beat of his heart.

"I want so much to believe in you," he said, his voice almost harsh.

"Don't you?" Cassie whispered.

His bottom lip touched her ear. "Not entirely, love." His hand slid down her waist to the fastening of her slacks.

"You should," Cassie said, her voice a bit ragged. "There's nothing about me you can't see. I'm just a woman. A very transparent woman," she added with a trace of self-mockery.

"I don't think that's really true."

He took his time undressing her. Cassie's eyes were trained on his face—the intensity of his tawny gaze, the steely restraint in the thrust of his jaw.

He wants me, she thought, and realized with a tiny shock how very important that was. Kurt had never fully wanted her, not this way, not the way Joel did.

His own clothes came off with swift urgency, and then he lifted her in his arms with elegant ease. There was something elemental and masculine about Joel, in the tension that rippled through supple muscles, in the angular planes of his face. She reached both palms to his nape and drew his mouth down to hers, kissing him deeply, her abandon suggestive of what they both wanted.

The feel of the satiny spread reminded her of where she was. "The honeymoon suite," she murmured, divided between laughter and desire.

"I have to admit to certain fantasies about this room." Joel's hand found the downy curve of her thigh. "Something about a hotel. All those beds, I suppose."

Her laughter never left her throat as his hands began exploring her curves and valleys. Instead her mouth softened, tenderly touching and kissing his face and neck. When she moved lower, tasting the saltiness of his shoulder and chest, she felt a tremor run beneath his skin. The effect she had on him gave her courage. Gently she moved her lips across his male nipple, kissing and biting softly.

The heightened desire that coursed through him was evident in his shifting muscles. Cassie saw their shadowed outlines in the moonlight, felt their poised supple strength. Joel had worked hard over the years and acquired the kind of fluid muscles weight lifters spent sweat and blood achieving. His position as head of Shepherd Construction hadn't turned him soft.

He suddenly twisted, pinning her beneath him. "My turn," he said simply, his mouth hot and hungry against skin already fevered with desire. Cassie moved convulsively as his tongue found hitherto unexplored areas, and she gasped at the pleasure this intimacy could give.

Her passionate nature ripped free of social constraint. She found herself responding to an unbridled primitive call that drove `her nails down his back; her body twisted restlessly, seeking his hardness.

"Joel," she whispered urgently.

"Shhh. Come here."

She was in the hard circle of his arms, partially atop him. Cassie's breath came in quick gasps, and she slid over him like honey.

A new possessiveness came over her. She lay on him, closing her eyes, simultaneously feeling a certain power and a terrifying subservience. A flash of insight made her realize the futility of her thoughts. She wanted this man, wanted a commitment that he was unwilling to give. But if he could just trust her . . .

She moved slowly, sliding like silk over his hardness. She felt his hands move convulsively, heard his uneven breath, then cried out at her own pleasure. She clung to him, saying things she'd never said, feeling him move with her in a muscular surge. Then she was on her back again, tension an unbroken wave that pushed his hips hard against hers.

"Joel!" she cried, feeling unable to say more, though words flowed from her lips.

He moved slowly, powerfully, until Cassie's pleasure gripped them both. She came apart in liquid waves of ecstasy. Joel saw her passionate, surrendering face and poured himself into her with a shuddering release he'd never found before and had doubted existed. Vaguely he knew his fate was sealed. Her silken spell had won.

"Cassie," she heard him say sometime later, his voice husky and far away, "did you mean what you said?"

Her soft dream evaporated as her words echoed through her mind. She looked at him, afraid, then relaxed at the expression on his face. "Yes." This honesty was harder than any other had been. "I love you."

He cradled her close. "Sweet, sweet Cassie . . ." Then, intently, "You'll have to give me some time."

It was more reassurance than she'd hoped for. Her face glowed with his promise. She wanted to tell him over and over again but understood that it wasn't quite time.

Her surroundings came back to her, and she looked around the cream, gold and rose room. "Should we really be here?"

Joel's laugh was dark and rich. "It's my hotel. Don't worry, love, no one will know."

"That's not what I meant."

"Isn't it?"

She shook her head, laughing. It was hard to express what she felt. Maybe he was right anyway. What better way to start a life of loving than the honeymoon suite?

She snuggled closer. She could think of no greater pleasure than being with Joel, entangled in his arms and legs as his lover. A realist, fully aware of her own charms and limitations, Cassie knew that she could make him love her. Given time, no matter what pain and anguish he'd suffered with Tali, Joel would let go and fall in love with her.

But it wouldn't be easy.

There was a lot of deception to work through yet. To accomplish her goal would take patience and finesse.

Joel turned lazy, satisfied eyes on her. "What are you thinking about?"

Cassie's lashes closed to hide from the invasion into her thoughts. He blew on her eyelids and she opened them again. "Think we could stay here all night?"

"Mmmhmmm." He teased the tip of her ear with his tongue. "But the work crew shows up at seven."

"No," Cassie groaned, reluctantly disengaging herself from Joel. "Forget it. I want to sleep in with you." Something nudged her brain. "The work crew? Does that mean you, too?"

He shook his head, then paused. "Well, yes and no. But I've got things I must do tomorrow. Much as I'd like to spend another day with you, I can't."

He sat up as if suddenly deciding something, and Cassie traced the smooth muscles on his back. "What do you have to do?" she asked curiously.

His glance was mischievous. "Talk to Roger. There are a few things that probably need discussing."

Cassie sat up. "About the hotel?"

He laughed and pulled her off the bed. "Maybe." Then he placed his finger over her lips. "No, now is not the time to play reporter. Come here. I want to show you something."

Feeling frustrated, Cassie let him lead her into an elegant, oversized bathroom. Peach and cream tiles covered the walls and shaped into a flowing rose on the far wall, its outline done in tiny fractures of gold tiles. Cassie marveled at the lavishness. The Maui Pacarro lacks nothing, she thought.

Joel was at the crystal clear glass door that led to the shower. With a loud snap he opened its door and Cassie watched him adjust the nozzle.

"I've been suddenly overcome with the urge for a shower. Now, if you'll just step over here . . ."

The startled sound of delight she made caused Joel to follow her gaze. She was looking into the shower at the raised dais of gold and magenta tiles surmounting a heart-shaped tub of eggshell ceramic. It was in an alcove sheltered from the spray, ostentatious and gleaming. Above, a leaded glass window glowed against the dark evening sky, its intricate design depicting a field of flowers in brilliant pinks and ambers.

"The great outdoors," he observed with a smile.

"Come on. Take a bath with me."

As she tugged at his hand, Joel asked blankly, "A bath?"

He followed reluctantly, and Cassie's lips turned into a sinful smile. The look of skepticism on his face made her laugh. "No one will know," she intoned gravely. "Come on. You'll enjoy it."

He'd stopped on the bottom step that led to the tub and Cassie stood on the step above his. They were nearly eye to eye and Cassie kissed him lightly. Her breasts touched his upper chest, her fingers ran through the mat of hair on his chest, her nails scraping lightly. "It'll be fun," she promised.

She let her hand slide down his muscular arm and entwined her fingers through his, drawing him up the last two steps. Mischief and seduction glowed from her aquamarine eyes.

The knobs were hammered brass and porcelain. Coaxing

Joel with her hand and featherlight kisses, Cassie twisted on the taps. The unused pipes groaned for only an instant, then a flood of crystal clear water rushed out. Cassie stepped inside, pulling Joel with her.

"Cassie . . ." Joel said dubiously, the water swirling around his feet.

"Stop being such a male." Cassie kicked some of the water so it splashed on his legs and thighs. Immediately she was grabbed and hauled into the water, laughing and squirming. Effervescent bubbles pooled over two bodies slick and wet, hands and mouths hungry and searching.

Cassie's mirth and mischief gave way to a soft surrender as Joel's hard but gentle hands washed her, finding every part of her, the tenderness of his touch reminding her how much she loved him, that only he could touch her soul and heal its hurt.

She took the rose-scented soap from his hands and began to clean him in the same pleasurable way he had her. Her fingers slid over him, lingering on supple muscles that shifted beneath her touch, examining the springy richness of his dark hair, tracing the sensual curve of his lips, the hard muscle that formed his thigh, his hair-roughened legs. Each time she discovered an area she wanted to know more.

Her hands were suddenly stopped; the soap slipped, forgotten, into the frothy pool. Water moved in silver sheets over their bodies as Joel pulled her to him.

It didn't matter anymore. She didn't care if she was overstepping her bounds. As his hands moved over her, his body flowing into hers, desire spreading outward in ever-expanding rings, Cassie bared her feelings, leaving herself open and vulnerable to the fates.

"I love you," she whispered, then the words were forgotten.

Chapter Seven

Cassie watched Joel walk across the ballroom floor to meet the silver-haired, round-shouldered man and felt a mixture of embarrassment and misgivings. This intruder couldn't know they'd just come from the honeymoon suite, yet Cassie felt positively naked. She was apprehensive until Joel said, "Roger!" in a surprised voice. He hadn't said so, but Cassie knew he'd been alarmed when they heard soft hammering coming from one of the mezzanine rooms. Neither of them imagined Joel's foreman would be working after midnight.

Thank God, she said inwardly. The last thing she'd been prepared to deal with tonight were vandals or burglars.

Joel's hands clasped warmly over one of Roger's, and Cassie heard them say a few words, laughter in the ring of Joel's voice. Then they came her way.

"Cassie." Joel's long strides brought him to her faster

than Roger's careful gait did him. He lagged behind as Joel's sturdy palm enfolded her upper arm, his familiarity unknowingly betraying the closeness of their relationship. Cassie felt oddly stiff. "I'd like you to meet Roger Caldwell, my foreman. Roger"—his head swiveled to include his friend and mentor—"meet Cassie Blakely. I forgot to tell you, love, Roger's a workaholic. But generally it's only eight days a week." His smile flashed, warmth in his gaze as he introduced his oldest friend. "Since when are you working nights, too?"

Suddenly, unexpectedly, everything stopped for Cassie —her breath, the moment, her elusive grip on happiness. The only thing that kept going was her heart, its beat loud and fast in her ears.

Roger Caldwell was someone she'd met before. The weathered lines of his suntanned face, the steel gray hair and sideburns, constant squint, and the irascible scowl that lifted only for his closest friends. Cassie had seen these before. She suddenly remembered the morning they'd been introduced. At the site of the Polynesian Village.

Like an electric warning in the air before a storm, she read the flash of anxiety that crossed his face and thought, He knows I'm Chris's sister.

Roger swept a slow hand across his brow, then ran it down his face contemplatively. "Since this place threatened to go past deadline, someone's gotta do it." He sighed, convincing Cassie that he knew her by the way he refused to glance in her direction. "There were a few things I wanted to check before I left today, but I got pulled away. Decided to come back tonight and finish. Didn't know you two were here."

"We haven't been here long," Cassie interjected, wondering why it seemed so imperative. Her heart was pumping double time as she considered the consequences. There was really nothing to worry about. Even if he remembered who she was, there was no earthly reason to panic. There was no cover-up about the accident; her relationship to Chris didn't matter.

Or did it?

She didn't miss how Roger's hand trembled as he searched his left breast pocket for the cigar stashed there. And the gaze that didn't quite mesh with hers was a red flag to whatever meager investigative instincts she possessed. But what did it all mean? Surely she was imagining the prickling along her nerves. Making mountains out of molehills, that's all it was.

As Roger lit his cigar he wet his bottom lip several times. Stress, Cassie thought. She wondered if she was as white as he.

For a brief frozen moment, Cassie had forgotten Joel. She nearly jumped when he suddenly asked, "What's wrong?" in a tense, tight voice.

Cassie turned dumbly, then realized it was Roger he was addressing. Joel's expression was part worry, part bewilderment. He seemed genuinely concerned.

"Wrong?" Roger's brow puckered. "In what way?"

"You upset about something?"

If Joel's studied scrutiny bothered him, he made an admirable effort not to show it. Roger might move slowly, Cassie thought wryly, but he was swift in other ways. She knew her appearance had stunned him, but for reasons of his own he wasn't going to advertise the fact.

His pause stretched endlessly. Cassie's nerves were screaming. She had no idea why she felt such fear, but Roger's whole demeanor was unsettling. Guilt, she decided. You're an expert at heaping guilt on yourself over nothing. Isn't that what Joel said?

"Delayed reaction," Roger said. "I heard noises and thought those young punks were at it again. I was ready to start screaming bloody murder and hope to hell they ran for it." His smile was wan, distracted. "Lucky I didn't scare you folks to death."

"There's been more damage?" Joel was quiet, cautious, sensing more than was being said.

"Some." Roger was noncommittal. The ash at the tip of his cigar threatened to spill, and he cupped his other palm under it. Cassie saw color begin to return to his ashen cheeks. "Have we met before, Miss Blakely?" he asked carefully.

Cassie wondered why lying, sometimes too easy, had become remarkably difficult for her. Self-preservation sometimes wasn't enough to smooth the way. She felt it nearly choke her. "I don't think so," she murmured, not bothering to correct his mistake. Let him think she had never been married; it would be harder for him to make the connection to Chris.

Joel was grappling with the shifting moods. He sensed lightning changes, utterly unexpected messages deliberately bypassing him. Thinking it was time to pin something down, he said, "Roger, why—"

"I think you'd better have a look at something, Joel," Roger cut in. "Somethin's been bothering me."

Cassie saw Joel straighten. With a curt nod to his friend, she was forgotten. Following doggedly behind them, she felt foolish and useless, a woman daring to tread into a man's world. Nothing had been said or done to make her feel that way, but she felt it nevertheless. Something about Roger . . .

He took them outside, down a stone walkway to the sheltered beach. A long pier was being built, stretching across the dark rolling water. There was scaffolding on all sides. Cassie, her forgottenness like an acute ache, lagged behind, hearing only fragments of their discussion. Roger's quiet voice was followed by Joel's incisive one. Roger spoke of vandalism at the pier.

Cassie scooped up some sand, its cool gritty texture real and firm. What had happened? In the space of an instant, something had changed. It was there, right there, just outside of her consciousness, but she couldn't name it.

Seeing Roger had been a shock she hadn't anticipated. She should have realized, should have remembered, but it had never occurred to her that she'd actually met him. But she remembered now.

Chris had proudly presented her to him. "My sister," he'd said gallantly. "The illustrious Cassie Blakely, the *Island Breeze*'s crack reporter."

She'd made some silly denial, and Roger had shaken her hand. "Just don't let the boss catch her here," he'd said teasingly. "He'll toss her off the property."

She hadn't understood Roger's connection; Chris had rarely mentioned his name. It was Joel whom Chris had admired and emulated. Cassie had always assumed there was no foreman other than Joel at that time.

Now Cassie pondered the uncomfortable position she'd been thrust in. Roger was sure to tell Joel of her relationship to Chris . . . if he remembered. But what else could his reaction have meant?

Still, she consoled herself, she'd been honest with Joel, only omitting her personal involvement in the accident. And that couldn't matter. Joel knew she wasn't after a story anymore. He would feel amazement, not betrayal, when he found out she was Chris Tanner's sister. He might even admire her for being able to put her anger in perspective to sort out the truth.

So why was she coiled as tight as a spring?

Cassie unclenched her hand, allowing sand to trickle through her fingers, the tiny grains lost forever to the beach. She cast an anxious glance toward the men, wondering what was being said. Their voices had lowered, their heads were together. Discussing her, perhaps?

With a frustrated sound directed solely at herself, Cassie crossed her arms and rubbed her bare elbows. She set out in the opposite direction of Roger and Joel, toward the mammoth rock ledge that supported the hotel. Lights were on at various levels, and Cassie wondered how many areas Roger had been working on.

Joel found her sitting on a lonely rock, waves swirling close to her feet. "Sorry," he apologized, dropping down beside her. "I didn't mean to get so involved." His gaze drifted down the beach. "Roger's worried about some vandalism that's been happening at the pier."

Is that all? Cassie didn't have the nerve to ask. "Aren't you?" His tone suggested that he wasn't.

"Not as much as Roger," Joel admitted. "It's pretty insignificant really. Just annoying. I suspect it'll stop as soon as the hotel's operational."

Cassie waited, half expecting him to bring up Chris. When he didn't, she looked down at her laced fingers, perplexed. Should she bring it up?

Joel peered down at her. The wind tossed a strand of fiery gold hair across her lips, and he carefully brushed it back, his cool finger grazing her cheek. Cassie sensed the tenderness and realized again that Roger hadn't given her away. She was at a loss to understand why he hadn't.

Cautiously she probed. "Do you think that's what's really bothering him?"

"Who? Roger?"

"Mmmhmm. He seemed so . . . tense."

Joel's hand had been absently rubbing her bare shoulders. Now it stopped. "What are you driving at?"

"Nothing. I just wondered if he was always that way."

Cassie was instantly sorry she'd brought it up. Joel shifted impatiently beside her, and she knew she'd overstepped her bounds. Joel and Roger's friendship was too strong for him to appreciate any interference from Cassie, no matter how good her intentions. She was the newcomer on the block, not Roger, and she'd inadvertently awakened Joel's protective instincts. Placing herself between Joel and Roger was suicide; she was forcing him to choose sides.

"What way?" Joel demanded.

"Forget it." Cassie looked out to sea.

"No, I won't forget it." She saw the anger on his face and felt helpless and frustrated. Damn! What was wrong with her? Why did she feel this need to stir up trouble?

Joel half turned, forcing her to face him, his mouth a tight line. "What the hell are you doing now, Cassie? Why Roger? Just what is it you're after?"

This last came out in a low hiss so that Roger, who was ambling their way, could not overhear. "Nothing," she said tightly.

"This reporter thing. Isn't anyone safe?"

Cassie could not respond, because now Roger came within earshot. She could only place a frozen smile on her face and wonder if Joel wasn't being just a tad too testy.

They went up the elevator in silence, Cassie feeling too raw and off-balance to participate in conversation. Joel ignored her, but several times she felt his eyes drop on her in a contemplative stare. What had happened to make them both so sensitive?

At the main lobby Roger snapped his fingers in afterthought. "I nearly forgot. A woman called. A reporter. She wants to cover the opening, and I said I'd have to speak to you." Bushy eyebrows raised inquiringly. "What d'ya think?"

Joel grimaced and Cassie gaped. They seemed never to be able to get away from her job. Like a splinter one couldn't quite remove, it annoyed and aggravated over and over again.

"I think," Joel sighed, "that reporters are a necessary evil." He slid a look toward Cassie, and she straightened her spine. "Sometimes, if you're lucky, you might even run across one who has some integrity."

His meaning was too obscure for Roger. Rubbing his nose, his expression darkening, Roger muttered, "I don't trust any of 'em."

Relieved by Joel's words, Cassie almost smiled. Fear of the press seemed to have infected all of Shepherd Construction.

Joel's eyes never left Cassie. "I'm trying to," he said for her alone. "Don't worry, Roger. She'll probably be from the society column. No pressure. And we need the publicity."

Roger looked at his employer as if he'd lost his mind. His mouth opened and shut in amazement, and Cassie was certain it was the first time Joel had ever been so kind to her profession. A glimmer of something crossed his face—that something she couldn't quite name.

Roger stared. "Are you sure, Joel?" Then, more intensely, "After what happened before?"

It took Joel several seconds to respond. A scowl crossed his lean face; his lips tightened.

What happened before . . . Something inside Cassie twisted uncomfortably, her instincts abuzz. A feeling of dread tightened her stomach.

Joel shot Roger a glance packed with meaning, then he turned to Cassie. "It's fortunate Roger doesn't get paid for worrying. I'd be broke." Very pointedly, he added, "Cassie's a reporter, Roger."

His face went white. "My apologies," he muttered. "I had no idea."

"It's all right . . . really." His distress was so obvious that Cassie sprang to his defense. It was automatic, an inherent urge to keep someone at ease. She reacted without thinking.

"No, no. It's my fault entirely. Please accept my apologies, Mrs. Blakely, I seem to have a knack for puttin' my foot in my mouth."

"Look, it's already forgotten," Cassie assured him. Vaguely she wondered why he was so upset. It couldn't be just because of his *faux pas*—his reaction was too acute. Then what? Had he remembered she was Chris Tanner's sister?

One gnarled hand worried the other as Roger said, "Well then, I'll see you both later. It was a pleasure meetin' you." Before Cassie could respond he went on, "I'll do some checkin' on what we discussed down at the beach. You'll be hearin' from me."

"We'll discuss it in the morning," Joel agreed.

Roger was inching toward the door as if he couldn't wait to make his exit. Disturbed, Cassie wondered what she was missing. Something . . . something . . .

Roger shook her hand and she smiled politely. The last thing she'd expected was this uneasy meeting with Joel's foreman, the man who'd guided him and been his friend for years. Unless . . .

Joel followed Roger to the door. "If that reporter really bothers you," he was saying, "just turn her down. Cassie'll be there anyway."

Roger made a sound of apology. "Sure. It's about time we got some good coverage." He laughed shortly. "Just keep Mike Casey out of it, right?"

"Right." The look Joel sent Cassie was electric. They both knew whom she worked for.

Joel turned out the lights. Cassie waited by the door, hearing the rumble of Roger's truck fade in the distance. It must have been parked farther up the road.

"You will come, won't you?" Joel inquired as they drove back to Kaanapali.

"To the opening? Of course."

Joel shifted gears, his eyes never leaving the highway. "Something wrong?"

Defeat was in the tight line of her mouth. Despising herself, she knew she couldn't completely trust him, not with Roger involved. There was no way she could ask about his foreman without stirring up trouble. There was too much between them. Yet something told her there were questions that needed to be asked.

Later, she told herself for the hundredth time. Not now. Not until she'd done some thinking.

"I think . . . I'm just tired."

It wasn't even close to a satisfactory answer, but Joel was forced to accept it. They drove the rest of the way in silence, Cassie trying to heed an inner voice of warning, Joel wondering why he felt caught in a dangerous undertow.

It wasn't that she really believed in a sixth sense or premonitions or that she considered herself gifted with ESP, but the cold feeling that had crept inside her bones at the hotel refused to be dislodged, and she couldn't ignore it. Wrapped inside the luxury of Joel's arms, Cassie had expected immediate sleep. Instead she was watching Joel's digital clock record each passing minute.

Let go, she told herself, irritation causing her to thump her pillow impatiently.

Drowsiness finally lowered her lids. Roger was just uncomfortable because he couldn't place where he'd seen her before. That was all. It was simple. After all, he'd called her Miss Blakely . . .

Cassie's eyes flew open. The first time! The second time he'd addressed her as *Mrs.* Blakely.

So he knew. It took several minutes for Cassie to get her

pulse under control. So what? she asked herself once more. What could it possibly matter?

Because it often helped to analyze a situation in order to put it in perspective, Cassie reviewed the whole evening. But the more she thought about it, the less sense it made. Was she overreacting, or was there something amiss?

She'd never been one to dramatize, yet she trusted her feelings. Roger's attitude had been inexplicable; he hadn't just been nervous, he'd been afraid. Of her?

Joel's arm was curved beneath her breasts; the feel of his breath on her nape was warm and reassuring. His trust in Roger was so implicit that Cassie felt like a traitor even thinking uneasy thoughts about him.

But they were uneasy. Roger was afraid. Once the idea took root, Cassie believed it as fact. But afraid of her? That hardly made sense; she wasn't certain he even knew who she was.

He'd acted strangely from the onset, almost as if they'd interrupted him, as if they'd caught him at something, as if he had something to hide.

Something to hide. The sick feeling in Cassie's stomach grew, and she automatically burrowed deeper into the safety of Joel's arms. He murmured and stirred but didn't awaken, and Cassie lay stiff beside him. Was Roger hiding something from Joel? How could he? Joel was the man in charge, and she knew from what her brother had told her that he was involved in every aspect of his business.

Then why was Roger frightened?

Suddenly she knew what had been hovering at the edges of her consciousness, the reason she'd felt uncomfortable with Roger from the moment they met. He *was* afraid of her. Maybe he hadn't remembered that she was a reporter, but the sight of her had triggered his fear. And how else could she be a threat to him?

Trying desperately to keep her thoughts in some kind of order, Cassie fretted out the answers. Being Chris's sister—did that fit in? Was he worried about her delving into the accident again?

Of course he was!

It made so much sense that Cassie couldn't ignore it. He did know her relationship to Chris Tanner. Maybe not in the beginning, but later, after Joel had explained that she was a reporter. Then he'd gone completely white, she recalled. Afterward, he'd addressed her as Mrs. Blakely.

And Joel had warned him—

No!

Cassie's pulse pounded in her temples. No. She rejected that instantly. She believed in Joel, and she believed in herself too completely to think she could be so utterly fooled.

But the nagging thought persisted. Joel had brought up her profession after Roger had said, "After what happened before?" as if there was something in the past to keep hidden from the public.

Joel shifted and Cassie curled close to him, feeling desperate. She loved him. Whatever was happening with Roger didn't necessarily involve Joel. There were ways to hide things within a company, many ways. Joel was just an innocent victim. That's all. Nothing more. And besides, just because her first meeting with Roger hadn't gone well, that didn't mean anything either. She was letting her imagination rule her.

Cassie's suddenly tight grip around his chest woke Joel. He stirred sleepily and murmured, "What?" because she'd said something.

She shook her head slightly, her cheek rubbing against the dark hair on his chest. "I was just thinking about mountains and molehills," she whispered, folding herself against him until his whole left side felt the warmth and softness of hers.

Joel's eyes opened in the dark and he frowned. Mountains and molehills? For some reason he couldn't quite fathom, that bothered him. Listening to her breathing fall into the regular rhythm of sleep, Joel stared at the ceiling. He'd been with Cassie a little over a day and a half, yet it seemed much longer, as if they'd been living together for years. Perversely, at the same time it seemed like one single shining moment, everything new.

Her head lay gracefully on his shoulder. Mountains and molehills. He sensed a message there somehow meant for him. The idea left him with a bad feeling, like the aftertaste of a bitter pill.

He didn't like the insinuating way she'd discussed Roger; that had been unfair and way out of line. If he didn't know better, he'd think she was trying to sniff out a story—that fell in with what he knew about reporters. But Cassie wasn't like the others. She was a thinking, feeling woman first—a human being.

So why the attack on Roger?

There was no ready answer to that, so Joel tried to drop it out of his mind. Cassie had awakened strong emotions within him, deep, treacherous emotions that he kept under careful control. Therein lay the problem, he supposed. She'd sprouted the seed of vulnerability inside him that he'd hoped had died. He knew it and almost resented it, aware how easily she could use it to her advantage. It was easier to be wary and save yourself from a trap than to try to find a way out once you were snared.

But it left things in an unsatisfactory limbo.

Blaming himself for caring too much, Joel fell into an uneasy slumber. His last thought was that he'd overreacted about Roger. They were both still uncomfortable enough with one another to suspect the other's motives.

Chapter Eight

*W*hoever said that things always looked better in the morning had to be a flaming optimist, Joel decided as he stared into Cassie's face. Devoid of any makeup, her lips pale, her lashes gold-tipped and sheer as a baby's, she looked more beautiful to him than he'd ever seen her. But the carefulness of her expression, the glimpse of defiance in her enormous eyes and the overall feeling that something was slipping away made him want to shake her.

"Say that again," he commanded in a quiet voice.

Cassie flushed, color spreading up her throat and staining her cheeks. But she'd made the decision; it would stand. "I have to go back to Honolulu today. I do have a job there, Joel."

"At the *Island Breeze*."

"At the *Island Breeze*," Cassie repeated, resenting his tone. "Look, Joel, it's not as if I want to leave."

"Or that I have any say over what you do," he cut in.

Cassie drew a wispy breath. She wasn't used to fighting with Joel, and she wondered how deadly he could be. And she understood his anger. She'd sprung the announcement on him when he was unprepared, throwing it out like some kind of challenge. Never mind that she'd lain awake half the night worrying herself numb over what to do; never mind that she'd made the only decision possible—to give herself some breathing room. All that Joel could see was that she was going back to the newspaper.

In reality she'd given it a great deal of thought. She had to end her assignment in person. That made sense and Mike Casey deserved that much from her. And she needed time to think and plan. Last night's meeting with Roger was still an uncomfortable memory, one Cassie had to tackle alone.

But she'd tossed out her announcement with a suddenness that took Joel by surprise. He was in the process of dressing for a meeting with a group of bankers and local investors, his tie half-knotted, forgotten, around his neck. She saw the muscles of his throat work as he fought down his anger.

"Damn it all, Cassie. Why are you going back now? I thought . . ." He paused, gestured irritably, then eased his shoulders back slowly. She admired his restraint. Given his situation, she would have felt utterly betrayed.

"Last night," he began slowly, walking toward her. She was lost in the deep folds of his velour coffee-colored robe, a tiny figure, proud and immobile. A daring glimpse of the valley between her breasts would have made him lose sight of his intentions at another time, but Joel was a man with a purpose. "Last night you said something that I believed."

Cassie's heart fluttered. A painful pressure built between them. "I said lots of things last night."

"You know what I mean."

"I . . ."

He waited, knowing he was pushing but unable to stop. He wasn't going to let her run out on him now.

Cassie's resilience was crumbling around her. Yes, she knew what he meant, but oh how unfair! How unfair of him to throw it at her now!

"You said you loved me."

Her breath was uneven, its ragged tempo a mimicry of his. "Yes, I know."

Joel's jaw worked, but his tawny gaze never wavered. "That's not something you say every day."

"No." Her answer was barely a whisper.

"Then why in God's name are you leaving?"

She felt totally incapable of explaining. "It's only for a few days."

"Is it?" Joel's voice was hoarse with frustration. "Why don't I believe you?"

In a deep inner part of her soul, she knew he was right. She was running, and she had no way of knowing when she'd be back. Like the refrain of a carousel, one message ran round and round her brain: The truth will protect you.

She loved him but was unable to bend completely until she spoke with and learned the truth about Roger.

Irrationality was new to Joel, but suddenly, irrevocably, he was gripped by the need to pin her down, to force her to stay. "Don't go, Cassie. Don't go back to Casey, the *Breeze*. It'll only cause us more trouble and, believe me, if he can, he'll destroy whatever faith you have in me."

Cassie's lips parted. "You can't be serious."

"Can't I? Listen to me. Mike Casey is in love with my ex-wife, Tali—still," he said firmly as Cassie stared. "When I met her, she was involved with him in some way. I don't know how deeply, at least on Tali's part, but Casey's held a grudge against me ever since. He's used his newspaper as a weapon many times. Many times, Cass.

And when you told me he was your employer . . ." Joel paused and sucked in a deep breath. His mouth twisted wryly. "Well, suffice it to say it's been difficult believing in you. I thought you were one of his tools."

Cassie was confused. "I work for him . . ."

Joel saw the tight line of her brow and felt a deep, driving pain. "Cassie, I want to tell you something. This cannot all be coincidence." At her swift glance he shook his head. "No, wait. Listen. You came here to get a story. Okay, it didn't work out that way, but that's why you came. And Mike Casey put you up to it. He's after me, love. Can't you see that?"

"He gave me a job when I needed it the most," she said tonelessly.

Joel's jaw tightened. He understood loyalty. God knew he understood loyalty! But Mike Casey didn't deserve Cassie's. "He's running that newspaper into the ground. A few more years and there'll be nothing left, Cass!"

She was swept up in the urgency of his plea, for a brief instant forgetting her identity, lost in his. The fact that she could be so pliable was a shock; she'd never lost sight of herself with Kurt. Yet she didn't totally disagree with Joel. The validity of some of his statements was enough to convince her that his interests weren't entirely selfish.

But it was *her* job they were discussing.

"I have a living to make, Joel. I'm a reporter, a good one I'd like to think—one who doesn't quit on a whim."

"This is no whim," he said quickly, but Cassie raised a quelling palm.

"Let me finish. To you, maybe not. But it is to me. I *owe* Mike Casey, Joel! I owe that man more than I can possibly repay!"

His hands pressed into the thick robe at her shoulders, as if he could change her thinking by holding her perfectly still. "You don't owe him anything."

"How can you say that? You don't know what he did for me. What a wreck I was when he salvaged me! If it hadn't been for him and—" Cassie caught herself before saying Chris's name, unwilling to bring him in now. She would have told Joel last night, before Roger, but now she couldn't. Hating herself for being so unsure, she whirled away from Joel's grasp. She didn't have a clue to her next course of action.

Joel had to fight himself not to grab her again. A crazy sensation of everything falling apart haunted him. His emotional state made him miss the subtleties in their argument, and he rushed forward blindly. "Damn it, Cass! We're talking about a job, not a penance of gratitude. You've paid your dues, love. Nothing more is required."

A righteous anger flared. "And what then, Joel? What am I supposed to live on? Love?"

Suddenly they were talking about the future. A day and a half of idyllic love was fine, but a far cry from perfection. They both wanted too much more; the day of reckoning had just come sooner than either had expected.

The urge to offer her his home and life was nearly irresistible. But marriage was a heavy proposition that he wasn't ready to consider, and asking her to live with him was too little. That he knew without asking. The other solution—offering to keep her—would be an insult.

"Get a job on Maui," he heard himself say. "There's a small paper in Kahului. Less glamorous than the *Breeze*, not as well circulated and a lot more folksy, but it's a place to start. I want you with me."

And what would he do if he knew that she was not the staff reporter she had led him to believe? Cassie's background and achievements were no small feat. Joel saw a move to an even smaller paper than the *Breeze* as acceptable. Careerwise, it was impossible.

The memory of the way Mike had treated her caused her to rethink. What was happening at the paper? What new direction was Mike taking? Maybe she didn't owe him anything. Maybe they'd both done each other a favor at a strategic time and now were free to go their separate ways.

Cassie was breathing heavily, her lips quivering but determined. She didn't know how this had all started, but she wanted it to stop. "I need to talk to Mike," she said, sidestepping carefully.

It was the smallest of concessions, but Joel let it stand. There was no forcing her. Cassie was independent and capable of making her own decisions, whether they included him or not. "Think about what I've said?"

"Nothing else," she sighed. She felt exhausted and offered no resistance when Joel's arms enfolded her, pressing her cheek hard against his chest, the button of his shirt a tiny discomfort she didn't mind. His hand slipped under the velour, rubbing her shoulder, caressing her fragile bones. They had no time for lovemaking; their discussion had already made him late. It didn't matter. Touching him was reassurance enough.

Later, after Joel was gone, Cassie showered and dressed, then went back to her villa. The dim outline of her future kept stealing her thoughts from their troubled pattern. She saw a chance for happiness with Joel. The possibility grew closer to certainty every day.

So why did trust seem so hard to grasp?

A surprisingly stiff gust of wind whipped Cassie's skirt above her knees as she descended the portable stairway from the Boeing 727. She scrambled to hold it down while at the same time giving Bryan a wave of recognition. He came toward her quickly, long strides crossing the still wet pavement, a reminder that Hawaii's skies were not always sunny. A sudden, furious cloudburst went hand in hand with the sublime weather. Rarely did a storm last long, and rarely did one wreak havoc.

"You didn't have to meet me," Cassie said a trifle breathlessly as Bryan insisted on relieving her of her shoulder bag.

"I didn't have to. I wanted to." His guiding hand gently touched the small of her back, turning her toward Hawaiian Air's terminal. "Any more of these?" he asked, indicating her bag.

"A suitcase. I checked it through."

His eyebrow lifted. "Coming home?"

"Maybe."

She had neither the energy nor inclination to apprise Bryan of the reasons she'd returned to Honolulu. She herself didn't know how permanent the move was. The decision had been one of reckless impulse, brought on by a hundred different things that made little or no sense.

She'd called Bryan as an afterthought, using him as a means to pave the way for her return. Mike would undoubtedly think that meant she'd completed her assignment. Cassie's mouth quirked. Well, in a way she had.

Bryan's offer to meet her at the airport had been a surprise. He'd sounded so anxious to see her that her ever-suspicious mind had started worrying overtime. Now, seeing his unusually sober expression, she asked, "Is everything okay?"

"One hundred percent."

Something about the way he said that sounded curiously flat. She waited, but Bryan was annoyingly closed-mouthed, a fact she didn't hesitate to tell him.

"I've just got some things on my mind" was his disappointing answer.

"Well, if it's about my story, I have a right to know."

"It's not."

Cassie was helpless against his stubborn stoicism and resented the feeling. "Then why did you insist on meeting me?"

The serious curtain lifted for just an instant. "Maybe I was just dying to see you."

Cassie's eyes were trained on the baggage carousel. "I'm sure you were," she said placidly. "But that really doesn't answer my question, does it?"

Her trim suitcase slipped into the parade of luggage, infant seats, backpacks and cardboard boxes that crowded the revolving conveyor belt. Bryan leaned forward and caught it as it passed. He shifted it easily from one hand to the other and gave her a penetrating look. "It answered the question the way you should have asked it, Cassie."

She was about to ask him what that meant, but the words never reached her lips. The look on his face told her. And the look of regret on her face told him how futile his hope was.

"Joel Shepherd," he said, his long breath whistling out in anger and resignation. "Damn the man. He doesn't deserve you."

Cassie wasn't about to tackle that hornet's nest again. Instead she made a move toward the door, suddenly feeling an absurd knot tightening her throat.

"Is Mike waiting for me?" she managed. Ahead of her a swaying elderly couple in wild red and orange Hawaiian shirts trudged carefully through the concourse, stopping every few feet to squint at one of the flight monitors. Lost in paradise, Cassie mused, but any thoughts she entertained of helping them were dismissed by Bryan's guiding hand. They swerved around the couple and headed for the door to the parking lot.

"Mike's been waiting for you for days," Bryan answered pointedly. "You'd think you'd cracked Watergate by all the tension he's worked up. Good luck, sweetheart."

"Now, what's that supposed to mean?" Cassie demanded.

"Nothing. You'll see."

"Bryan, don't you dare go secretive on me now. I need you to keep me straight!"

. His firmly chiseled jaw worked tensely. Then he slanted her a smile. "But that's all you need me for, right?"

The fissure in Cassie's composure widened, her heart wrenching painfully. Bryan had to know the pressure he was applying, had to see that it was pointless. But he refused to let it go. He was asking and she had to answer.

"Don't belittle our friendship, Bryan. It's important to me. If . . . if you're expecting something else, something more, then I can't say I feel the same. I'm sorry."

The silence that followed was like the low rumble of thunder—it threatened. Cassie unconsciously braced herself for some kind of explosion. Bryan struggled, then swore pungently.

"I'm not going to tell you you're making a mistake," he said angrily. "You know that already. You also know you can't have it both ways: your job and Shepherd. Mike won't be able to understand."

Cassie felt her temper rise. The men in her life kept forcing their opinions on her, whether she asked for them or not. "Mike," she answered through her teeth, "is sounding more and more intolerant. I'm beginning to think I don't know him at all."

Bryan's unexpected silence drew a quizzical look from her. Feeling her eyes, he roused himself. "Maybe."

Cassie made an angry sound. "Bryan . . ." she warned.

"Are you in love with him?"

The conversation jumped so fast that Cassie blinked. "Joel?" she asked cautiously.

Bryan's lips tightened, but he nodded curtly. Cassie,

who was in no mood to have a full-blown argument, felt the strongest desire to lie. But Bryan deserved better.

She stared out the window, seeing the familiar buildings and hotels down Kalakaua Avenue. She could catch only glimpses of Waikiki; ostentatious hotels blocked the view. Cassie's gaze fastened sightlessly on the distinctive, winged Sheraton Waikiki; a flash of dusky pink amid palm trees was all she saw of the Royal Hawaiian. "Yes," she said simply. "I love him."

Bryan parked the car and helped her out her side, the strength of his grip on her hand evidence of his mental state. As they approached the doors to the *Breeze*'s offices, he touched her shoulder. She turned, wary, and he managed a faint smile at her expression.

"Does it ever occur to you, Cassie, that you fall in love with the wrong kind of man?"

She sighed. "Often."

"But it doesn't make any difference."

Cassie shook her head. "No, but not the way you think. Joel's nothing like Kurt. We have our problems, but he's an entirely different man. And my eyes are open. If I get hurt, it won't be the same way."

Bryan looked disgusted. "You talk so bravely. Why bother at all, Cass? Unless you're looking for heartbreak."

"I don't think you understand—"

"Oh, I understand perfectly," he interrupted, waving her words aside. "I understand a helluva lot more than you do."

Cassie heard the undercurrents there. He was hinting at something but wouldn't come straight out and say it. "Now, what does that mean?" she asked narrowly.

Bryan recognized the limits of her patience and pushed open the door. "Ask Mike," he suggested.

* * *

Cassie didn't have much time to prepare before she was hustled into Mike's office. She'd just dropped her purse at her desk and signed into her computer when her inner office line buzzed. With trepidation she lifted it to hear herself ordered into his inner sanctum at once.

Lynnette Cosgrove was already inside; the swift look of commiseration she gave Cassie was instantly masked when Mike stood up from behind his desk.

"All right," he said congenially, indicating a chair. "Sit down and tell me all about it."

Cassie did as she was told, put slightly off balance by Lynnette's inclusion. This was just between Mike and herself. She considered a moment and decided it wasn't worth fighting about. The battle would be hard enough without making a scene about Lynnette.

"Before I begin," she said carefully, conscious of how closely attuned Lynnette was (she'd leaned forward avidly, poised, her eyes sharp and eager), "I'd like to clear the air a little. I want you to know my personal position on this story."

Mike smiled. "Certainly, Cassie. This isn't an inquisition, you know."

That was a matter of debate, Cassie thought wryly. "First of all, I think you're barking up the wrong tree," she began briskly, allowing no time for interruption. "I'm convinced Joel's not personally responsible for the accident. It was just that—an accident. There's no evidence of anything else." This was said with a twinge of guilt as she had certain instincts that told her differently. "Even if there were," she amended hastily, "he's unaware of it. Our suspicions—yours and mine—are way off base."

Mike linked his hands together, steepling his fingers and pointing them in her direction. "Our information came from your brother," he reminded quietly.

Cassie was prepared for that. "Chris never mentioned Joel," she answered just as quietly. "In fact, he never mentioned anyone. It was just a feeling he had, that's all. I've been remembering his change of attitude toward Shepherd Construction and basing all my theories on that—hardly concrete evidence."

"Sometimes it's enough to start an investigation."

They were circling each other like crafty wolves, testing one another's weaknesses. Cassie, never one to attack the jugular, disliked the analogy immensely. "Which brings me to my second point—or, rather, question. Those are my reasons for going after Joel. What are yours?"

Mike's spine stiffened. "The same. It's news, Cass. Real news, and news sells."

Cassie curved her nails around the arm of her chair. "What about Tali Paccaro-Shepherd, Mike?"

Mike moved sharply, throwing a glance in Lynnette's direction as if he suddenly wished she weren't listening in. Lynnette arched one thin eyebrow but said nothing.

In an even, deadly tone, he said, "Joel Shepherd's done a number on you. You're starting to mix up your priorities."

"Not me, Mike."

Out of her peripheral vision Cassie saw Lynnette's head jerk in surprise, and she felt a brief flash of triumph. She wasn't about to be cowed by Mike's interrogation, nor would she change her mind. It was about time they both understood that.

But her triumph was short-lived, for Mike gave up his treacherous little game of parry and thrust. He nodded his head at her, as if he'd been proved right on some issue they'd previously disagreed on.

"I take it you aren't going to reveal what he said in the interview, then."

"I didn't get the interview, Mike."

The smile that touched his lips said he didn't believe her. "Where's the cassette?"

Cassie felt cold panic. "It's . . . in my purse. I'll bring it to you." She looked him right in the eye and lied with everything she was worth. "The tape's blank. I didn't even use it."

What was the point in explaining that all she'd gotten were a few confessions on the waste of his marriage? It was hardly newsworthy. Its only benefit would be to salve Mike's ego, and that was no benefit at all. Cassie wished she'd had the sense to destroy the tape after all.

"So what did you and Shepherd talk about? You must know something!"

Cassie seethed. So far she'd been congratulating herself on the way she'd dealt with Mike's insulting attitude, but she was reaching her limit. She wasn't a child, although it certainly wasn't evident from the way he treated her. "I can do without your sarcasm, I think."

Mike sighed. "Look, Cassie. I'm trying very hard, really. But I'm feeling totally frustrated! Since when do you up and decide the outcome of a story before the end? That's not fair to any of us. We need facts, not wishful thinking! This is real, for God's sake!" He shook his head sadly, as if expecting better from her. "There are no fairy tale endings."

Cassie was quiet. The tiny clock on Mike's desk ticked off the seconds. She didn't know how to tell him he was wasting his time; she was immune to this particular song and dance. He was not going to make her continue this assignment by loading on a pile of guilt. She knew what she was capable of. And she knew what she wasn't capable of.

"I want off the assignment, Mike," she said at length, determination in the tilt of her chin, in the direct blue of her eyes. "I didn't get the interview you wanted because I can't. I don't want to. I am too personally involved."

"Because of Chris?" he threw in swiftly.

"No."

The air was loaded with expectation. Cassie could almost breathe it. Mike was waiting, so was Lynnette. She shrugged, her cavalier attempt not coming off quite right. "Because of Joel."

"Damn it!" Mike's hand slammed onto his desk; the clock rocked to its side and several pencils rolled off the edge. Cassie reached forward to catch one, then froze in the act. "Damn it! You're crazy! Absolutely crazy! Just what the hell do you mean by 'personally involved,' Cassie? Sexually?"

"That's not your business, Mike." Cassie's voice was taut and angry.

But Mike was angrier. "The hell it isn't!" he exploded. "I sent you there, to him, to get a story, and you come back with this 'personally involved' nonsense that doesn't wash. Hardly a professional job, Cassie."

"The whole thing was hardly professional—"

"The whole thing was an assignment that you refuse to complete! Why? Because you've succumbed to the much-vaunted charms of Joel Shepherd!" Mike sat back heavily, his fury waning. Cassie clamped her lips shut and forced herself not to point out the flaws in his arguments. He, too, was personally involved—with Joel's ex-wife.

"Can't you see what he's doing?" Mike asked wearily. "He's blinding you. Putting on a charming facade to do just that—charm the pants off you!"

Cassie winced at Mike's lewd message. "Now, get this straight—"

He leaned forward abruptly and jabbed a finger in front of her face. "No, *you* get this straight. I like you. I care what happens to you. I *cared* what happened to Tali!'' He stopped, watching her reaction. Cassie was rigid, her breath frozen. She thought Mike was going to break down and confess his deepest feelings, but after a long, painful pause, he simply said, ''Don't let it happen to you.''

It was Lynnette who stirred first after Mike's impassioned speech. Cassie couldn't. She was swamped by feelings: anger, annoyance, regret, helplessness. One moment she wanted to shriek at Mike, the next she wanted to reassure him. Life was far too complicated.

''Bring me the cassette,'' Mike ordered gruffly as Cassie, feeling her unspoken dismissal, headed for the door. Lynnette was already there.

Cassie could only nod. She'd made her position pretty clear. Mike would have to take it from here.

''Oh, and Cass . . .'' The frown etched on his face made him look extremely weary. ''Do me a favor, will you? Don't tip him off to the investigation.''

Cassie's hand was on the knob. She gripped it with sudden emotion. ''Does that mean it's ongoing?'' she asked cautiously.

Mike's stare was steady. ''You're off the assignment, Cass. Maybe it's better if you don't know.''

The feeling of being a traitor to all sides weighed heavily, but Cassie was powerless to change newspaper policy. ''I won't say anything,'' she promised, feeling a steel gate close on her future.

She spent the rest of the afternoon convincing herself that it couldn't matter either way, because Joel had nothing to hide.

Joel stripped the tie from his neck as he strode across the carpeted anteroom to his office. He gave Penny, his secretary, a brief wave of acknowledgment but didn't break stride. She knew him well enough to divine his mood: no calls, no interruptions, no problems—nothing.

A pulsebeat throbbed in the back of his head. A warning. He couldn't ignore the signal nor the knowledge that he had very little time to set it right before a full-blown migraine ensued.

His jacket came off next, and he lay down on the leather-covered couch against the back wall. Rest. Don't move. And don't think.

But the last—and probably most important—order was impossible to follow. His brain was a whirl of information and messages, a storm of impressions that left him feeling unsettled and tense.

The meeting at the bank had started it. Five investors from the mainland, and not one of them seemed eager to part with their carefully earned money. He'd known it the instant he'd walked into the room. It was a situation he'd met often in the past.

The big question this time was Why?

He could have understood it before, when he was still scrimping and saving and sweating each expenditure. But now? His success ratio was extraordinarily high. And the hell of it was that they'd requested the meeting, not he!

He'd had a prickling along his nerves that boded trouble. The banker who'd arranged the meeting was perplexed. His speech had started out firm and decisive, filled with high expectations and assurance. When it was received with stony silence, he hesitated, wavering. Joel knew right then he'd lost.

It wasn't that he was in dire need of their funding. True, being in a business that tied up tons of capital, at times he found himself cash poor. But that was expected. Always—*always*—he had to seek outside financing. The new project on Molokai—the next island expected to attract the ever

increasing influx of tourists, as yet fairly undeveloped—
needed a stunning amount of investor capital.

But they'd come to him! So why the shutout?

Joel moved his neck gingerly, wishing he could trust his
head to hang in there and allow him to have a drink. Sparks
of pain shot along his nerves, and he froze instantly. So
much for that idea.

He'd been troubled about the meeting and had dwelled on
it during his late morning rendezvous with Roger at the
hotel. Possibly because of lingering anxieties over the
offbeat encounter with Roger the night before, or maybe
because of the memory of Cassie's not too subtle questions,
or more probably, both. Whatever, the headache had started
then.

He'd been anxious to get away, and Roger had seemed
just as eager to be alone. They'd parted quickly, but Joel
had been snagged by one of the architects who'd worked on
both of his most expensive projects, the Maui Paccaro and
the Polynesian Village. He'd listened to the man's worries
with only half an ear. The architect was an unbridled
alarmist whom Joel had soothed over and over again. When
he finally could, Joel had escaped from the man's real and
imaginary problems, asking himself if this man was really
worth it. Roger didn't think so. He'd wanted to boot him for
a long time. But then Roger didn't always make the
decisions Joel wanted.

His biggest mistake was missing lunch. When a potential
migraine threatened he never, never, missed a meal. But
today couldn't be helped and now he was paying for it.
Damn it all! He thought he'd licked these blasted headaches!

He closed his eyes and tried to concentrate on not moving
a single muscle. Memories of his worst attacks kept him
still. The headache was bad enough, the nausea worse. If he

could just get through this without an unexpected trauma . . .

By far the worst shock to his system, however, had been returning home and finding the note from Cassie. He'd lied to himself all morning, believing she would change her mind. But her message was brief and to the point: She had to go back.

The worry this had caused him was something he didn't want to analyze too closely. His feelings were dangerously tied up in that woman. He had the urge to control her but knew it was the worst and weakest thing he could do, that is, if she let him.

He questioned if she would come back.

The telephone on his desk buzzed faintly. For a second Joel didn't move, more stunned that Penny hadn't gotten the right message than annoyed. It rang two more times before he rose from the couch. Swaying slightly, he realized he wasn't lost yet. Another hour or so of rest and he'd be past the worst.

"Yes?" he demanded harshly, pressing the intercom button. He would have been smart to take the afternoon off, but Cassie's note had depressed him, driving him from his house.

"Sorry to disturb you, but Mrs. Paccaro is on line two. She just wants to be assured that Scott got home safely." Penny paused as Joel absorbed this disturbing news. "She sounds upset," she apologized once more.

Joel didn't bother to answer, he was already picking up the other line. "When was Scott supposed to be home?" he asked his former mother-in-law tersely, forging straight to the heart of her anxiety.

He heard her breath catch. She let out a faint cry. "Yesterday, Joel. He said you were picking him up at the airport yesterday!"

Chapter Nine

Cassie touched the space bar of the computer, thought about what she'd just written, then erased it. In frustration she signed off. Her crisp, incisive style was missing, and the article on government funding that had widened one of Honolulu's busiest streets by adding a greenway in the center, thereby eliminating local parking and putting the surrounding store owners out of business, was a terrible hodge-podge. The wit and irony she was famous for were not evident. Instead the story circled around the key points and ended up drab and uninteresting—words on paper, nothing more.

Cassie hoped her lack of imagination was a passing thing. Her mind was occupied by more pressing problems. She still hadn't given Mike the cassette recorder, nor had she destroyed the tape. She intended to hand the recorder over just before she left, minus the tape, so that he couldn't harangue her the rest of the day about her lack of professionalism. There was no way she was going to put ammunition in his hands, and seeing there was no sane reason to hang onto it, Cassie pulled the recorder from her purse, flipping out the tiny tape.

She weighed it in her hand. What if there had been something incriminating on it? What would she have done then?

In all honesty she couldn't say. She fiercely believed in Joel's innocence, yet she sensed other things, things he wouldn't talk about. But his reticence could be for a hundred different reasons.

The magnetic ribbon was still looped out from when she'd yanked on it at Joel's. It was crinkled and useless-looking but Cassie felt compelled to ruin it further. She searched through her drawer and found a pair of scissors. One quick snip, and it was severed forever.

The instant it was done she felt like a fool. Who would really care? There was nothing newsworthy on the tape; there never had been. Even Mike's smoldering antipathy wouldn't allow him to print anything recorded on it. He was too good a newspaper man to do something so pointless.

So why all the paranoia?

"Destroying the evidence?"

Lynnette's voice so close to her ear caused Cassie to gasp in surprise. Her hand closed protectively around the tape and she turned a startled head to meet Lynnette's inquiring gaze.

"You nearly scared me out of a year's growth," she accused, her cheekbones coloring in anger.

"Sorry." Lynnette shrugged lightly. Her eyes traveled to the ruined tape, observing the smoothly cut ends of the ribbon slipping through Cassie's fingers. She picked up the scissors. "For someone who didn't get an interview you seem awfully worried about what someone might find on that tape."

Cassie leveled her a look. "You want the truth?"

"You mean you didn't give it to Mike?"

There was something about Lynnette that grated on Cassie's nerves. Cassie paused, controlling her anger, then said, "Yes, I told Mike the truth. I didn't get that interview. All the tape had on it was a private conversation between myself and Joel. I figured Mike wouldn't need to hear it after all. When I listened to it, I realized there was nothing there of importance, not even a hint about the accident."

Lynnette was frowning down at her beautifully manicured nails. "Have you ever thought you might not be the right judge of that?"

"No." Cassie was definite. "There was nothing there. It was just about his son, Scott, and a little about Tali. Some about how he got into the business. Really, Lynnette"— Cassie turned away, her voice dismissive—"it was all a waste of time."

Lynnette had been leaning against the edge of Cassie's desk. Now she straightened, smoothing down her skirt. "If you say so," she muttered, unconvinced.

Cassie's breath came out in a frustrated rush. "Why does everyone around here treat me like I don't know my own mind. I'm the only one who does!"

A tired smile lifted Lynnette's lips. "Because you trust the man, Cassie. All that shows is that you can be fooled." As Cassie stiffened with affront she waved a pacifying hand. "Relax. We're all fooled at one time or another. Once I trusted someone," she went on, startling Cassie, "a man. I knew deep down I shouldn't have, but I just wanted to so badly. Know what I mean?"

The room felt suddenly close. Cassie's pulse hammered, the uncomfortable doubt that refused to be dislodged pricking up its ears at Lynnette's words. There were too many corollaries for her to ignore. Cassie waited in dread for the rest, and Lynnette's words began spilling faster, like a pent-up confession.

"I had a story to do. He was involved. When he learned I was part of the press, he offered to help me." Lynnette's mouth twisted ruefully, bitterly. "I had all this evidence pointing right at him! But I couldn't believe it. I wouldn't." She stared into Cassie's distressed eyes, hers for an instant shadowed by old misery. Her voice was flat when she continued. "He used me, Cass. Used the best part of me."

Cassie swallowed against a dry throat. "Don't think that way, Lynnette."

At the empathy in Cassie's voice, Lynnette moved sharply. Her face hardened. Within seconds it was as if it had never happened. She gave Cassie a sympathetic, almost regretful look. "Listen, we all have to do what we have to do to survive, right? You go your way, I'll go mine." She tapped her fist lightly on Cassie's desk and added, "I can live with myself."

And with that obscure message as a closing thought, she turned one hip and moved away, leaving Cassie with the feeling she'd missed something of vast importance.

An evening alone was something Cassie thought she needed badly, but after several hours of her own company she began to wonder if she was right. She felt so up in the air about everything. A few weeks ago her life had been unhappy but staid and turning on a comfortable schedule. Now she knew some happiness but her life was in turmoil. She didn't know where or how to begin to sort it through.

Even unpacking her suitcase gave her uncomfortable moments. She hadn't completely told Bryan the truth. She had left some things at the villa on Maui; she hadn't checked out. It was like a fragile link between herself and Joel, one she couldn't break. If she quit her job, she would need a place to stay . . .

The thought was a revelation, freezing her hand in the act of folding her clothes. When she'd argued with Joel that morning, she hadn't really given serious consideration to quitting; she'd been far more concerned with his opinions on Mike. But now?

Cassie sat down on the edge of the bed, hunching her shoulders against the frightening self-realization. Would she really give up everything for him? Everything? That was so incredibly foolhardy she hated thinking she was actually capable of it. All those warnings—from Bryan, Mike, Lynnette . . . Was she reckless enough to dismiss them without a backward glance?

No.

Cassie stood up again, the painful doubt deep inside too huge to ignore. First she had to know everything, every last little thing about that accident. It would be like a purge to have her beliefs hardened to reality.

She thought about confronting Joel with all her theories and fears. No. The chance of success was practically zero. She needed something more concrete than a few words of assurance.

With a grimace Cassie realized she was back at square one. Well, not quite. She loved Joel; now she was on his side. But convincing him of that while sleuthing for the truth was an impossible task.

There was a way, however—Roger Caldwell. Last night's meeting had shown her that he was a likely candidate for information. Without Joel around to protect him, Cassie had the feeling Roger would say more than he meant to.

And Joel?

She believed he was innocent but felt something was going on somewhere. All she had to do was start searching.

It didn't occur to her that she was doing just what Mike

Casey wanted, planning a way to dig into Shepherd Construction. For Cassie it was a personal quest that had nothing to do with newspapers or assignments. This was for her and for her alone.

Her doorbell sounded as she was preparing a light meal of tossed green salad and sourdough bread. Frowning, she wiped her hands on the small apron that covered her skirt and blouse, then as an afterthought untied it and draped it over the counter. She wasn't expecting anyone, but her state of mind was such that she wanted to be prepared just in case . . .

"Bryan!" Cassie's stomach instantly fluttered nervously. He never just dropped in uninvited. Looking at his face, she had a feeling of impending doom. He'd hinted at trouble that afternoon. She knew without being told that he'd come to explain.

"Sit down," she invited, gesturing to one of her kitchen chairs. "Have you eaten? All I've got is salad . . ."

"No. Thanks." Bryan hesitated. "I'm meeting Mike later for dinner. You go ahead. I only came over for a few minutes."

Cassie was in the process of tying on her apron again, but she paused. Bryan looked like a man struggling with a monumental problem. She suddenly couldn't wait any longer. She had to know what it was.

"Why come at all?" she asked. "Unless it's something important."

His eyes flickered in her direction, but his lips compressed in an obstinate line. He picked up her salad fork, twiddled it, then realizing what he was doing, put it back carefully. Cassie watched this, half angry, half amused. Was he afraid to confide in her? Or was his male ego injured because she hadn't waited for him to unfold his story?

Cassie sighed, pulled a bottle of chilled wine from the

refrigerator and plucked two glasses from the cupboard. Without a word she poured them each a glass, then sat down across from him, putting a silent pressure on him, refusing to budge until he opened up.

Bryan shot her a swift look, accepted the cold glass, then cleared his throat. "I know you probably think I came here to lecture you again."

"If you did, you're wasting your time, but no, I don't think that's why you're here."

That got his full attention. He stared at her. "Why do you think I came?" he wondered.

Cassie's impatience surfaced. "I have no idea. But you look as if you're full of news—none of it good—and you can't decide where to begin. Stop stalling, Bryan. I'm ready to listen."

He rubbed his hand across his jaw, and Cassie read the indecision on his face. Finally he took a long swallow of the wine and set the glass down with the air of someone who's decided an important matter. "All right. There are some things happening at the office I don't like."

"Like what?"

He shook his head. "I don't know. Just feelings, mostly. Mike seems"—he broke off, searching for the right word—"under a lot of pressure. He's tense."

Cassie sipped her wine, savoring its cool tartness. "I've noticed."

"There's a rumor floating that he's having trouble making ends meet, Cass. Circulation's way down."

This wasn't any real news; circulation had been decreasing all year. But it triggered a thought in Cassie's mind, something Joel had said about Mike and the *Breeze*— "Mike Casey's a scandalmonger from way back . . . He's running that newspaper into the ground."

"It's the recession," Cassie answered automatically,

falling back on the well-worn excuse everyone used when their business failed.

"Then how come Shepherd hasn't been affected? New construction should be the first thing to fall off, and he's been making money hand over fist!" For a moment his bitterness over Joel Shepherd made his lips tighten, then he exhaled and sat back, his mouth wry. "Sorry. I really don't have anything against Shepherd personally. Not like Mike, anyway. It's just the man's so damn lucky!"

"I don't know if it's all luck," Cassie disagreed cautiously. "Joel's a hard worker."

Bryan snorted. "And a smart operator." He looked penitent once more. "Sorry again. I guess I just don't like the idea of him with you. I still don't trust him."

"Or anyone by the sound of it. Tell me more about Mike and the paper."

Bryan's eyes narrowed thoughtfully. He looked at Cassie's intent expression and considered. Not a man to heed unfounded rumors, he felt the urge to warn her. He shook his head. "Ever get the feeling there's something going on that no one's telling you about?"

"Always," Cassie answered dryly.

"Mike's up to something, Cass. Some kind of last ditch attempt to put things right with the paper."

"Financially?"

"I think so."

Bryan's anxiety was infectious. "And that worries you," she suggested, putting out careful feelers. She couldn't see that there was any problem with Mike getting alternate financing, but he'd been acting so strange lately that she wasn't about to dismiss it altogether. "What kind of financing, Bryan?"

Cassie's tense voice penetrated Bryan's preoccupied mind. He made a deprecatory sound and leaned back in his chair. "Maybe I'm wrong. Hell, I'm no reporter! I've just been getting bad vibes ever since you took the Shepherd assignment."

"What kind of vibes? And I'm off the Shepherd assignment, by the way."

Bryan blinked. "He pulled you off?"

"I pulled myself off. I couldn't go on with it, Bryan. Not the way I feel."

He digested that silently. "So what are you doing now . . . at the paper?"

"Marking time." Cassie lifted one shoulder. "I don't think Mike knows what to do with me. He asked me not to let Joel know that there might be an investigation."

"Now that's interesting," Bryan said, his eyebrows rising. "And are you going to keep mum?"

Cassie nodded. "Joel has nothing to hide and, to be frank, I'll be glad to get the air cleared once and for all. There's too much speculation. It's almost claustrophobic."

"Cassie."

"What?" The tone of Bryan's voice had altered, and Cassie automatically steeled herself for what was to come. She was developing a sixth sense about trouble, she told herself wryly. Maybe because there'd been so much of it.

"Are you sure, really sure, Shepherd's not involved?"

Her pulse jumped, and she hoped her fear didn't show on her face. "Of course I'm sure," she answered in a neutral voice. She was, wasn't she?

"What if . . . Mike should uncover something? How would you feel then?"

She smiled, showing her even white teeth. "I'll just have to cross that bridge when I come to it, won't I?"

His gaze never left hers. "You'd better make sure you know how to swim."

If she'd been more sure, if she'd really had the conviction of Joel's innocence that she purported to have, if she weren't inwardly afraid, then she would have jumped all over Bryan for his superciliousness. But she couldn't. So instead she defused the bomb. "You were talking about Mike's financing for the *Breeze*."

"I was talking about you."

"Don't, Bryan. Really. I've had enough." She got up, grabbed another plate and fork and placed it in front of him. She kept her eyes averted, wishing Bryan would stop balancing their friendship on the fine edge of romance. She wasn't interested, and she had no other way to tell him that.

They ate in silence. Cassie finished her wine and poured herself another. She had polished off half the glass when she felt it suddenly go right to her head, blurring the edges of her awareness. She set the glass down. This was not a time to miss the subtleties of conversation. She needed her wits about her.

Then, because it suddenly seemed the right thing to say, she said, "I've been thinking about quitting."

Bryan, his glass at his lips, suddenly put it back down. The seriousness of his expression surprised Cassie. She'd expected denouncements, even jealous raging, but he simply said, "I think that could be a very good idea."

"Why?" Cassie's head cleared instantly. "For Pete's sake, Bryan! It's time you came straight out and told me what's wrong. And I don't care if it's all suspicion and rumor. Tell me!"

Bryan moistened his lips. "Look, Cass, I probably shouldn't have come here at all with a lot of half-baked theories." He stopped at her heated expression, and his hand came up, warding off the angry protestations hovering on her tongue. "Okay, okay. Mike seems different these days—I'd go so far as to say desperate. Haven't you felt that?"

Had she? She wasn't completely certain. Part of her problem with Mike these days was because of Joel. An innate honesty made her admit that she'd been partially turned against him by Joel's opinions. "He's been tense," she agreed cautiously. "He's a busy man, Bryan."

"I think it's a whole lot more. Yesterday a group of men in three-piece suits showed up, and Mike hustled them into his office."

"The financing?" Cassie guessed.

"I'd bet on it. But after they left, Mike looked so relieved."

Cassie, sensing she was approaching the heart of what was bothering Bryan, pointed out the obvious. "Well, he would be relieved if the deal went through. It sounds like he needs money."

"But that's just it," Bryan said vehemently. "He looked too relieved. Almost smug. Like the cat who swallowed—"

The soft buzz of Cassie's kitchen phone stopped Bryan in mid-sentence. It disturbed Cassie, too. It broke the tense camaraderie that had developed. She determined to dispense with whomever was on the other end of the line as quickly as possible.

"Hello?" Her voice was crisp, brusque.

"Cassie? It's Joel. I've been sitting here for hours, debating on whether to call you or not, and need won out over pride. I need you. Tonight. Is there anything I can do or say to get you to come back here?"

Cassie's mouth opened in surprise. She was overcome by a sudden tide of love and desire that left her speechless. When had it happened, this feeling of total commitment and love? And how could it happen with so many things unanswered between them?

"Joel . . ." she responded at last, a trifle unsteadily. "Uh, tonight?" She was suddenly dying to see him. "I don't know if I could catch a flight this late." She felt Bryan's anger and turned her shoulder, knowing she should be stronger, not wanting to be. There was a tightness to Joel's voice that spoke of strain. Because of her? Her heart leaped at the fantasy that he was desperate to see her.

His breathing sounded irregular. She was about to ask if anything was wrong when he interrupted abruptly, "Scott's gone. He left Hawaii yesterday and told his grandparents that I was picking him up at the airport. No one's seen him since."

"Oh, Joel." Cassie sat down hard, her heart thumping. Bryan, her own feelings for Joel, problems at the paper— everything faded to instant oblivion. Her mind raced ahead, following a terrible route of its own. Kidnapping. Joel was a wealthy, well-known man in the islands. The idea, once implanted, refused to be dislodged.

Her hand shaking, she reached for the telephone book. "I'll get there as soon as I can," she heard herself say. She didn't care if she had to swim now. The need in Joel's voice drew her as if Scott were her own child. "I'll be there. Wait for me."

"What the hell do you think you're doing?" Bryan demanded as soon as Cassie hung up the phone.

She scanned the fine type of the telephone pages, only half hearing. "I've gotta go, Bryan. Joel's son—"

"I don't give a damn what it is!" he roared. "Cass, for God's sake! He crooks his little finger and you come running!"

She raised her head, befuddled. For a moment she couldn't understand why Bryan should be so angry. "His son's missing," she said calmly. "He's missing. Joel's sick with worry."

Bryan's face dropped. "Does that mean you have to fly to Maui, Cass?"

"Yes." Was there really any question?

Bryan Kerr was not a reporter, nor did he consider

himself the type of man who had insight into human nature. If he wanted something, he generally just bulldozed his way in until he achieved it. But once in a while he knew defeat, real defeat, and then he backed off gracefully. Her words hadn't had any effect on him; he'd believed Cassie would get over Joel Shepherd as soon as she was apart from him for a while. But the look on her face just now—worry and love and even selflessness—was the signal of his own defeat.

"I'll drive you to the airport," he said softly, taking the phone book from her nerveless fingers.

"Bryan, you don't have—"

"Shhh. Yes, I do. Come on. If we hurry, we can catch the last flight on Hawaiian Air."

Cassie had the presence of mind to ask Bryan what he'd been leading up to before Joel's call, but he just wagged his head and told her she had more important things to worry about. There was no arguing with the truth, so she just sat back and waited, the seconds interminably long hours, the minutes eons.

She was lucky enough to catch the nine o'clock flight and even luckier to find a helpful car rental agency with a lot right next to Kahului airport. Precious minutes were saved, and finally she was driving the road that bisected east and west Maui, the road to Joel's house.

It didn't bother Cassie that she was back to the same situation she'd escaped from mere hours before. Now everything was different. Nothing mattered but finding Scott. Nothing was important except helping Joel.

It was funny, Cassie thought detachedly, how ordinary and familiar everything looked even in a crisis. She'd half expected some visible change, but as she hurried up the walk to Joel's home the house and grounds were just as she remembered. An outside light told her he was waiting. She shivered in its amber glow. Had he heard any more news?

One look at Joel and Cassie's heart plummeted. The strain on his face made her want to cry and, pushing other thoughts and fears aside, she reached for him. His arms crushed her to him; the feel, the smell of him, the tension that ran like a current from him to her—all of it made her clutch him desperately, wanting to give, hoping she could make it right.

"Any news?" she queried, her voice muffled against his shirt.

"No."

His chin was next to her temple, his cheek pressed against her hair. Cassie suddenly noticed he was trembling. She pulled back gently, concern written on her face. "Are you telling me the truth, Joel? Please, please tell me the truth. I don't need to be protected."

His mouth quirked in irony. "There's no news, Cass. Really. And no news can be good news," he added without the slightest trace of humor.

"But you're expecting the worst, aren't you? You're trembling."

Slowly he released her from the warmth of his arms, then he pressed his finger hard against his left temple. "It's this blasted headache," he muttered. "Damn it all. I can't function."

Cassie was perplexed, then worried, then downright frightened as she followed him down the hall to the solàrium. The careful way he moved and the sweat that beaded on his forehead as he cautiously maneuvered himself onto the couch terrified her. "What is it, Joel?" she cried. "Tell me."

His sigh was one of utter disgust. Eyes closed, perfectly still, he said wearily, "It's a migraine. I get them once in a while, but I thought I'd licked them." He slowly opened his eyes and looked at her. "Lately they've been back with a vengeance."

Cassie felt helpless. She perched herself carefully beside him. "Because of me?"

"No. I don't know why exactly. Sometimes pressure brings them on, or lack of sleep, or skipping meals." There were deep shadows under his eyes and a gaunt, pained look around his mouth. His pallor showed beneath his tan. "With me it's usually pressure."

Cassie reached for an afghan tossed over a wicker chair, but Joel waved it away. "I'll get up in a minute."

"No you won't," she said severely, amazed that he would even try. She was no expert, but she could easily read the signs of acute pain. "Relax. My God, Joel. There's no reason to get up, especially on my account."

"But there is because of Scott." Joel moved in frustration. "Where the hell is he?"

"Have the police been notified?" Cassie asked.

"Yes, but it's been just a little over twenty-four hours, so they've just begun to search. I think they're talking to Tali's parents now. I've tried to get hold of Tali, but she's not home."

Joel stared at the ceiling. "Actually I'm more angry than worried. This is so like Scott. He's so damned arrogant and selfish!"

And you're worried sick, Cassie thought silently. He was justifiably angry, but no matter what he said, his fear was real and overpowering. He started to struggle to get up, and she placed a firm, gentle hand on his chest, pushing him back. "Lots of teenagers are arrogant and selfish." His hair was rumpled, as if he'd been lying down before she arrived. It was impossible for Cassie not to push it back, the tenderness in her caress more explicit than words. "It comes with the age, Joel, like rebellion and an interest in sex. Thank God we only have to go through it once!''

Joel focused on her again, amazed. Cassie had a source of strength he'd never found in a woman before. She was flexible and had incredible insight into Scott's problems, though she'd never had children of her own. She was fair when unfairness would have been understood and accepted. Feeling the vast disloyalty of it, Joel wished Scott's mother had been Cassie, not Tali.

"You want children, don't you, Cassie?" Joel cradled her face in his palms and pulled her close, so their faces were bare inches from one another. His words brought a flicker of surprise, almost alarm, to her eyes. "You should be a mother," he whispered intently.

Cassie's heart somersaulted. His uncanny way of reading into her soul worried her. He knew her so well, maybe too well. She took a careful step into uncharted waters. "With me marriage comes first," she whispered back.

It was a statement of fact, not a condition she was imposing, but she half expected Joel to take it as such. There was a vulnerability in his face she hadn't seen before—perhaps because of the migraine—that made it easier for her to speak about such potentially explosive issues. And after all, he'd brought it up.

Joel's gaze was locked to her. He picked his words carefully. "I haven't been thinking about marriage. I don't know that I'm ready for that again. Are you?"

Cassie's breath caught in her throat. Her head was rushing. "I—I don't know."

There was the tiniest airspace between their lips. With a minimum of effort Joel closed the gap, his mouth melting into hers, his hands sliding around her, down her back. Passion simmered just below the surface, but Cassie moved gingerly, conscious of Joel's headache.

She kissed his mouth and face, aware of a new dimension between them, an understanding that went beyond the moment. She sensed his need of her, and she wanted to give. It was like a blossoming self-realization; she loved being needed.

Joel accepted the warmth of her body against his passively, letting Cassie make all the moves. She witnessed an emotion she dared not really consider in the murky depths of his eyes. Love? Was it truly possible Joel cared for her as deeply as she cared for him?

"What brought this headache on?" Cassie questioned softly, thinking she needed to slow down the flickers of desire and deal with the very real issue of his health. "Scott?"

Joel flashed back on the events of the day. "No. Scott's disappearance just brought it to a head." His lips curved. "Actually, you were partly to blame. Your note was very disillusioning."

"I'm back." Her eyes probed his, her priorities suddenly falling into place. "To stay."

The only sound was the breathy hum of the overhead fan. Joel sucked air in between his teeth, hardly noticing that the pain of his migraine had faded to a dull, bearable ache. "What happened in Honolulu?" he asked.

Cassie sat up, Joel's hands falling from her back to his sides. She looked out at the ocean then back to the man she loved, aware that she was moving too fast, angry she couldn't run with her instincts. "I took a stand against Mike. It may cost me my job." She paused. "Then again, I might just quit."

She'd drawn herself up in a regal pose. Her look challenged him to say anything, anything at all. It had been her decision, not his.

"Know something?" Joel's finger traced the line of her chin, then traveled to the softness of her mouth.

"What?" There was a slight resentment in her voice. She half expected him to congratulate himself on a job well done.

"You have the most luscious mouth."

Cassie felt a warm, melting feeling, a kind of security—like coming home. Her lips curved, unknowingly seductive. "You have a way of winning an argument," she scolded.

"What argument?" His hands parted the neckline of her blouse, his thumbs exploring the hollow of her throat. He pressed his mouth to her throat, felt her heartbeat against his lips.

She felt him shudder as he muttered hoarsely, "Oh, Cassie!"

Neither was in the frame of mind to make love, but a driving, aching passion held them together. The desire to curl up beside Joel and shut the world out was very strong, but other pressing problems couldn't be ignored.

His voice muffled, Joel said, "I think I'd better call the Paccaros again, they've probably—"

The telephone on the bar rang, and Joel and Cassie both looked at it for a frozen second. Then, with lightning speed, Joel was upon it, one long arm grabbing the receiver.

"Yes?" he answered tersely, and Cassie leaned against the back of the couch, trembling.

The succession of emotions on Joel's face was indescribable. Cassie clutched her hands together with bone-crushing force. She was afraid to guess what had happened.

"Damn it all, Tali!" Joel suddenly exploded. "Couldn't you have let me know? We've been half out of our minds. Your parents—" There was a long pause during which Cassie could hear a rapid voice firing back at Joel. She saw him flex his fingers very slowly. Then, "How'd he get there? Who paid for the ticket?"

Cassie was blessedly relieved. Scott was in Los Angeles

with his mother. But as soon as she absorbed this good news, anger took over. Like Joel, she was outraged that Tali hadn't called.

As Joel listened to his ex-wife's explanations, his face set in cold fury. Whatever was being said obviously wasn't something he wanted to hear, and Cassie held her breath, seeing a rather frightening and deadly side of Joel. His voice was quiet when he finally answered, an unspoken rage behind the words. "You do whatever you have to, Tali. Fob this off on me, buy another lawyer, try to get a judge in your pocket. But understand this: You're gonna have one helluva fight! Whatever it takes, Tali. I'll fight dirty for my son. I'll bring up things you'd rather forget. I'll crush you."

Cassie listened in growing horror. It was obvious that Tali was threatening for custody, but Joel's granite face and cold demeanor took her aback. Flashes of remembered warnings crossed her mind. There was the hardness to Joel's nature that she'd wondered about before; it worried her.

Yet didn't he have the right to be furious with Tali?

"Put him on the phone. Yes. Right now." Another long pause, then angrily, "I don't care, Tali! Get him. Put him on the phone, or I'm flying to the mainland tonight!"

For just a second Cassie's eyes collided with Joel's. His were dark and full of fury, his jaw taut and thrusting, the set of his body one of a man prepared for battle. Cassie could only offer silent commiseration. She wasn't sure how to deal with this Joel, how to offer comfort or advice.

"Scott." The terse acknowledgment of his son made Cassie's heart hurt. Father and son were poles apart in understanding.

Joel shifted his weight, running a weary hand around the back of his neck, his shoulders locked in tension. "Maybe you ought to explain why you decided to fly to L.A. without telling anyone. Maybe you owe that to me.''

Whatever Scott's explanation was, it went on and on. Cassie thought she heard sullen undertones but wasn't sure. She started to feel uncomfortable listening in. Worrying about Scott's welfare was one thing; witnessing a father-son battle was quite another.

Cassie left Joel alone, disappearing quietly down the hall to give him some privacy. Seeking a place to retreat to, she happened upon his office. She stopped just inside the threshold, looking around with interest.

A bookcase lined one wall, filled mostly with paperbacks. The lower shelves were cluttered with papers and blueprints, notations of every kind scribbled along the margins. The desk was strictly utilitarian: small, sturdy and metal. Neat stacks of notes and bills sat beside an impressive pile of legal-looking documents. Cassie picked one up abstractedly.

It was a proposal for a shopping plaza on Molokai. She scanned it with interest, flipping through the pages until she found the architect's drawings. A piece of blue paper stuck between the pages fluttered to the floor and landed by her feet. Cassie stooped to pick it up. She read it once, then filled with dread, she read it a second time. Words glared at her—''. . . need to reinforce east building . . . far more risk than hotel . . . faultline . . . this requires immediate attention . . . can't afford another accident.''

''Cassie?''

She whirled around, the note burning her fingers. Joel's voice came from down the hall. With nerveless hands she replaced it, memorizing the architect's name—Daniel.

''I'm—I'm in your office.'' Hoping her expression wouldn't give her away, she put an expectant look on her face. ''What happened?'' she asked when Joel appeared.

Joel cast a swift glance around the room. "Couldn't you guess? Scott's been in L.A. since yesterday. Tali wants custody and Scott . . ." A flicker of hopelessness crossed his face. "Scott wants to live with her."

With the distinct feeling of being in the wrong place at the wrong time, Cassie said helplessly, "I'm sorry."

Joel sucked in a ragged breath. "Well, it can't be helped now. I called the authorities and told them where he was. At least we know."

"Yes."

Joel eyed her closed expression and wondered briefly if she was even listening. That old feeling that he was missing something crept over him. "Come on out of here," he said brusquely, holding the door wide. "I think I need a drink."

Chapter Ten

It was interesting how, when the heat of the moment had passed, one's mind could begin to arrange the facts in a more acceptable pattern. Cassie found that to be true, and not for the first time since she'd begun her investigation on Joel. She thought about the scrap of paper and wondered what she'd gotten so worked up over. An architect's recommendation to a contractor? Hardly incriminating evidence.

You're looking for trouble, she told herself. Give it a rest.

Joel was exhausted but seemed disinclined to go to bed. "Unless you come with me, of course," he drawled, and Cassie, after a moment's hesitation, followed him into his bedroom.

He backed toward the bed, holding her hands; she followed willingly enough until he urged her down beside him. "What about your headache?"

"Trust me. There's a simple cure."

He pulled gently and she lay on his chest, her palms braced on either side of his head. "I'd venture that what you have in mind isn't documented in any medical book."

Joel's mouth slanted wisely. "Every new theory needs research."

Cassie had serious doubts about the wisdom of going to bed with Joel at this particular stage. True, she loved him, but love could be blind, after all. Until she rid herself of this deep-rooted doubt she couldn't give all her trust. And trust and love were entwined too completely ever really to separate.

Then there was the matter of his headache.

"Have you been faking?" she accused, resisting the pressure of his fingers massaging the base of her neck.

"Faking?" Joel's laugh held no humor. "Hardly."

"How long does a migraine usually last?"

"Depends on the severity." His mouth moved closer as the pressure increased. "Hours, sometimes days. It's been a while since I've had one, love."

"And this one?"

Instead of kissing her, Joel's mouth tugged at her bottom lip, sucking on it until it was warm and wet. Cassie sought to fight the incredible sensations this started, the quiver in her stomach, the wave of weakness that tumbled over her. Trust and love weren't the only inseparable feelings, she thought wryly, so were love and sex.

"This one's over," Joel breathed against her parted lips. He shifted her body against his, the contours fitting neatly. "You're the cure for all my ailments," he whispered in her ear. "I have never felt this way about a woman."

When his mouth finally claimed hers, Cassie couldn't fight; she didn't want to. I love you, she thought, but didn't say it. Instead, as he slowly unbuttoned her blouse she concentrated on pushing everything to the back of her mind except the joy of being with him.

For Joel it was a moment of truth. Fighting her was the furthest thing from his mind. He loved her. Wholly and completely. If that made him a fool, then so be it. Tangling his fingers in her fiery hair, he whispered harshly, "I love you, Cassie. And I want you. No, don't say anything. Just love me. Now."

The beach looked long and endless, the gray hues of dawn not yet bright enough to gild the grains of sand, the striped umbrellas near the cafe still folded and damp with dew. Cassie decided all over again that running was not her sport, and through panting breaths she told Joel the same.

He was barely winded. "Four miles is only one more than three," he pointed out.

Cassie glowered at him, regretting having told him her limit. "And a mile is five thousand two hundred and eighty feet, speaking of which, mine are killing me." She collapsed onto the sand, thinking the three miles she'd just put in were more than enough for someone her age and condition.

Joel didn't seem to be showing her the proper empathy. "I'll meet you back at the house in half an hour," he said, glancing toward the north. Rays of sunlight formed a halo over the rock wall that enclosed the Sheraton Maui and brought Kaanapali Beach to an end.

"You ought to be resting today," Cassie grumbled. "Anyone who was as sick as you claimed—"

"Exercise is therapeutic," Joel cut her off, grinning. "You should try it sometime."

Cassie just shot him a baleful glance. Somewhere in all that was a challenge she wished she had the energy to meet. Even with Joel shortening his strides to meet hers, she was painfully inept at keeping up the pace.

Cassie wiped away a rivulet of sweat that threatened to run down the side of her face. "One more mile?"

"Only one."

Muttering to herself, she accepted Joel's outstretched hand and got to her feet. "I want you to know right now that I have no intention of becoming a jock. This preoccupation with physical fitness is a disease that I, for one, am going to avoid."

Joel looked amused. "Then why did you take up running?"

"To meet you," Cassie answered promptly, dusting off the seat of her pants. "Haven't you figured that out yet?"

"It had crossed my mind," he said dryly, a comment on her tactics Cassie could have done without. "But now that you've started . . ." His unfinished sentence hovered like a threat.

"Oh, no. No, no." Cassie shook her head and gave him her most determined look. "Don't think you're going to convince me to keep this up. First off, I'm happy with my body. I think there's a point of being too fit. Really. And what other reason is there to run? I'm not going to race!"

The grin on Joel's face slowly faded to a resigned smile. "Sometimes I use running as an escape. It's a way to work off tension."

Cassie just looked at him. "Is that why we're running this morning? Because of . . . Scott?"

"One of the reasons." Joel flexed his shoulders, his expression hardening. He looked thoughtful for a moment, then narrowed his eyes on her. "What do you think I should do?"

The question nearly bowled Cassie over; its implications on how far their relationship had progressed were stunning to consider. Joel was asking her advice, trusting her decisions. Cassie, who suddenly felt at sea with the weight of the question, answered him as truthfully as she could. "I think . . . Scott should stay with Tali for a while, to see if it's what he really wants.'' She chose her words carefully, knowing Scott was Joel's most sensitive nerve. "It's what I would do if I were you.''

Joel didn't answer, but Cassie knew he was mulling over her words the rest of the run. To Cassie's way of thinking, what other choice did he have? Dragging Scott from the mainland by force wasn't going to ease the tense situation between father and son; its effect would be just the reverse. And though living with Tali and her soon-to-be husband wasn't ideal, there wasn't an alternate solution unless Joel alienated Scott.

Cassie was half convinced Tali was using her son to get to Joel financially. But if that was the case, maybe leaving Scott in her care for a time was the answer. Scott was no fool. And if he could back off from the situation a little and be honest with himself, then he might come to the same realization about Tali that Joel had.

A couple of big ifs to expect from an angry, disillusioned teenager. Cassie was well aware of the intricate emotions involved, as was Joel.

Whoever said the last mile was the hardest knew what he was talking about, Cassie concluded later. The steps from the beach to Joel's solarium were an impossible hurdle, one that her tired legs balked at. Her knees wobbled, but she gritted her teeth and climbed the carved rock stairway, deciding that asking Joel for help would be the ultimate defeat.

In the end she had to admit it was worth it. The hot, stinging shower with Joel pushed weariness away and brought back her sense of humor.

"I may even have the strength to make breakfast,'' she announced airily, toweling her hair dry with one of the plush towels folded on the wicker stand beside the sink.

Joel grinned. "Such willpower. What an athlete.''

He was lucky he could move so quickly, Cassie thought later as she was searching through his cupboards. She'd actually considered tossing something at him.

Her lips curved, her thoughts bright and gleaming. Arrogant male! When he came back from retrieving the paper, she'd have to set him straight on a few things.

Later, when Cassie thought back to those moments in Joel's kitchen, she realized she should have foreseen the events that followed. But she was too deliriously happy to wonder what took Joel so long, too wrapped in a cocoon of self-deception to consider what riveting story in the *Breeze* might delay him.

It was the sound of his footsteps on the teak hallway floor that first alerted her. They were purposeful, determined, angry. Cassie hesitated in the act of breaking eggs into a bowl, then half turned.

In the split second before his hands clamped fiercely on her shoulders and spun her around, she sensed trouble. She was whirled between his capable palms, trapped under the bruising force of his fingers, pinned by his dark blazing eyes.

"Wh-a-a-t?" she asked tremulously, confusion mingling with fear. The *Breeze* sat like a confession on the counter, but Cassie was too distraught to notice.

"Damn you!" he rasped through clenched teeth. Cassie's eyes strayed to the paper. Joel, seeing her glance, shook her once hard, then pushed her away, scooping the offending paper up in the same motion and slapping it into her startled palms. He impaled her with a furious glare, his face contorted with an indictment of betrayal.

Under attack for a crime she couldn't fathom, Cassie's eyes dropped from his, landing on a story under Lynnette Cosgrove's by-line. The headline leaped out at her: "Joel Shepherd's Ongoing Battle."

Her temple pulsed, the paper shook in her trembling hands. Joel's silence was almost as disturbing as the article. For a moment she could hardly concentrate, then the story grabbed her, squeezing her heart with fear. It was about Joel's turbulent marriage to Tali and the ensuing custody battle.

"It can't be," she murmured, feeling the weight of Joel's silent anger. Insinuating and clever, the story slashed Joel's character, making Tali out to be a victim. Several direct quotes glared, belying the trust she'd begged Joel to give her. His quotes. From the tape!

Cassie's breath came in frightened gasps, her mind whirling. The tape was in her purse! She'd purposely held onto it, her trust in Mike too weak to leave it lying around the office.

Fearful eyes turned to Joel's angry amber ones. "I can explain—"

"No!" The bitter anger on his face stopped her heart. "No, you can't."

"Please!" Cassie was desperate, the world slipping away from her.

Joel shook his head, outrage etched on his face. "And I knew it," he muttered fiercely. "Damn it! I knew it!"

"You don't understand—"

"The hell I don't!" Joel's fist smashed into the counter, causing the stoneware Cassie had placed there to jump and clatter. A glass tipped over and rolled off the edge to splinter into a thousand pieces. Cassie didn't dare look.

"You damn lovely little liar!" he said through his teeth. "All that clever sidestepping. All that deception! For this!" He grabbed the paper from her unresisting hand and stared at it in mute disbelief.

Cassie's throat was dry with shock. Lynnette must have taken the tape. Who else could have? Lynnette was the only one who knew what was on it; she was the only person who knew Cassie still had it. And Mike had printed it!

Helplessness hit her like a wave, inundating her, making her anger at Lynnette and Mike far less important than the despair at losing Joel's love and trust. "I can live with myself," Lynnette had said, and Cassie now understood the full meaning of that remark. But could she live with herself?

"I didn't want it printed," she whispered, sick with self-reproach. "The tape was stolen from my purse."

With a laugh full of so much bitterness that Cassie felt a physical ache, Joel tossed the newspaper to the same fate as the shattered glass. "Didn't want it printed?" he sneered. "God, Cassie! It's a little late for excuses."

"I'm sure Mike was behind it, Joel. You're right. He is after you."

"Of course he is!" Joel raged. "But you supplied the ammunition. Why? *Why?* Didn't it ever occur to you what the consequences would be? Or didn't you care? Was all that talk of love just a vile way to get me to believe in you?"

She understood his shock, his disillusionment. But she was desperate to hold on, to make him see her feelings were real. "No, Joel. I do love you. I couldn't lie about that.".

"Couldn't you?"

Joel's anger was turning to disgust, at himself for being such a willing fool, but at Cassie, too, for playing such a sly, wretched game. Her white face touched his conscience, but her betrayal made him want to hurt her in return. "You wanted trust, Cass, and I gave it. And I was dead wrong. I should have known it's not something that can be given. You have to earn it!"

"Joel, I never wanted that story printed. Believe me, please. The tape was taken from me."

"The tape?"

Cassie felt a burning in her throat and behind her lids. His words were a painful jolt of reality. She'd taped him. She'd used him. She'd willfully set out to destroy him.

"They knew I didn't want it printed," she whispered.

Joel's caustic response lashed back at her. "Maybe you should have thought of that before, Mrs. Blakely. Maybe you should have practiced a little professional restraint instead of reaching for publishing glory. Maybe you should have divided what's news from what's just trashy gossip. My life"—he broke off, clenching his jaw for one horrible moment—"my life isn't for sale. And it's not for print. Now get out of it." He paused briefly for the full impact to penetrate Cassie's mind. "Get the hell out!"

There was nothing she could say in her own defense. Worse, some of what he accused her of was justified. But Joel's anger, his loss of trust, his contempt broke her heart. Her throat hurt with the effort not to cry.

When she spoke it was with a calmness she didn't feel. "I don't blame you for what you think of me. I probably deserve it. But if it makes any difference, I never wanted to hurt you."

"You haven't." A coldness had invaded Joel's voice; the hardness that had frightened her before surfaced once again. But now it was directed at her. And that made it a thousand times worse. "All you've done is open my eyes. The real tragedy is that they were closed for so long."

Cassie watched him walk through the solarium and onto the deck, the tenseness of his spine testimony to his dangerously suppressed emotions. Unable to think, she stood dumbly by, waiting for God knew what. She couldn't even muster up any rage at what Lynnette and Mike had done to her. She'd done it to herself.

"Joel . . ."

Joel's fingers dug into the wood railing. "Get out, Cass," he said harshly, refusing to turn around, unwilling to look into those treacherous blue eyes. Once he thought he'd seen something inside them, some hidden message for him alone. God! His naiveté made him sick.

Cassie's hand tentatively touched his upper arm, and Joel flinched. He heard her uneven breathing and knew she was affected at least on some level. It was small satisfaction, but it was all he had and he fed it with all the anger he'd saved up during his years with Tali. The two women were alike after all.

"I'll get a retraction from Mike," she was saying, speaking in a tight, worried voice, the ever-turning wheels of her mind speeding onto the next step. For Joel it was the last straw.

"I don't give a damn about that!" he threw back scornfully, wheeling around to impale her with blazing eyes. "I only want one thing right now—solitude." The flash of pain that crossed her face would have stopped him once, but Joel was past caring. "Now I'm leaving. If you recall, I've got a few things on my mind right now. I want you gone when I get back."

Without waiting for an answer, he brushed past her and walked straight through the house and out the front door.

"He'll be with you in just a moment," the *Island Breeze*'s receptionist informed Cassie in her carefully modulated voice. "I'll put you on hold."

The faint beep she heard preceded the stringed harmony of Muzak, and Cassie had a few seconds to marshal her thoughts before Mike was put through. While fretting at the delay, she recognized the need to arrange her accusations carefully lest she come off sounding like a shrew. She was furious, yes, and she had a right to be. But she had some self-respect left, and she intended to hang onto it while she nailed Mike to the wall.

She hurt all over. Upon searching through her purse and

finding the tape, Cassie had sucked in her breath in surprise. Then she realized just how crafty Mike and Lynnette had been. They'd lifted her tape, taken a copy, then replaced it. She'd never even known it was gone, and there'd been ample opportunity to do the deed while she was engrossed in her work.

Had it really been necessary to go to so much trouble just for a story on Joel? Suddenly she saw that all Joel's suspicions about Mike were true. How had she failed to see that earlier?

"Mike Casey."

"Hello, Mike. It's Cassie. I've got some news for you. I saw Lynnette's article in this morning's paper."

"And?"

His voice was wary, cagey. Cassie felt a cold stab of fury. How could he? How could he! He'd ruined everything for her, yet there was no hint of remorse.

Blaming him brought her around to her senses. It was her fault as much as his.

She took a deep breath. "And I think it's one of the shoddiest pieces of journalism I've ever seen. Joel Shepherd agrees with me, by the way. We had quite a discussion about it."

"I see."

"I don't think you do, Mike. What you and Lynnette did was little short of criminal."

"That tape was my property," he replied.

Cassie was amazed at his cool. She felt an unpleasant crawling sensation and shivered. Just how well did she know Mike?

"I think you've got blinders on when it comes to Joel," she went on carefully. "What I don't know is why. An age-old grudge over Tali doesn't quite cut it, I'm afraid."

Mike's response was sharp. "What do you mean?"

His reaction broke her train of thought. She really hadn't meant anything by it; it had just popped into her head. Now she wondered what the significance was.

"I don't know, Mike," Cassie said slowly, her resolve growing, "but I intend to find out. That's what investigative reporters are for, aren't they? And oh, by the way, I quit."

Even though it had been her intention to say it, Cassie was a little surprised she'd had the strength to deliver the message so calmly and completely. Emotionalism was running at an all-time high, and she felt as wild and miserable as she had during her divorce.

Mike's response was almost a snarl. "He's got you all turned around, Cass. I'm warning you, you'll get hurt."

Cassie laughed silently, her bitterness a living thing deep inside her. "I couldn't be more hurt than I already am, Mike. It's difficult to know who your friends are."

"Cass, listen—"

"No." She clenched her teeth together until the pressure was a throbbing ache. "I'm through listening, Mike. You broke a trust—a very valuable trust. You won't get another chance."

Her last words were little better than a whisper, and she hung up before Mike could reply. There was nothing he could say to change her mind anyway. And it was long past the time to believe in flimsy excuses.

Cassie rose from the chair and walked to her bedroom. The villa was dreary and lonely, and she needed to get out. Mere hours ago she'd been running down the beach alongside Joel; now the silence of her solitude was unbearable.

What could she have done differently? Trusted Joel more? Mike less? Was there anything she could do to make it right?

Never having been a quitter, Cassie considered that

challenge. She saw her reflection in the vanity mirror and was appalled by her appearance. Her blue eyes were bleak and shadowed, her mouth drawn and unhappy. Defeat was so clearly evident in her hunched shoulders that she straightened and tried for a smile. It hovered uncertainly on her lips before sliding away. With a muffled oath, Cassie lifted her chin, challenging the bleak image. It hurt but she managed to sustain the determined smile. No matter what happened, she couldn't give up on herself.

Joel was furious with her and hurt, no matter what he said to the contrary. She'd done to him what Mike had done to her—she'd destroyed his faith.

Cassie shifted away from her reflection, repressing the urge to fling herself onto the bed and cry herself into oblivion. She couldn't pander to her self-pity, or she'd never be able to win back what she'd lost.

If only there *was* some way to regain his trust.

Trust. There it was again, that horrible, double-edged word that mocked her over and over again. She'd broken the tenuous bond of trust developing between herself and Joel. She doubted that it could be repaired.

Cassie changed clothes and walked into the kitchen, lost in thought. She poured herself a cup of coffee and flipped on the air conditioning as she began to feel the late morning heat.

She sat a long time, thinking over everything, painfully remembering the scene she'd had with Joel. Would he ever forgive her? Not likely. Unless . . .

Cassie set her mug down carefully. Maybe all was not lost after all. What she'd done, though a monumental betrayal in principle, had actually wreaked very little damage. Even Joel would have to admit that. The article was sleazy and insinuating and a blow to his pride, but in actual fact it said next to nothing. She understood his anger, especially his fury over her deception, and she knew how much he loathed that type of press. But when all the dust settled and he cooled off, wasn't it possible that he might forgive her? Or, at the very least, just listen to her?

"You're grasping at straws," she muttered, but her mind spun onward. She knew Joel cared about her—had cared about her. Feelings like that refused to die away, no matter how hard one tried to kill them. There was a chance. There was still a chance.

Cassie was never sure when the idea germinated and became a conviction, but suddenly she knew she couldn't just sit by and watch her life fall apart. She needed to see Joel, to talk to him, hoping that she could convince him to hear her out before it was too late. Grabbing her purse, Cassie headed for the door. One way or another they'd have this out.

After all, she thought, her mouth drawing into a determined line, what have I got to lose?

Joel was not at his office, and his secretary informed Cassie that she didn't know where he was or when he'd be back. Privately, Cassie was of the opinion that the woman was very well trained at putting off uninvited guests, but she accepted the information with a polite thank you and left without giving her name.

After dialing his home number several more times, she got back in her car and headed toward the Maui Paccaro, figuring the hotel site was as good a place to try as any other. It wasn't the ideal place for a heated discussion; the workmen would surely be a distraction for both of them and vice versa. Still, it was the only other place he could be . . . unless he'd rejected her advice and flown to the mainland to get Scott.

Cassie pushed that notion aside, refusing to consider it. He had to be on Maui. He had to.

Bad luck seemed to follow her like a black cloud, she mused as she parked in the gravel lot beneath a banyan tree. There was no sign of Joel's car amid the half dozen trucks, pickups and vans. She hurried up the stone walkway to the hotel's imposing double doors.

A man she'd never seen before was down on one knee near the curved stairway, a carpetlayer's kneepad protecting him as he slammed the stretched fabric under the rise of a stair, the rich cerulean hue a mimicry of the beautiful sea that surrounded the islands.

Cassie walked up to him, watching as the carpet was pounded and hooked on rows of narrow strips of wood studded with tiny, deadly looking nails. "Excuse me," she said, winning herself his bored attention. "Is Mr. Shepherd at the site? I need to speak to him."

The man turned back to his duty. "Nope. But Roger's here. The foreman. He can probably help you."

Cassie didn't feel like telling him her business was with Joel and Joel alone. And the thought of facing Roger right now was unpalatable. So much for her investigation into the accident, she mused wryly. Even if she unveiled the mystery that surrounded it and was able to trust in Joel completely, so what? The urgency of it was gone; it had disappeared with Joel.

She murmured a thank you to the workman and rotated on one heel, then heard heavy footsteps coming from the south tower's connecting hallway. She knew it was Roger even before his silvery head appeared.

"Hello, Roger," Cassie greeted him, a hesitant smile on her lips. She really wasn't in the frame of mind to delve into the whys and wherefores surrounding the man but was forced, for the sake of politeness, to acknowledge him.

Roger stopped dead in his tracks. Harsh, uneasy lines creased his forehead, and he cleared his throat before answering. "Mrs. Blakely." He nodded to her, keeping a wide distance. "What brings you here?""

"I was looking for Joel. Has he been here today?"

"No."

There comes a time, Cassie decided, when skirting the issue is far more difficult and destructive than meeting it head on. She and Roger Caldwell were at that impasse, neither willing to reach for the hot potato between them. They each knew or sensed something about the other that they wished they didn't.

Cassie seized the moment, albeit reluctantly. "Could I talk to you? Somewhere private?"

Roger glanced apprehensively at the workman. "It's sort of a difficult time for me right now. Maybe some other time?"

It was an avenue of escape that Cassie nearly accepted, but Roger's nervousness kept her pushing doggedly forward. "It'd be just a few minutes. Please. I know . . . how much you and Joel mean to each other. He holds you in very high esteem." Cassie swallowed, the weight of unspoken words and regrets threatening to engulf her. She wished there was a way to explain things to Roger without explaining. In a hushed voice, she added, "I care about him, too."

A muscle beside his jaw twitched. There was no doubt this man was carrying some terrible burden. She prayed it had nothing to do with Joel. Wordlessly he led her to a reception anteroom, a closet, lockers and time clock indicating its intended use for the Maui Paccaro's employees. "What exactly is it you want?" Roger asked, giving her a quick glance.

Cassie regarded him helplessly. "I don't know."

His forehead puckered. "If it's something about you and Joel, I'm afraid I can't help you. He goes his own way."

"It's not that exactly." Cassie drew a steadying breath, wondering how much to reveal.

"Mrs. Blakely—"

Cassie looked up when he stopped. Roger Caldwell was frightened, and she knew she had to find out why.

It was at that moment that she realized she did not want to be an investigative reporter. The kind of interrogations that required brushed too close to sensitive nerves. But she was too deeply involved with Joel and the problems surrounding his company to give up now. She owed it to him to believe in him fully, she owed it to herself to learn the truth, and she owed it to her brother to make certain that if there was a cover-up, it would never happen again.

Cassie lifted her chin, attempting to hold Roger's shifting gaze. "I won't mince words, Mr. Caldwell. I think you and I know each other from other circumstances." His face darkened in denial. "Otherwise why would you address me as *Mrs.* Blakely. No one told you I'd been married."

The silence was deafening, the only noise being the sporadic thumping of the carpetlayer's hammer. Cassie wondered if she'd met another wall, then Roger's shoulders slumped. "You're Chris Tanner's sister," he muttered, searching his breast pocket for a cigar. "And you're a reporter."

Cassie waited quietly. That about said it all, she supposed. Nodding, she gave him some time, feeling closed in by the pungent odor of the cigar and the anxiety of the man in front of her.

"You're after Joel?" he asked suddenly.

Cassie's stomach lurched. "No, I'm after answers."

Roger's mouth twisted. "They're one and the same, Mrs. Blakely. Don't you know that?"

"I just want to know . . . what happened," Cassie pursued, her pulse fluttering in alarm. Half of her had always known, but now that she was so close, she had the violent urge to back away. She didn't want to know—not if it was bad, not if her worst fears were confirmed.

"You're talking about the accident." Roger didn't wait for her to acknowledge this statement. "That's Joel's company, his decisions. If he made a mistake, well . . ." Roger gave her an uneasy look, noting her white face. He paused. "Look, you said you care about him. Maybe you should lay off and just go with that. Don't think he doesn't have regrets, because he does."

Cassie felt her heart stop cold. She couldn't breathe or move. No, no, no! She would not believe it! Roger was saying there was something to find and that Joel was responsible. Her voice shaking, she said tautly, "I need to have facts, Mr. Caldwell, not hearsay. I need documentation."

"Then you're talkin' to the wrong man." As he brushed past her, Cassie grasped his arm, fingers tense.

'Who's the right man? Joel? Or someone else?"

Roger refused to look her way; his eyes were trained straight ahead, his mouth clamped into a stubborn line. Cassie, her insides torn apart, knew a moment of intense pain. How could this be happening? She loved Joel.

She persisted. "I can always ask your architect, Daniel."

Roger tore away from her grasp; his usually slow steps were tight and hurried. Cassie leaned back against the wall and closed her eyes, spent. It was time to face the truth, and she didn't want to, couldn't do it. Her breath came in strangled gasps. How could something so horrible be true?

"You all right, ma'am?"

Cassie's eyes flew open. "Yes . . . yes . . . fine," she murmured, turning away from the concerned face of the carpetlayer. She pushed herself away from the wall.

"Let me get you a glass of water."

"No, please. I'll be fine. Thank you."

She stepped away as quickly as possible, suddenly desperate for fresh air. Her footsteps echoed on the hardwood floor like a mocking laugh. Desolation was nothing new to Cassie, but this painful agony of indecision was.

How could she love someone guilty of such heinous negligence?

Chapter Eleven

Cassie stared blindly across the incandescent, silver waves, waiting for the sun to turn them into shades of blue and gold. She didn't know what time she'd risen—sometime way before dawn—and she wasn't certain how long she'd been sitting at the bistro before the management closed the bar and opened the umbrellas. But the cold cramp in her lower back warned her it had been hours.

And it would undoubtedly be hours more before she came to any decision. Her head throbbed and her shoulders ached; her brain was dull and fuzzy. Too much had happened in too short a time.

She hadn't seen or heard from Joel in two days. She'd lost count of how many phone calls she'd made, how many times she'd heard that he wasn't in and wasn't expected back anytime soon.

Confronting his secretary hadn't helped either. She was polite, crisp and completely uninformative. Once Cassie had caught a pitying look, but the woman had quickly masked it.

There was no question that Joel was avoiding her.

So where did that leave her?

Cassie thanked her waiter for the cup of tea he set before her, squeezed a lemon section into it, then stirred listlessly. Her warning to Roger about the architect—Daniel Lessing —had been no idle threat. She'd pursued that lead, finally catching up with him on Molokai via long distance.

It hadn't taken Cassie long to realize she'd have to sort through a lot of alarmist theorizing on the part of Daniel Lessing to come up with any real specifics. Lessing knew how to milk a situation for the worst. He feared everything, especially the thought of being sued. Still, he seemed knowledgeable in his profession and, somewhat surprisingly, genuinely respectful of his employer.

Encouraged, Cassie had asked him about Joel. Lessing had given her a picture of a man who was conscientious and careful, exacting but learned, helpful and patient. But when she brought up the fire at the Polynesian Village, he suddenly stopped talking. It was as quick as turning off a spigot. Cassie was left high and dry. Rather coldly, Lessing informed her she'd have to check that out with Joel himself.

She'd tried, but Joel refused to return her calls, a fact that boded poorly for his innocence. Yet Cassie still hadn't given up her belief in that entirely . . . until she confronted Shepherd Construction's accountant and heard a chillingly horrific story told in the most matter-of-fact manner.

She disliked Paul Gaston on sight. He had the superior attitude of one who resignedly puts up with the little people of the world. At first he stonewalled her, but as Cassie revealed what she knew and suspected, his cool persona cracked. He didn't actually fall apart, but he started to sweat, enough to convince Cassie she was on the right track.

Her heart plummeted. She felt like a character in a badly staged play, forced to react on two levels. One part of her was clinical, detached, like a wooden mannequin collecting data. The other part was denying the proof Gaston showed her: the note from Roger asking if they should really buy cheaper material and risk a fire hazard, the invoice for that material signed with Joel's slashing signature.

Proof enough. Maybe not criminal, but certainly negligent. Cassie was sick, a victim of her betraying heart.

She gulped her tea, wishing it could thaw the frozen agony within her. It was a vain hope. Joel was guilty; his actions had directly caused her brother's death.

She was locked within a prison of her own making, faced with a terrible dilemma. Even now, with the bald truth staring at her, with evidence of Joel's weakness—even now she felt the flame of love burning on. She'd never really understood what would happen to her if she found out Joel was involved; she'd never believed he was. Now that she knew, she was immobilized, unable to commit herself one way or another. Revealing what she knew would destroy Joel; keeping it to herself would eventually destroy her.

Why had she insisted on finding out the truth? It had been far easier to live with her suspicions. Now she was forced to make an unbearable choice; she would lose either way.

So many people had warned her: Bryan, Lynnette, Mike, Roger. Even her own conscience had nagged her. But she'd been heedless, reckless in her newfound love.

How could she expose him now? How could she not? With a heavy heart she remembered how dutifully Joel had tried to destroy her perception of Mike. He'd almost succeeded. Painfully, she recalled Mike's last warning: "He's got you all turned around, Cass."

Sunlight fell across the table, turning the drops of dew to glittering gems. Cassie ran her finger across the top in agonized circles, knowing what she had to do, refusing to do it, hating herself for being such a fool.

There really was no choice at all.

Feeling as if she had aged a lifetime in just a few moments, Cassie slowly rose from her chair. It was early but not too early. Mike was undoubtedly already seated behind his desk.

She captured the attention of her eager waiter. "Excuse me, could you show me where there's a phone I could use?"

"Thanks. No. I'm not interested. I don't care who it was, I'm not—"

Joel broke off in midsentence and sat bolt upright. Disbelief and shock vied for control before the rigid anger he'd felt the last few days covered his dark features. "*Who* called?" he demanded harshly, cutting through Daniel Lessing's hysterical soliloquy.

". . . . and as if that weren't enough, she brought up the Polynesian Village tragedy—"

"Who?" Joel bellowed. "Cassie Blakely?"

Lessing paused. "Yes, I believe that's what she said her name was. I told her she'd have to speak to you. Look, Joel, I don't know what happened there, but I don't want to be involved."

"Nothing happened. *Nothing*. And if Mrs. Blakely's looking for another story, she's in for a nasty surprise."

Joel slammed down the receiver before his rage vented itself on the unsuspecting architect. His anger was for Cassie. Damn her! Damn her treacherous lies!

He raked his hands through his hair, then clasped them behind his neck. There was no headache now, just a crystal clear fury that forced him to sit back and think carefully. This bizarre fiasco had helped him understand something

about himself: His headaches stemmed from personal problems he was helpless to control. Cassie Blakely was a whole
different story.

The hell of it was, he'd almost forgiven her! He was
furious with her for printing that article, yes, and he was
hurt, too. He could admit that now. He'd trusted her,
believed in her, and she'd slapped him in the face with her
duplicity.

But when he thought about her—the silky feel of her
skin, the lurking humor and seduction in her eyes, her
throat, her intelligence, her soft sighs—the thought of
giving all that up wrenched his soul.

You have to have something before you can give it up, his
conscience mocked.

Still, what really amazed him was his own ambivalent
feelings. He'd been dangerously close to forgiving her.
He'd seriously considered overlooking the trashy article
she'd had printed in the *Breeze*. After all, the damage to his
reputation had been minimal, just more speculation and
unfounded rumors. He could live with that. But the damage
to his pride—that had been tricky.

And yet, even with everything that had transpired—even
with her purposeful deception!—he'd been ready to put it
all behind him for the sake of love.

Lessing's call had obliterated that chance. Now he had to
deal with her the way she really was. In the end her
weakness for success had shown itself. She wanted her
name written boldly in black and white under a story, any
story, whether it was fact or fiction. His already low
opinion of reporters took a sharp dive.

The telephone jarred him from his self-recriminations. In
the brief second before sanity intervened he knew it must be
Cassie calling again. He'd refused her calls to this point;
now he'd give her the brutal truth of what he thought of her.

"Joel Shepherd," he answered tersely.

"Dad?"

The tentative tone of Scott's voice rendered him speechless. He couldn't believe his ears. "Scott? Are you all right?"

"Yeah. Sure. Hollywood's great."

Joel winced, wondering if he was in for another lecture on all the benefits of living with Tali. "I'm sure it is," he answered dryly. "How's your mother?"

"Okay."

There were heavy messages being sent over the line that Joel hadn't known Scott capable of. There was hesitancy, carefulness, even fear. Was Scott afraid to talk to him? Joel found the idea actually reassuring. Unsurety had never been something Scott would own up to; belligerence was more the norm. "I'm glad you called. I've been thinking about you."

Scott snorted disbelievingly. "Really? You're probably thrilled to death I'm out of your hair."

This attack was more Scott's style, but Joel refused to be baited. "I'd rather you were here with me, that's all."

"So you can keep better track of my comings and goings?"

Joel was noncommittal. "Maybe."

Scott swore pungently, but Joel ignored it. Scott was reaching out to him for the first time in years. Why, Joel wasn't sure, but Scott had phoned. Something was happening.

It was just frustrating that Scott felt compelled to push away even when he was begging for help. "You like living with your mother, then?" Joel suggested casually.

"Yeah. Why?"

"No reason. Tali wants me to let you stay with her. I'm just checking to make sure that's what you want."

"Of course it is! Why wouldn't it be?"

"You tell me."

There was a gigantic pause. Joel realized he was holding his breath and wondered if he hadn't imagined the whole scenario. Expecting Scott to change was like banking on winning the lottery. The odds against it were enormous.

"If you ever wanted to come home, you'd let me know, wouldn't you?" Joel asked.

"You mean I can stay?"

"I'm considering it, yes. But only if it's really what you want. On the other hand, if you wanted to come back, well . . ." Joel hesitated, listening. Scott hadn't flown into a rage of defensive objections. "I could wire you some money for a ticket."

Scott seemed to think that over for a minute, but Joel had the feeling the decision had already been made. "Yeah. Do that," Scott said. "I could use the money."

"Sure," Joel answered, stealing from his son's vocabulary. "I'll do it today."

"Great. Okay. Talk to you later."

"Good-bye, Scott."

Joel hung up and stared at the receiver for several seconds. He couldn't help feeling jubilant. He understood Scott well enough to realize this had been a major breakthrough. Maybe things in California weren't as great as Scott had imagined they'd be.

Scott couldn't quite admit that he wanted to return. Acknowledging that he'd been wrong would be too humbling. Nevertheless, Joel was greatly encouraged. It was a relief to block out his explosive feelings about Cassie with the pleasurable knowledge that there was light at the end of the tunnel as far as Scott was concerned.

There was also a side benefit to Scott's change of heart: Tali couldn't use him as a tool. Joel was certain she was trying to use Scott as ammunition, a way to apply pressure. Tali wanted something else, and he was pretty sure it was money. He'd had a lengthy discussion with her parents when Scott was visiting them, and he'd learned she'd asked them for financial help. Even being their daughter, they'd refused her. They felt, as Joel did, that it was time for Tali to start accepting some responsibility for her own actions.

Maybe, Joel thought, blocking out the image of Cassie's appealing face, things were finally coming together. Maybe. Just maybe . . .

Cassie sat at the villa's kitchen counter, notes and letters strewn in a haphazard semicircle around her. She'd written and examined and dissected and written some more, trying to make some sense out of all the facts about Joel, failing at every turn. It was just too obvious: Joel was guilty.

It was a conclusion she'd drawn days before but one she desperately wanted to disbelieve. Calling Mike hadn't helped; his elation over her findings made her feel desolate. Lynnette was going to follow up.

She looked down at the questions she'd listed for herself. Why? *Why?* Why would Joel cut such important corners? He was wealthy, had been for years. There was simply no need . . .

And why hadn't anything turned up during the initial investigation right after the accident? True, she'd always felt that it had been hushed up, that somehow people at Shepherd Construction had paid off those who really mattered.

Why, then, had it been so easy for her to find the truth? Looking back, Cassie had to admit the road had been remarkably smooth. First Roger, then Lessing, then finally Gaston. Her only stumbling block had been Joel.

Did that make sense?

Cassie rubbed her hands across her face. Even with all the facts it still seemed improbable, and this was her head talking, not her heart. She'd believed in Joel's innocence once, and part of her still believed in him.

Cassie stood up and stretched, relieving the strain on her back. She was completely isolated, an island in the stream, cut off from her job, her friends and her lover. She supposed it was little more than she deserved, yet she had the uneasy feeling that she was being had.

"You're crazy," she muttered angrily, wondering at herself. How had she ever become so paranoid?

Cassie paced the confines of her small apartment, thinking how soon she was going to have to give it up and move back to Honolulu permanently. Mike had offered her a position on the staff again, but Cassie had demurred. She needed time to think things through before she went back to the *Island Breeze*. Joel had been right about the paper's finances. Mike was on a downhill slide that would be difficult to arrest.

There was another reason she hadn't accepted the temptation of a steady paying job on the paper. Bryan had quit. Mike had given her that stunning news after she'd unloaded the truth about Joel. When she'd asked why, he'd been enigmatic. "He's moving back to the mainland," Mike had said. "That's all I know."

That almost more than anything had hurt the most. Cassie remembered Bryan's vague worries about Mike and felt the need to keep away. She'd informed Mike she'd think about his offer.

In the meantime she was left in a painful limbo, wanting to see Joel, knowing she couldn't, aware that whatever they'd had together was gone forever. It had been her folly to believe in the unbelievable, to want something so much that she ignored the obvious. She'd been taken in, just as Lynnette had warned, and now she was paying the price.

She'd known it from the beginning, of course, but she'd been fooled by Joel Shepherd, the man himself. He'd convinced her that he was incapable of the kind of gross negligence she suspected him of. He'd made her believe him. He'd even made her love him.

She'd hidden all her fears and doubts, pushed them away until they seemed insignificant and remote. Running into Roger that night at the hotel had been the turning point. From then on, whether she'd admitted it to herself or not, she knew that Joel was involved in—responsible for—her brother's death.

Then why was it so hard to accept?

Cassie sighed and walked onto her patio. Tonight was the night of the Maui Paccaro's grand opening. It seemed like a million years since•Joel had invited her. It seemed like forever since she'd seen him.

The layer of sand on the patio floor felt gritty beneath her bare feet. It was a good feeling, one that reminded her she wasn't completely numb or desensitized yet. Joel would be at the opening. There was no way he could avoid going.

Cassie bit savagely on her lower lip. And there was no way he could avoid her if she decided to show up.

The thought of facing him again made her stomach quiver. What could she say? What could he say? By now he had to know about her inquiries into his business affairs. What would seeing her do to him?

With sudden decisiveness, Cassie walked back to her bedroom. It didn't much matter. Anything was better than leaving things as they were.

She had one adequate dress, a cream sheath with thin gold threads that glimmered when she moved. It draped over one shoulder; the loose folds of the bodice tucked into a narrow waistband. For Cassie it didn't matter what she wore. Her mind was on a tortuous path of its own that wouldn't end until she cleared the air between herself and Joel once and for all.

Her resolve nearly fled when she saw the lines of

expensive cars and waiting limousines outside the front entrance of the hotel. Lights blazed everywhere. She handed her keys to the parking attendant, aware that hers was the only automobile in the lot selling for less than $20,000. How did Joel like moving in these circles? she mused. From what she knew of him, probably not a lot.

Then again, what did she really know of him?

The doorman took one look at her and asked politely, "Invitation?"

Cassie stared at him, nonplussed. It hadn't occurred to her she would need to prove her inclusion in this function. "I forgot it," she lied beautifully, "but if you check with Mr. Shepherd, he'll okay me."

Her smile was just a little tight, a touch regal, as if she'd tolerate his boorish manners because she understood he was just doing his job.

"That's not necessary, Miss . . . ?"

"Blakely. Mrs. Cassie Blakely."

"Mrs. Blakely," he answered smoothly. "I have a list of the guests right here."

He dug inside the carved oak desk for a loose leaf notebook, and Cassie waited with a nervous stomach. She had the doomed feeling Joel had neglected to add her.

She was right. The man checked several times, his brows pulling together in a frown.

In a burst of inspiration, she said, "I'm with the press. Are you sure I'm not listed? Mr. Shepherd specifically invited me to cover his grand opening."

The doorman gave her a searching look, then flipped to another page. His eyes scanned it briefly and Cassie's heart sank. "Ma'am, the only woman listed here who's with the press is Ms. Lynnette Cosgrove," he stated flatly. "I'm sorry."

Cassie's lips parted. Lynnette? She was the reporter Roger had talked about? From the society page?

No. Joel had *thought* she'd be from the society page. But Lynnette was after something far larger. She was after Joel's blood.

Suddenly Cassie's choice was clear. No matter what happened, no matter who was at fault, what crimes had been committed, she had to warn Joel about the investigation. She couldn't let it come crashing down on him unawares. She owed him that much—at least that much.

"I must speak to Mr. Shepherd," Cassie said firmly. "It's very important. Please let him know I'm here."

"I'm very sorry, ma'am. But Mr. Shepherd is unavailable."

"What do you mean, unavailable?"

"I mean it's impossible to reach him. He's showing guests around the hotel."

Cassie knew she'd been put off but was incapable of pushing the man. She was entertaining ideas of renting a boat and pulling up to the pier when a rather doubtful savior appeared—Roger.

He stopped dead when he saw her standing in the foyer. Mustering her courage, Cassie waved, the smile feeling cold and stiff on her lips.

Reluctantly, he came forward, looking almost absurd in a dark gray suit and tie. He was as uncomfortable as he appeared.

"Hullo, Roger," Cassie drawled. "I seem to be having some trouble. This man can't find my name on the guest list. Would you please tell him that I have a personal invitation from Mr. Shepherd?"

It seemed an eternity before he answered. Cassie knew he was dying to get rid of her, and her suspicions about him mounted. But she kept her eyes trained on him, and finally he met her gaze. "Mrs. Blakely is a personal friend of Mr. Shepherd's," he announced, his jaw tense. "She must have been accidentally omitted."

"Thank you," Cassie murmured as she walked past the desk. Roger didn't acknowledge her, he just turned toward the reception counter. Piqued, Cassie followed. "You don't like me very much, do you?" she accused tightly.

Roger's shoulders stiffened. "I don't know what you mean."

"I frighten you, because you're afraid I'll expose Joel." When he didn't say anything, she went on, "We're talking about covering up criminal negligence—negligence that killed my brother! I have no choice but to disclose what I know."

Roger's pallor was a sickening shade of gray. "Think about what you're saying. You'll destroy Joel."

Cassie's chest hurt, her lungs were tight and aching. "Your warning's a little late. I called my editor yesterday."

"Casey?"

Cassie nodded. "I talked to your accountant a few days ago and to your architect. I've tried to talk to Joel, but he won't take my calls. Now I'm telling you."

She expected him to attack her for her disloyalty, but Roger Caldwell was a beaten man. He didn't even look at her as he turned and walked away. Somehow that was far worse.

Cassie's battered heart almost turned her into a coward. After Roger, she didn't know if she could face Joel. She walked to the elevators and pushed the button, her earlier anticipation fading to uneasiness.

The ballroom was packed with gorgeous gowns and dark suits. Cassie felt intimidated by the glamor. There were important people here, influence and money evidently the prerequisites for receiving an invitation. Cassie glanced at the faces. The crowd read like a *Who's Who* of the islands.

A waiter, deftly maneuvering a tray of champagne glasses, weaved his way toward the bar. He stopped gallantly in front of Cassie, and she lifted one of the fragile glasses. Her mouth was dry as ash. She felt like an outsider, like a spy and a traitor. Her uncomfortable thoughts caused color to run up her throat and flush her cheeks.

Cassie was unaware of how appealing she looked. She hadn't had time to fix her hair, so it fell against her shoulders like a silken curtain of red gold. Her eyes were wide and worried, her mouth vulnerable. Her heightened color only added to her unconscious allure. She had the air of a woman who'd been forced to build character on an unhappy past. In this room of vapid luxury and wealth, she was an unexpected treasure, a glittering gem amid paste.

"Care to dance, beautiful lady?"

Cassie jumped at the voice in her ear. She turned slowly and examined the older gentleman who'd offered the invitation. There was a speculative gleam in his eyes she didn't like. With a polite smile, she shook her head and moved away. Where was Joel?

She found a quiet corner at the far end of the buffet table. So far the guests weren't interested in the exotic delicacies covering every inch of the row of tables lining one entire wall. Cassie, for lack of something to do, picked up a wafer-thin cracker covered with cream cheese and smoked fish and topped with a delicate, pungent red sauce.

She watched a man fill a tiny plate, two fingers reaching up periodically to loosen his collar. She felt an instant camaraderie; he looked as uncomfortable as she.

He caught her look and smiled, his movements quick and birdlike. "Helluva place to be," he muttered, sensing a friend.

"Why don't you leave?" Cassie wondered.

He laughed shortly. "I just wish I could." He shrugged. "It's part of my duty to be here."

The voice, the manner, seemed familiar. Curious, Cassie asked, "What duty's that?"

"I'm the head architect for the Maui Paccaro." Before

Cassie could mask her surprise, he extended a hand. "The name's Daniel Lessing. What's yours?"

Very dryly, Cassie answered, "Cassie Blakely. Still want to talk to me?"

Lessing's mouth dropped, then he shut it with an angry click. "So . . . you're still investigating. I had no idea you were so—" He broke off and frowned down at the food on his plate.

"Persistent?" Cassie supplied, taking a liking to her companion. He was about as far removed from her mental image of an architect as possible.

His face went red. "Attractive," he corrected formally. "I think you should leave Joel alone."

"That seems to be a universal opinion around here. Why?"

Lessing drew in a long breath, his chest expanding like a proud father. "Joel Shepherd runs one of the fairest and cleanest operations around. He's won all kinds of beautification awards. Before the Polynesian Village, that piece of property was an eyesore—rundown, decrepit buildings that couldn't be and weren't worth saving. Why can't you people just be satisfied with that? Why are you always looking for sensationalism?"

"I'm not looking for—"

"Sure you are. That's what you called me for." Lessing began pontificating on the mistakes of the press, and Cassie was helpless to deter him. In elaborate detail he went over all the safety considerations Joel insisted on using, each above and beyond the legal requirement. Cassie was unable to keep still.

"Then what about the Polynesian Village?" she cut in when Daniel paused to take a breath. "How come Joel signed an invoice for cheaper, less safe material when he'd been warned against it?"

Lessing blinked. "Who told you that?"

"I saw the invoice with my own eyes. Paul Gaston showed it to me."

"Gaston did?" he asked blankly.

Cassie nodded. She could practically see Daniel Lessing's faith in Joel crumbling; his face was a mask of disbelief, his shoulders sagged. Like a pestilence, she was sweeping in to destroy Joel's life. Cassie fought back an urge to cry, loathing herself and the role she was cast in.

Lessing cleared his throat. "I think you'd better talk to Joel, Mrs. Blakely."

"Thank you. It's what I want, too."

For several hours Cassie wandered around the fringes of the ballroom. She received many invitations to dance, but apart from Daniel Lessing, no one bothered to talk to her. Roger Caldwell, she knew, was acutely aware of her; she caught him watching her more than once. But neither he nor anyone else sought her company.

She was half convinced Joel had been warned away from her. If she hadn't been so depressed, she would have been furious. What kind of man was he that he couldn't face her?

She was just about to leave when she sensed him. Turning quickly to the sound of new voices, she saw him step off the elevator with a group of serious-looking men. Businessmen. Potential investors, she guessed.

In direct contrast to her own, Joel's company was eagerly sought after. In minutes he had a group of enthusiastic supporters surrounding him.

Cassie was hit by a wave of emotion, none of it anything easy. Love, desire, betrayal, helpless rage—she felt them all. She could only stand transfixed, her gaze centered on the man she loved.

Joel looked as unapproachable and foreign to her as she'd ever seen him. Dressed in a black tuxedo, his face stern, lines around his mouth, he appeared as out of place as she and Daniel Lessing. Too sober, too tense, he wasn't enjoying himself either.

His range of interest didn't extend beyond the small group of businessmen. Elegantly turned-out women and influential but self-important men weren't his cup of tea. His eyes roamed the room as if looking for a route of escape.

Cassie's heart stopped as his gaze caught and held hers. The well of love and sadness she felt hurt like nothing she'd ever known. Loneliness, aching loneliness, hammered at her. She knew her pain was in her eyes but couldn't hide it. She still loved him. It was one of the impossibilities of her life.

The guests milling near Joel suddenly became aware that his attention was riveted on something. As if of one mind, they stepped back, leaving him room to walk across the floor to Cassie. He stopped a few feet in front of her.

"I—I need to talk to you," she managed, quaking inside. She hadn't realized how much depended on this, how much hope still lingered despite impossible odds. Why, she couldn't understand. Love wasn't blind, she mused resignedly. It was all-forgiving.

Joel's eyes raked over her, leaving her feeling absurdly naked. His face was rigid and cold, and her senses cried out against it. Anger, rage, hate—those she could accept. That was passion. But detachment, disdain, loss of respect? How could she live with all of that?

"Please, Joel," she begged humbly.

Joel was also fighting a losing battle. He'd told himself time and again that he wanted to kill Cassie for the extra trauma and disruption she'd caused him. He'd tried of late to treat her solely as a problem, not as a woman. He'd forced himself to concentrate on her betrayal and deceit.

But he hadn't been prepared enough. Seeing her wide, trembling mouth and sensitive to her vulnerability, her needs, Joel couldn't force himself to hurt her. He was held to her by some invisible chain he couldn't weaken.

"Let's go somewhere quiet," he suggested tensely, lightly touching her arm to guide her to an outside door.

There were a few guests scattered across the patio and beach. Joel dropped his hand, breaking the brief contact they had, and headed in the direction of the pier. Cassie followed half a step behind, her mind completely blank, void of all the important questions that had plagued her for days. She was too numb, too off balance.

Small, impudent waves slapped the pier, its structure repaired of all damage and vandalism, the scaffolding removed. Cassie stared across the inky waves and felt Joel's warm presence beside her. She was truly at a loss for words.

Joel was forced to coax her. "Go ahead, Cassie," he said, his voice level.

Her hands were clutching the luminous folds of her skirt. Slowly she unwound her tense fingers. "I don't know where to begin," she answered honestly. "I know what you must think of me, and you have a right to feel that way."

"Thank you," Joel said dryly.

Cassie winced. He was making her feel more guilty than she already did, and it wasn't fair. Everything—*everything* —was because of him.

Because there seemed no good way to broach the subject, Cassie decided to start at the beginning. Sighing, she asked, "Does the name Chris Tanner mean anything to you? He was my brother."

Lights from the hotel gleamed across the dark water. In the several seconds of silence that followed she watched their moving, glimmering patterns.

"My God," Joel swore behind her, his voice shaken.

Cassie hugged herself closer. "I had to know the truth, Joel," she said quietly. "I had to know for me, for Chris." She gnawed on the inside of her lip. "And I had to know for us."

The tension in her shoulders was a living thing, making her feel the shocked force of his gaze on her back. She couldn't move, didn't dare breathe.

Joel stared at Cassie's huddled figure, stunned. He couldn't believe the enormity of it all. Cassie hadn't been after a story, she'd been after revenge! As he realized how badly she'd wanted to hurt him, he felt a dull amazement that he'd come off so unscathed.

"You thought—" He stopped and corrected himself. "You think I'm responsible for your brother's death?" His voice was a stranger's, foreign to his own ears.

"I didn't know what to think," Cassie answered tonelessly. "I was on assignment to find out the truth."

"From Mike Casey?" Joel's query was quick.

"Yes." Cassie paused. This part was the trickiest. It was too close to the raw edge of her emotions. "Your fondness for the press is well recorded," she added bitterly. "Nobody could get near you."

Joel's penetrating glare was deadly. "But you did."

"Oh, yes. I did. Only it didn't go quite as planned. It backfired, as you well know. I—I fell in love with you."

Her words fell like stones, heavy, hard. It was a torture to be so honest. Cassie waited, her gaze fixed straight ahead, her senses crying out for understanding.

Behind her, Joel was tense and rigid. She heard his uneven breathing. "Lies fall too easily from your lips, Cassie."

She probably deserved that, she thought fatalistically, but she'd already heaped more than enough blame on herself. Some of it—maybe most of it—belonged to Joel. "What about you?" she accused, turning slowly. "Why couldn't you tell me the truth? Why did I have to find out from someone else?''

"What truth?'' His hands descended on her shoulders, hard fingers pressing into her flesh. She was like a stiff mannequin, refusing to betray the slightest quiver of emotion, wanting to say what she had to say without the destructive interference of feelings.

"What truth?'' Joel demanded again, his tone harsh. "About your brother? Just what is it you expect me to say, for God's sake? That I'm sorry? That I should have known?'' His words lashed at her with the sting of a whip. Cassie's eyes widened in shock as Joel raged on, "He was in the wrong place at the wrong time. What more is there to say?''

"Stop it!'' Cassie's shoulders shook. She felt hysteria closing in on her. "How can you be so cruel and unfeeling?'' she shouted. "What kind of man are you?''

She'd never wanted to hit another human being before, but suddenly she wanted to batter Joel and all he stood for. Blinded by a hurt too strong to understand, she balled her hands into tight little fists and struck at him with a vengeance, beating his chest with all her strength, loosing the anger and loneliness she'd held inside for years. Her teeth were gritted, silent tears of rage coursed down her cheeks, her chest heaved. She pummeled him as if she wanted to break through the wall of his chest.

Joel's hands clamped around her upper arms, restraining her from inflicting serious damage. He let her go on for a few tense minutes until her sobbing of grief overwhelmed her and she suddenly sagged against him. He folded his arms around her tightly and waited.

After a moment she sucked in a deep breath, then expelled it with a shudder. Then for long moments neither one of them moved.

"I don't know what you think I've done,'' Joel said

quietly, picking his words, "but your brother's death was just an unfortunate accident. I'm sorry, I—"

Cassie stiffened instantly. "I know what you've done," she accused, her words muffled against his shirt.

Joel pushed her back as far as his arms would allow, his brows drawn into a harsh line. He was baffled and a little annoyed at her stubbornness. "Look, Cass—" he began, only to be cut off by her sharp movement. She backed away, stopping when she felt the support of one of the pier's posts against her knees.

She was determined not to let him foil her attempts to get everything out in the open. She held her palm up as if to ward off an advance. Joel didn't move a muscle.

"I want you to know that I called Mike and told him everything I know. I . . . couldn't keep it hidden." Cassie swallowed hard. "I think you probably understand."

A heartbeat passed. "What are you talking about?" he asked evenly. "What did you tell Casey?"

Cassie wished she could sit down. This confession— or interrogation—was sapping her of strength. It was far harder than she'd imagined. "I told him about the accident . . . and about the invoice your accountant showed me."

"Gaston?" Joel's sudden, intent look alarmed her.

She nodded jerkily. "I couldn't go on with the story myself. I think the reason's obvious. I've been too emotionally involved from the start because of Chris." Cassie hurried on, oblivious to the subtle change in Joel's demeanor. His face was tense, shaken, disbelieving. "And, let's face it, I let myself get involved with you, too."

"Go back to Gaston. What invoice did he show you?"

"The—the one about the wiring. I saw Roger's note, too."

"What wiring? For the Polynesian Village?"

Cassie hesitated. Joel was tense, coiled. She knew a moment of fear at what he must be thinking. "Yes," she answered painfully, "I saw your signature okaying the cheaper material."

"What?" Then, after an explosive moment, "God!"

Cassie watched as the color receded from Joel's face. She saw his jaw slacken in disbelief, his eyes focus on some faraway point as if she'd just dropped from his consciousness. Cassie felt herself lose him and wondered why it had happened now, when she should have experienced this feeling days before.

Suddenly Joel was in motion, jogging, then sprinting back to the hotel.

"Joel!" Cassie cried, truly frightened now. What was he running from? Her?

She tried to keep up, cursing her weakness and his speed. She stumbled once, caught herself, then ripped off her shoes, racing after him in stockinged feet. What they were running to or from didn't cross her mind. She just needed to be with him, to share and face whatever problems there were together.

She yanked on the door to the ballroom, her eyes anxiously scanning the crowd for Joel's tall form and dark head. Uncaring of the raised eyebrows her disheveled appearance created, she pushed her way frantically through the crowd.

"Joel!" she cried, spying him near the elevators. A man with a wide belly blocked her path and she swore at his unwitting interference.

Then suddenly, before the noisy conversation had a chance to dim, a terrifying shudder rocked the building. Cassie looked up, heard a woman's high-pitched scream, then staggered backward in horror as an ear-splitting wrenching noise tore from the overhead skyway. The bridge buckled slowly, inexorably. For the space of a silent pulsebeat it hung, its elegant arch looking ponderous and malevolent, people scrambling for their lives. Then, as if seen through a slow motion lens, it broke at its centermost point, falling with a deafening crash upon the crowd below.

Chapter Twelve

The hushed quiet that descended lasted one brief, eternal moment. Stunned, the crowd was frozen into silence. Cassie could only stare through horror-widened eyes for those few seconds, her fingers pressed against her mouth.

Like statues brought to life, the guests slowly began to back away from the broken skyway. Cassie felt them brushing past her, a slow-motion exodus that started to rev to a fever pitch. They bumped and jostled her, and she had to fight to retain her footing.

Joel. Where was he?

She began struggling in earnest, pushing madly through the crowd. Luckily, most of the people who'd been under the bridge had had time to run to safety. Still, the low moaning Cassie could hear filled her with fear.

Pieces of wood and concrete littered the floor. Cassie's sandals crunched over them, her eyes fixed on the back of a dark haired man in a black tuxedo, prone on the floor. With a steady nerve she didn't know she possessed, she bent down over him, realizing even as she did so that it wasn't Joel. Her shoulders slumped with relief. Trembling fingers searched for his pulse, and at that moment his eyelids fluttered open.

"Don't move," she warned shakily. "You're all right." She felt helpless and swallowed desperately. One of the waiters, a sober-looking youth with a strong jaw, was suddenly beside her. As she cleared her throat to ask what he thought they should do, he bent on one knee; his ministrations soon convinced her he'd had some kind of medical training.

No one lay beneath the twisted wood and steel. Of that she was certain. Cassie squeezed her face between her palms, trying to remember. Had anyone fallen from the skyway? She shuddered as she recalled one body clinging to the bridge as it plummeted.

She picked her way through the wreckage, heartened by the few guests who remained inside to help the injured. A woman with an arm bent at an impossible angle was groaning, and Cassie rushed to her, forcing herself to control her anxiety over Joel. She was helpless to do more than assure the woman that she would be all right.

"Shhh. An ambulance will be here soon," Cassie soothed, wiping beads of perspiration from the woman's forehead. Her stomach was twisted in knots of worry.

A surging crowd around the elevator caught Cassie's eye. People were trying to escape the disaster, turning a cold shoulder on the injured, their only interest being to save themselves. Cassie had the urge to scream at them. Then she saw Joel.

Apart from looking deathly pale, he was unhurt. Coolly, authoritatively, he allowed only a safe number of people to crowd into the elevator at one time. One desperate man was jerked firmly back by his lapels. Joel's harsh expression kept the hysteria from spreading.

Suddenly his gaze collided with hers. She trembled at the relief that filled his expression, tears clouding her vision. He was all right. So was she.

The icy hand of fear lifted its grip, and Cassie concentrated on soothing her patient's agony. "They're coming. Hang in there. See? The elevator's coming down now."

Cassie stepped wearily around the debris, oblivious to the pop of flashbulbs and the eagerly snapped questions of the press. She leaned her back against the wall and let out a heartfelt sigh, wondering vaguely what time it was. Very few people remained, only those willing to sacrifice their sleep to answer the hundreds of questions that were on everyone's mind. How had it happened? Who was responsible? Would there by an inquiry into the accident? Was anyone seriously hurt?

The last question was the big one. As far as Cassie knew, no one had died, but one man, the one who'd fallen with the bridge, was in critical condition. Another man had a broken hip and was still unconscious.

Cassie watched Lynnette Cosgrove interviewing people and felt her weariness increase. Mike was going to get more than he'd bargained for. Joel didn't have a prayer.

Lynnette saw her and smiled grimly. Cassie realized she had an "I told you so" coming, but Lynnette, showing unusual graciousness, didn't rub it in. "Are you all right?" she asked.

"I'll live," Cassie answered unsmilingly.

"And Shepherd?"

Cassie pushed herself away from the wall, a sudden lick of anger turning into a raging flame. "Joel Shepherd," she said evenly, "deserves whatever happens to him."

Lynnette's eyebrows raised. "Can I quote you on that?"

"Just do what's necessary, Lynnette."

Cassie brushed past her, walking to the glass doors she'd chased Joel through only hours before. Once outside she gulped for air, fighting back an overwhelming feeling of nausea. Her stomach quivered, and she rested her feverish forehead against one of the columns supporting the patio roof.

Whatever I felt for him is dead, she told herself. It's dead and buried. There is nothing left.

Cassie didn't have the strength to test the mettle of her thoughts. She knew that even if it weren't completely true yet, she would make it true. She'd been fooled, tricked by her own desire, and she never would be again. She would kill her love for Joel somehow.

There was no way this disaster was an accident. She knew without a shadow of a doubt that as soon as the truth was disclosed, some kind of underhanded dealing would come to light. And the blame would be Joel's.

Her mouth curved downward bitterly. Love *is* blind . . .

With sudden clarity she remembered the first evening she'd met Kurt—how he'd dazzled her, romanced her, turned her into a lovesick fool who refused to see his bad points. She'd been eager to love him, marry him. She'd been angry with her brother for his cautious advice and concern. Before her mind could be changed, before her own doubts could be realized, she'd rushed into a doomed marriage with a man she barely knew.

Now she'd almost done it again. Against impossible truths she'd rejected Joel's dark side and concentrated on loving the good.

How could she be so foolish? A second time!

"There you are." Joel's voice sounded near her ear, the door closing softly behind him. "I've been looking for you."

Cassie turned slowly, a cold fury suddenly chilling her. All that hurt, all that hate, suddenly had a direction. She let it come on stronger to quench the ember of love that wouldn't quite die.

She saw the lines of fatigue and remorse that bracketed Joel's mouth but ignored them. Like a vengeful angel she swooped down on him. "How could you? How *could* you?" She swept a wrathful arm toward the ballroom. "You did this, Joel! You risked people's lives, for God's sake! Why? *Why?*"

His tie was gone; his elegant clothes looked used and wrinkled. He just stared blankly toward the ocean.

"I loved you," Cassie said bitterly. "I believed in you!"

Joel managed a bleak glance in her direction. "Did you really?"

Cassie sucked in a sharp breath and jerked her eyes from his. "Yes. I tried to," she added more honestly. "I really wanted to. Everyone warned me, but I wouldn't listen." Her mouth twisted. "I never listen."

There was no one on the beach. They were alone, away from the furious activity inside the hotel. A breeze fluttered off the ocean and Cassie turned her face to it, trying to hold in her raging anger.

"It couldn't have been for the money you saved, Joel," she said through tight lips. "I have a right to know why."

"Yes." His answer was slow, tortured. "You do."

"Then why? Why? Tell me why!"

"I trusted someone too much," he said softly after a brief, painful silence. "Someone I loved." His head sank back wearily against the pillar next to hers, and he emitted a short, mirthless laugh. "You should appreciate the irony in that."

Cassie's voice was cold. "What are you talking about?"

"I don't know." Joel let out an uneven breath. "I just don't know."

"Well, you'd better find out," Cassie threw out, drawing herself up angrily. "And you'd better find out fast. You've ruined lives, Joel. People have died!"

Joel's white face went paler yet. He looked so utterly lost that Cassie paused in wonderment. Regrets? At this late date? No, she wouldn't let herself fall victim to that trap! The man had a unique talent for making her believe in him even when she knew he was guilty. She shook her head in self-disgust. He'd practically confessed, and she still nourished that doubt deep inside!

"The *Island Breeze* will crucify you," she said tonelessly. "You're not going to be able to buy yourself out of this one." A wave of pain squeezed her heart. "But nothing will bring my brother back," she whispered.

"Cassie . . ."

"Don't." She stiffened against the entreaty of his tone. "Just . . . don't."

Joel looked at her hopelessly.

"I'm going to make sure you get what you deserve, Joel. You've hurt people. You've hurt me. And I'm not going to let you hurt anyone else."

There was a painful silence between them. Cassie felt its crushing force and shrieked, "Well, aren't you even going to say anything? Won't you even try to prove me wrong?"

"What could I possibly say?" Joel asked bleakly. "You've already tried and convicted me. Would you believe me if I said I had no idea? If I told you I probably feel worse than you do? No"—Joel held up a palm against the furious disbelief on her face—"I didn't think so."

Cassie examined his ravaged face and felt a deep, driving pain. "Maybe you ought to try something more concrete," she whispered.

"Anything I would say in my own defense would sound lame to you."

"Try me."

"I just did."

Cassie's chest was heaving as if she'd just climbed ten flights of stairs. "Go ahead," she said, her voice quaking. "Convince me. I want you to convince me."

"Oh, Cassie . . ." Joel's voice was tortured. "I didn't know about the skyway."

"Liar!"

Her lips were quivering, her back tight and hurting. She couldn't listen anymore. He was right. Nothing he could say would make her believe him.

Tears burned in her widened eyes. She felt them begin to drizzle slowly down her cheeks, but she never blinked. She saw how badly he was hurting but was unable to help. He'd done this. He'd destroyed both her love and himself.

"I can't love you anymore." Cassie choked on a sob, then caught herself. "I can't forgive you."

Joel closed his eyes.

Cassie turned blindly away, filled with unspeakable despair. At that moment the door to the hotel burst open; reporters spilled out. She felt a quick twist to her heart, a last regret as they descended upon Joel like a pack of hungry jackals. She looked back, saw the silent defeat in the line of his shoulders, the fatigue in his face, and then his eyes met hers.

She turned away, stumbling toward the hotel door. Trying desperately to block it out, she nevertheless saw that last ravaged look again and again in her mind's eye. There was a message there, one of regret and good-bye.

It was seared into her brain and held in mental focus long after her tears had dried on her pillow.

Any illusions Cassie had that time would help ease her pain were quickly banished. A week after the accident she was still huddled inside her Honolulu apartment, listlessly wondering what she ought to do with the rest of her life.

She was no closer to an answer now than she had been that last fateful night with Joel. Dozens of ideas had been considered and rejected; nothing seemed right.

The one bright spot had been Bryan's unexpected call. He was back in Los Angeles, working for one of the major newspapers. After feeling Cassie out about her position, he'd casually suggested there might be room for her on the staff, too. Cassie, warmed by his thoughtfulness, had said she'd call him back. It was time to make that decision.

She'd left Maui without a backward look, gathering all her belongings and releasing her apartment. In a rather bizarre gesture that now embarrassed her, she'd thrown her running gear into the trash. No more new horizons, she mused defeatedly.

So what now?

Her morning copy of the *Island Breeze* was still folded on the coffee table. Cassie, who hadn't had the heart to read it earlier, reluctantly picked it up and settled onto the sofa. Since it was a major island paper, she still subscribed. Most people she knew did—even Joel—but it was fast losing its audience. Joel had been right about one thing: Mike was ruining its reputation.

One look at the morning headline and her stomach revolted. The words almost made her physically sick. Then anger saved her. Damn Mike Casey! He'd stopped only a hair's breadth short of calling Joel a murderer.

Cassie flung down the paper and fell back against the cushions of her couch, feeling exhausted. She picked up her cup of spiced tea and absently turned the cup around on the plate. When was she ever going to be rid of this ambivalence? she wondered tiredly. One moment she hated Joel; the next she loathed Mike for attacking him.

What on earth did she really want?

Sighing, she got up and walked into the kitchen, oblivious to the golden, late morning sunshine that poured into the room. A vase full of hot pink plumeria and scarlet anthuriums dazzled the eye, but for Cassie the beauty was lost. Too many memories; too much unrealized hope. She didn't want to live here anymore.

The one thing she did know was that she wasn't interested in working for Mike or the *Island Breeze*. Her confidence in it as a newspaper was completely gone.

So what did that leave her?

When she'd come to Hawaii she'd had her brother. Now she was alone. There was nothing left for her in the islands. Thinking she should have made the decision long ago, Cassie sat at the kitchen counter and reached for the telephone, her eye on the scrap of paper with Bryan's number. There really was no other choice.

The doorbell intruded before the second ring. With a muffled curse, Cassie dropped the receiver into its cradle and stared wrathfully at the door. She didn't feel like seeing anyone. The thought that it might be Mike's or Lynnette's gloating face on the other side made her feel wretched. Her head pounded.

Catching a glimpse of herself in the entry mirror did little to hearten her. Her hair was a tousled mess of red and gold; deep blue rings circled her huge, tired-looking eyes. She looked as weary as she felt. With a feeling of self-disgust, she was glad she'd decided to move back to Los Angeles. There was nothing for her here; she was turning into a person she didn't like very much.

Cassie cinched the sash of her blue velour robe, giving herself a moment to collect herself. If it were Mike and he started in on Joel . . . Her teeth clenched.

"Joel!" Cassie was so surprised his name came out in a gasp. He was standing in the slanting sunshine on her porch, his face haggard and exhausted. So he's been doing some soul-searching, she thought, but the idea gave her cold comfort.

"May I come in?" he inquired carefully. "I'd like to talk to you, explain some things."

Cassie just stared at him. She toyed with the notion of just closing the door in his face. She owed him nothing—nothing! And she already knew how adept he was at changing her mind, convincing her of the unconvinceable.

Because you want to be convinced, she reminded herself.

"I don't think there's anything that can be explained to me that I don't already know or haven't at least guessed," she answered coldly, refusing to acknowledge the flash of pain in his tawny gaze. She pulled the lapels of her robe close to her throat.

A muscle worked beside Joel's jaw. "I'd like to try."

Cassie hesitated, then moved aside wordlessly, her throat hot and hurting. She couldn't allow him to touch that part of her that only he could. She refused to let it happen.

He walked across her living room and stared through the narrow copper-colored blinds to a wildly overgrown garden of trees and flowers tucked between the apartments.

He sighed, pushing his hands into his back pockets. Cassie watched him warily, keeping a wide distance between them, afraid of the pull of her emotions. His shirt was stretched across his broad shoulders, and the sight of his lithe, tough frame made her react crazily. Tears scalded her vision. She brushed them away angrily, thankful that Joel's back was to her. She was beginning to loathe her own weakness for him.

Joel's shoulders dropped slightly. He cleared his throat. "I wanted to tell you some things—about me and Shepherd Construction—before you read them in the paper."

Cassie's breath was strangled. What was this? Some kind of delayed confession? She laughed harshly. "You mean there's more?"

Joel raked a hand through his hair, letting out a ragged sigh. He half turned. "There's lots more, Cassie. You don't know the half of it.'' He swung around fully and regarded her with somber eyes. "Neither did I until this week.''

"I don't want to hear it." Cassie suddenly wheeled around, her eyes searching wildly for an avenue of escape. She had the strongest desire to bury her head in the sand like an ostrich and let the world pass her by. She sensed he had a lot to say, and she was certain it wasn't anything good.

Her withdrawal stopped him cold. "None of it?"

Cassie could barely stand the defeat in his voice. He really wanted to tell her now, when it was all too late. She swallowed hard, squeezing her eyes shut. She couldn't bear any more misery. "No, none of it. It takes me half a day to find the courage to open the paper, Joel. Let me learn in my own time.''

A fine tension spread between them. Cassie sensed it and felt her resolve weakening, breaking down from the powerful silence of Joel's presence.

"I need to tell you about the accident, Cassie—why it happened.''

Her jaw ached from holding her teeth together. "Was it your fault, Joel?" she asked shakily.

He didn't move. She felt him weighing his answer. "Partly,'' he admitted.

Cassie's shoulders slumped. She wanted to sink into dark oblivion. She wasn't even aware that Joel had moved until his strong arm encircled her. The temptation to sag against him was enormous, but Cassie dragged herself away, walking unsteadily to the couch, her knees already buckling before she sank down. "Then there's nothing else to say, is there, Joel?" she whispered, her eyes wide and dry.

"There is for me."

Cassie's lips pressed together. "I don't really care about you," she said tautly. "It's over. It's all over. Nothing you can say or do will ever change that." She paused, counting her heartbeats. "Perhaps you should leave."

Joel heard the tremulous quality of her voice and felt her pain a thousandfold. He wondered if he wasn't out of his mind, risking wounding each of them even more without changing a thing. Hopelessness was new to him and he loathed it. But he felt, rather arrogantly he supposed, that if there was even one chance, he was compelled to take it.

"You once asked me why, Cass. You wanted to know why everything happened the way it did. I want to tell you. I *need* to tell you."

Her chin came up stubbornly. "You ask a helluva lot."

"Yes," he agreed, holding her gaze. "I do."

For days he'd refused to think about Cassie and about his deep, unshakable feelings for her. Any anger, all bitterness, that he'd felt at her deception had died. He understood her reasons totally. He understood everything now.

"There was a time in my life when I couldn't cope with my own personal problems," he began, staring at the vase of flowers in the kitchen, knowing she didn't want him looking at her. "Tali was . . . very sick. She did some very self-destructive things that made me furious. Once she was in a car accident—her fault because of drugs—and Scott nearly lost his life. I wanted to kill her."

Cassie's nails were torturing the roughly woven texture of the couch. She was screaming inside. Part of her was fascinated, still fascinated. The other part was backing away. Holding control of her shaking voice, she murmured, "Pretty paltry excuses for causing my brother's death, Joel."

"I'm not looking for excuses. There wouldn't be one large enough."

Cassie chanced a glance in his direction. His face was drawn and serious, his mouth curved down. He looked so unhappy. She pulled her eyes away.

Joel sighed resignedly. "I had a lot of stress. I started

getting migraines. I was ordered by my doctor to find a way to relieve that stress or suffer the consequences. It meant turning my back on Tali—and that meant Scott, too—or giving up the business.'' His mouth twisted in self-mockery. "Or better yet, both. I was unwilling to do either.''

Joel paused, unsure of Cassie's reaction. Her skin was pale and tight, her face a studied effort of control. She was listening, but it was costing her to do so.

Her eyes flickered his way. "So you compromised,'' she suggested thinly.

"In a manner of speaking,'' Joel admitted, memories of that time vivid. He thought of Tali, her weakness, her childish viciousness. He remembered Scott's wide-eyed watchfulness with a dull, regretful ache. And he recalled his own momentous decision. "I put Roger in charge of the Polynesian Village project,'' he continued tiredly. "I okayed anything and everything he slid across my desk.''

Outside, the light twittering of birds and the distant hum of traffic made Cassie aware that nothing had changed. Inside, the air was so charged Cassie thought she'd stopped breathing. She heard Joel's words, understood the electrifying message. She looked up sharply and saw the bleakness in his eyes. When he nodded to her questioning, disbelieving gaze, she looked away. She felt hope surge like a bird preparing for flight and desperately tried to bank the feeling. "It's not enough,'' she whispered, struck cold by the magnitude of Roger's crime. It was, after all, Joel's company.

"No, I'm sure it's not. Nothing can bring your brother back.''

The sincere regret of his simple words pierced through the icy wall surrounding her heart. She hated herself for wanting to believe him. But Roger? Roger! Fleetingly,

Cassie sensed Joel's smoldering, helpless rage at his closest friend's betrayal. It was far worse than hers because complete trust had been given so long ago.

Now she was desperate to hear more. With pain-filled blue eyes she asked, "Roger? How, Joel? Why?"

It was a question he'd asked himself over and over again and one he'd eventually posed to Roger. His friend—the man he thought was his friend—had been hard pressed for money and had seen a way to get it. In reality, Roger had felt the safety requirements to be too high anyway; he'd been convinced that shaving a few dollars here or a couple hundred there would never make a difference.

Joel shook his head. "For the money. He thought it was a way to get extra capital without harming anyone." Joel's face hardened, his recollections too clear, too vivid. "The accident at the Polynesian Village proved him wrong. I remember now how devastated he was, but I thought it was just normal grief." Joel sucked in a long, unsteady breath. "You know, I could have prevented it. I knew, even back then, that there was something wrong, but I . . ." His voice trailed off in self-loathing. Cassie felt an urge to offer solace but squelched it. Couldn't this be just a well-rehearsed act? Couldn't it?

Twice burned, she wasn't eager to make another blind mistake. "He blamed you, y'know," she murmured, watching him.

Joel hadn't known, but he'd suspected as much. When confronted, Roger hadn't immediately broken down and confessed. Only Joel's overwhelming evidence of Roger's deceit—written statements from Daniel Lessing; confessions from Paul Gaston, who was also involved in the cover-up; and conversations with several individuals from the insurance company that had originally investigated the accident—had forced the whole story to come out.

But to hear Cassie's words was still a blow, an aftershock

to an already devastating quake. Joel looked around for a chair in which to collapse. He didn't trust that Cassie was ready to sit next to him, so he chose the well-worn rust velveteen armchair across from her.

"I spent so much time comforting him." Joel's self-blame was in his voice. "I should have known there was something more, but I just didn't take the time. I was half out of my mind about Tali—worrying about her next move, praying that Scott wouldn't be an innocent victim. It was an incredible relief when she ran off to L.A." Cassie's heart contracted at the aching torment on his face. "You see, you're right. It is my fault."

Cassie, even in her cautiousness, couldn't let him shoulder that burden. The ring of truth was too disturbingly self-evident. "No, it's not your fault. You were as much a victim as any of us."

His head came up slowly, his eyes searching hers. Cassie tried to keep her expression neutral. She wasn't about to rush fences; Joel needed to know that.

Her blue green gaze held his, honest, open and direct, but not ready to bury the past. Experience was a teacher one couldn't easily forget or ignore. Her hurt was too fresh. For that matter, so was Joel's.

But it was time to explain a few things to him that he didn't yet know. "I pressed Roger about you . . . and Gaston and Lessing."

"I know. I talked to all of them."

Cassie gnawed at her lower lip, thinking. "Did Roger also tell you that when I got too close he shifted the blame to you? He didn't deny it; he just pointed the finger at you."

Joel stared silently at his hands, feeling like half a man. How could he have trusted Roger so implicitly?

"I . . . I don't mean to . . . hurt you."

"No, it's okay. Really. I know what you mean."

Cassie's stammered apology did more to restore Joel's

equilibrium than all the answers to the harrowing questions of the last week had done. The barren emptiness inside him lessened a little.

"I think," he said at length, offering an answer to the question furrowing Cassie's brow, "that he understood our relationship—yours and mine—better than even we did. He believed you loved me enough to stop digging. Pushing you in my direction was just a matter of self-preservation. Your love for me would keep you quiet."

Cassie hugged her arms tightly around herself, a chill of regret sliding down her spine to settle uncomfortably in her lower back. "There is a matter of living with oneself." That sounded pathetically feeble as an explanation. "Roger didn't know me very well."

"And I didn't know him very well." Joel rolled his eyes toward the ceiling in a gesture of tortured disbelief. "God!" he expelled, anguish in the lines on his face.

The subject was far too grim for Cassie to feel even vaguely relieved at Joel's innocence. It was almost beyond belief that Roger could be so wickedly callous, yet she knew it to be true. She'd been struck by his odd attitude from the first, had wondered more than once what motivated him. Now she thought she knew. "Do you think Roger resented working for you?" she asked cautiously. "All those years of being your tutor, then suddenly he's out of money and needing a job. You offer it to him. He never really gets over it."

Joel observed her blankly. He rejected her scenario without thinking. "Roger's not that petty. He wouldn't—"

Cassie got up and walked to the kitchen, unable to witness Joel's disturbing realizations about his once closest friend. He'd cut himself off as he recognized his folly. He didn't understand Roger anymore.

She turned up the burner under her teapot and waited for

it to heat. She needed the diversion; Joel needed the diversion. Within minutes a high-pitched whistle announced that the water was boiling.

Cassie poured them each a cup of tea. She handed one to Joel, careful not to let her fingertips meet his. She wanted to touch him, but she was too afraid. In the deep recesses of her mind she'd forgiven him, but dark mysteries and motivations remained. After all, the skyway across the ballroom floor had collapsed long after Joel had settled his marital problems and gotten his migraines under control. He couldn't easily blame that all on Roger. He was not a man to be duped so completely.

Joel had quietly pulled himself together while Cassie was out of the room. "After the accident at the Polynesian Village, there was an investigation by the insurance company. Nothing was found to be out of the ordinary. I was convinced it was just a horrible accident. I never thought it was anything else, and all the hype in the paper just disgusted me. Scandalmongers. Mike Casey." He snorted derisively. "I couldn't handle those circling vultures.

"But, as it turns out, I was wrong. Wrong, wrong, wrong. And Casey was right. That was hard to take until I delved a little deeper. God!" he muttered fervently. "Does everyone have a darker side?"

"What do you mean?"

"Never mind. It's not important for the moment. There are so many other things."

Cassie stirred lemon into her tea, absently watching the swirling amber liquid, counting the circles. "Like the skyway?" she probed softly.

Joel set his cup on the coffee table with inordinate care. His eyes captured hers. "Do you really believe I was responsible for that?" Her silence, the way her gaze slid from his, was answer enough. Joel stared at the profile of her face, deciding to continue, though there seemed to be little reason. "You didn't realize it, but when we were talking on the dock, you said things that hit me like a thunderbolt."

Cassie smiled faintly. "Oh, I realized it. I just wasn't sure why."

"I suddenly knew! Gaston, Roger—the whole thing fell together, and I didn't want to believe it. I couldn't! When the . . . enormity of it struck me . . . well . . ." Joel leaned tensely forward, wishing he had the power to make her understand. "I had to find Roger," he finished. "I had to know."

Cassie's look was sharp. "Before something else happened?"

"Maybe. Though I don't believe I was thinking that rationally. I just had to know." His brows drew down. "Can you understand that?"

Oh, yes. She could understand. She'd spent weeks vacillating back and forth, telling herself if only she could just know. Now she was afraid to know. Six days ago, if he'd come to her with these revelations, she would have welcomed him with open arms, gloried in the proof of his innocence, planned a shining future together. But after the skyway collapse, the injuries . . . Even though no one was fatally hurt, she couldn't forget that scene or completely absolve Joel.

Joel sensed her hesitation and knew instinctively that she was balanced on the knife's edge of indecision. "The girders weren't strong enough to support the bridge," he said in a quiet clinical voice. "Roger, with the aid of Paul Gaston, siphoned money off the top there, too. When I found that out I ordered another complete investigation. They're checking invoices with purchase orders." His jaw tightened. "They've already found a few other dangerous cuts. I doubt the hotel will really open for at least two more years.''

"Oh, Joel!" Cassie's cup clattered in its saucer as she set it on the table with trembling hands. She suddenly, belatedly, saw the full extent of Roger's duplicity, the savagery of his crime. He'd used a friend's trust, then deliberately set out to destroy that friend, whether he understood his own motivations or not.

"Roger ordered inferior-grade products from at least twenty different sources. It's just a matter of seeing what can be done to reinforce or replace them.''

Cassie could only shake her head slowly from side to side. She felt drained yet relieved. Ordering the criminal investigation, ferreting out the confusing details of the deception, bringing the case to the attention of the authorities—in Cassie's eyes, these actions absolved Joel.

He was watching her closely. "If it's any interest to you, Roger never brought any of the invoices for the Maui Paccaro to my attention. He had complete control. After the Polynesian Village accident I took over again for a while, but Roger asked to be solely in charge of the hotel. I couldn't see any reason to play big brother. After all," Joel added quietly, poignantly, "he trained me.''

Cassie's heart was in her eyes. She loved him, and she ached to read the disillusionment on his face. Roger's selfish deception had shattered his faith, but she'd contributed a lot herself.

"I'm sorry. Oh, Joel, I'm so sorry.''

"Don't be. It certainly wasn't your fault." After a thoughtful moment he stood, then moved to sit down next to her. "Actually, I'm amazed you even believe me, what with Roger's note and all. I never saw it," he assured her, mistaking the sudden look on her face as apprehension. "It was written after the fact.''

"It's not that. I should have known that note was a phony. It's all the horrible things I said to you. Joel, I—"

"Shhh." His warm finger shushed her apologies. "Not now. God, not now."

"But I want to. I need to." She smiled to hear herself echoing his earlier words. "Every time I turned around someone was telling me it was you, *you*. One minute I'd believe you, the next I'd listen to Mike or Lynnette or Roger. I've hated myself for being unsure. I should have known, Joel. I did know, I just wouldn't listen to my—"

The contact of his mouth on hers effectively stopped her string of apologies. His lips moved softly against hers, and Cassie slowly closed her eyes. They had time, lots of time. All the fears and doubts that had been held in so long could wait a little longer before they were explored then banished forever.

Cassie's mouth grew hungry under Joel's. All the desperation she'd felt seemed expressed in that one simple contact. She wrapped her arms around his shoulders, pressing herself tightly to his chest.

"I always said you talked too much," he muttered against the supple skin of her throat.

Cassie's mouth curved into a smile. "You were right. I think talking's highly overrated."

"Like running?"

"Exactly like running."

His hands swept over her robe, pulling it free, exposing an ever-widening triangle of smooth flesh. She had nothing on beneath the robe; she'd been planning to take a shower before the morning paper was delivered. Now Joel's hands discovered that secret, and he tensed in surprise. He drew a long breath in between his teeth. Cassie couldn't keep the corners of her mouth from twitching. She loved him so much. Nothing mattered but that.

"I've been so awful," she said, pressing his hard jaw

against her temple. "Believing the worst of you. The very worst."

Joel laughed softly, his hands on her warm skin possessive yet incredibly gentle. "You had enough reason, love. If I hadn't known better, I would have blamed me, too." He covered her face with tiny kisses. Cassie's eyes fluttered closed. Beneath the heavy layers of deception that were now stripped away, something shifted and moved, something beautiful that she'd always known was there if only she could find it. It was trust, wonderful and complete.

The warmth of his body against hers melted her doubt. Cassie's eyes told Joel that eloquently, but he clasped her face between the palms of his hands nevertheless, anxious that she understand all of it. "I feel a responsibility for Chris's death, and the others'. I trusted Roger too much, even when he made decisions I didn't agree with."

Cassie's tender kisses smoothed the grim lines around his mouth. Wordlessly she shook her head, letting him know that her brother's death was not his responsibility. Roger had a lot on his conscience. She imagined the burden he carried was crippling him.

Her thoughts were on Roger's betrayal and Joel's shattered trust. "I was thinking earlier that love can be so blind."

"Is that how you feel about me?" he asked cautiously.

"No." Cassie smiled wistfully, reassuring him. "I used to feel that way—that I was blindly overlooking your faults, wanting you so badly that I ignored the bad. But now I think I was wrong." The pressure of his hands and the warmth of his body made Cassie stretch out beside him. He followed her down onto the cushions of the couch, his arms on either side of her, wanting but waiting.

"What do you mean by *wrong?*" he asked.

She closed her eyes. "I didn't overlook, Joel. I did just the opposite. I dug and dug and dug, not being able to trust you, convinced you were hiding something. I was so certain I'd find something that I couldn't trust my feelings.'' She pressed a hot cheek against the cool strength of his chest, listening to the steady beat of his heart. "I was afraid to love you,'' she whispered, "afraid I'd get hurt again.''

The look on his face told her he felt he'd already hurt her far too much. She couldn't wipe away the incredible responsibility he felt with mere words. Only time would help.

In silent mutual consent the questions halted. Cassie felt him shudder as her hands explored him, pulling buttons free, finding the zip of his pants, helping him out of his clothes until his lean body was pressed against hers, hearts close together. Her robe fell open until every part of her was covered with his supple warmth.

For an endless moment they were still, each thinking of what they'd almost lost. She felt his tongue touch her ear. "I was afraid I'd never be able to touch you again,'' he muttered, the torture of that thought evident in his uneven voice.

A tremor shook her. "What would you have done?'' she whispered.

"Gone quietly out of my mind.''

Her flesh was quivering, not from the coolness of the room, but from the pulsing desire just beneath her skin. She, too, would have withered without his lovemaking.

"I love you, Joel.'' The time was finally right for her to say it. "I have from the beginning.''

"Oh, love,'' he groaned. "I've never loved the way I love you.''

Cassie cried out as his hands began touching her as only he could. His fingers moved hungrily, and she turned and twisted to meet each sensitive stroke. Her wantonness brought his urgent mouth to meet hers, his tongue moving slowly, deeply, until her desire flamed and she arched her restless body to his.

But he wasn't finished. His hands continued their seduction, moving from her heaving breasts to the silken down of her abdomen, then on to explore her quivering inner thighs until he felt all of her and she was lost in dazed pleasure.

"Joel," she murmured, "I'm weak."

"We're both weak." Then, "I love you, Cassie," as he moved swiftly, possessing her, uniting his hardness to her softness. She closed her eyes and made an incoherent sound as Joel brought her to a pleasure that was almost painful.

In the throbbing moment of complete love Cassie found an inner peace. The loneliness that had held her soul captive for so long was gone. She loved and was loved in return.

Time would heal all the other pain. Now she and Joel had a chance.

When finally the moments of silent union had slipped away and they became aware of one another as separate entities again, Joel shifted his supple weight and curved Cassie against him. With loving eyes he examined the smooth texture of her skin, the little wisps of hair that feathered her temple.

"There are still a few things to clear up," he said a little regretfully.

Cassie stretched and curled contentedly. "Not now, Joel," she said huskily. "I'm too loved up to talk."

"Then just listen," Joel said, unable to resist tasting her. His tongue licked the flesh behind her ear, feeling the subtle rhythm of her pulse. He wrapped his arms protectively, possessively, around her. "It's time you knew how you were duped."

"Duped?" Cassie's eyes flew open. "Me? What do you mean?"

"Relax." Then, reading her mind, he added with a soft

laugh, "It's not anything about me. No more confessions. It's about Mike Casey."

Cassie groaned. "Sounds like more bad news."

It was difficult for Joel to keep his mind on his theme with the glowing seductiveness of Cassie's aquamarine gaze focused so closely. Force of will kept him talking in an even voice. "Yes and no. Everything's already been straightened out, although I doubt you'll be able to read about it in his paper."

Cassie's curiosity mounted. "What's straightened out?"

"I had a long talk with your old buddy, and he told me some very interesting facts."

"Ex–old buddy," Cassie corrected him.

"Ex–old buddy, then. Did you ever wonder why he suddenly decided to go after Shepherd Construction now, two years after the accident at the Polynesian Village?"

"No."

"Well, there's a reason, love. He wasn't just trying to nail me; he wanted something far more tangible than revenge."

Cassie struggled to sit up, but Joel held her down with strong arms, his slashing grin telling her he was enjoying the battle. But Cassie's mind was on his words, on the unspoken message they held. "What was he after?" she questioned tensely.

"Money. The same as Tali." For a moment he looked extremely bitter.

"That's what you meant about everyone having a darker side?"

Joel nodded. "The property the Maui Paccaro is on originally belonged to Tali. She sold it to me, legally, right before our divorce. But, as I said before, Tali has a way of burning money that can't be equalled. When she realized she'd run out, she started thinking up ways to get more."

"Like using Scott," Cassie prompted.

"Exactly. Oh, by the way, I had a long talk with my son. He's coming back to Maui."

"Oh, Joël! That's wonderful." She saw the easing of tension on his face, and her heart glowed with happiness. She hadn't realized what a weight Scott had been on her own shoulders until that moment.

"But what has this got to do with Mike?" she questioned, remembering how their conversation had begun.

Joel's mouth curved derisively. "A lot. Mike and Tali knew each other a long time ago, and apparently they've kept in pretty close contact over the years. I knew some of it, because I can remember times when I'd catch her on the telephone, crying her heart out to any sympathetic listener there was. Mike was always available."

"Why?"

Joel shrugged his shoulders. "Who knows? Unrequited love, perhaps? Anyway, I thought that was all over when she moved to L.A. I didn't much care one way or another. But when Tali's money ran out, she started calling Mike again, and they came up with a plan that would benefit both of them."

Cassie was beyond intrigue; she was riveted. "Go on," she urged, half dreading what she suspected was yet to come.

"You can guess the rest. Mike used his newspaper as a weapon against me every time he could. He hoped to discredit me and help Tali regain title. That way they'd both become winners."

"Bastard!" Cassie spat viciously.

Joel regarded her with amusement. "Well, well. So there's a side of you I've never even seen."

"Mike put me on the case because I was already biased against you," Cassie said bitterly. "I always knew there was another reason! God! How could I have been so blind!"

"I think that's a question we've asked ourselves to

death," Joel soothed, liking the way she bristled to his defense. "Mike was afraid he'd lose the newspaper without some new capital. He tried getting investors, even managed to turn some away from me," Joel added, remembering the bank interview. "But he's so mired in personal debt there's no way he'll see the light of day."

"How do you know so much?" Cassie asked suspiciously.

"Don't trust me?"

"Of course I do! But short of breaking all of Mike's arms and legs, I don't see how—" Joel's sudden burst of laughter cut her short. "What's so funny?" she demanded.

"Nothing. Everything." Little spasms of laughter rocked his chest and Cassie, curled next to him, was infected by the mood.

"Okay, wise guy. What did you do? Put him in the hospital?"

Joel kissed her once, hard, full on the mouth. He grinned. "No, but I sure as hell threatened to! I was half crazed over what Roger'd done to me. By the time I got hold of Mike and realized what he'd been up to, I was ready to kill. Luckily, he started talking so fast I could hardly keep up with him."

"Lucky for him," Cassie muttered dryly.

"I also managed to squeeze your address out of him, although I must admit that was the hardest part. I think he thought I'd try to kill you when I was through with him."

Cassie's chin tilted thoughtfully. She allowed herself a kind thought for her ex-employer. "Maybe he's not such a villain after all. I mean, he thought he was saving my life."

"Hardly. He didn't hold out *that* long."

For a few minutes they both fell into a moody silence, thinking of the magnitude of deception and greed that had nearly ruined their lives.

Eventually Joel said grimly, "It was just too bad there

was a cover-up for Mike to print. Things would have been a lot simpler if there hadn't been.''

"What will happen to them—Roger and Mike?"

"Only time will tell."

There was a gigantic pause. Cassie couldn't help feeling a deep, yawning regret. "And what about you, Joel? What about your company? You've been slandered and attacked and used from all sides."

"I'll survive," he assured her. His eyes captured hers and he added softly, "With you."

Cassie gave him one of her quicksilver glances of blue green, the kind that once he'd imagined held a promise for him alone. "Is that a proposal?"

"If you want it to be. Whatever you want, Cassie, that's all I need. I'd love to marry you, have children, share a life together. But I'll settle for whatever you're ready for."

His honesty was so beautiful it almost hurt. For a moment she couldn't speak. Then, "Once I told you I wanted everything, Joel. I still do."

His grip around her tightened; their hearts pounded in unison. "We'll have Scott, too, you know. I couldn't let him stay with Tali, especially—"

"I know that. You know I do. I want to live with both of you."

Joel raised a skeptical brow. "Scott's not exactly easy."

"So you've said." She started a line of kisses down his cheek and throat, each one a little deeper, each one a little longer. "But everyone's got to have a challenge in their life, don't they?"

Joel's pulse pounded beneath her seductive touch. "I thought yours was that 'extra mile.' If we're going to get married, you're going to have to improve—What are you laughing at?"

"Never mind," Cassie said, her mirth-filled voice muffled against his hair-roughened chest. A picture of her discarded running gear, tossed to the trash in a fit of despair, was imprinted on her brain. "I'll tell you later . . . much, much later. But right now it seems that I have something better to do . . ."

And Joel, benefactor of Cassie's slow, purposeful love-making, decided she was completely right.

Silhouette Special Edition

MORE ROMANCE FOR
A SPECIAL WAY TO RELAX
$1.95 each

2 ☐ Hastings	21 ☐ Hastings	41 ☐ Halston	60 ☐ Thorne
3 ☐ Dixon	22 ☐ Howard	42 ☐ Drummond	61 ☐ Beckman
4 ☐ Vitek	23 ☐ Charles	43 ☐ Shaw	62 ☐ Bright
5 ☐ Converse	24 ☐ Dixon	44 ☐ Eden	63 ☐ Wallace
6 ☐ Douglass	25 ☐ Hardy	45 ☐ Charles	64 ☐ Converse
7 ☐ Stanford	26 ☐ Scott	46 ☐ Howard	65 ☐ Cates
8 ☐ Halston	27 ☐ Wisdom	47 ☐ Stephens	66 ☐ Mikels
9 ☐ Baxter	28 ☐ Ripy	48 ☐ Ferrell	67 ☐ Shaw
10 ☐ Thiels	29 ☐ Bergen	49 ☐ Hastings	68 ☐ Sinclair
11 ☐ Thornton	30 ☐ Stephens	50 ☐ Browning	69 ☐ Dalton
12 ☐ Sinclair	31 ☐ Baxter	51 ☐ Trent	70 ☐ Clare
13 ☐ Beckman	32 ☐ Douglass	52 ☐ Sinclair	71 ☐ Skillern
14 ☐ Keene	33 ☐ Palmer	53 ☐ Thomas	72 ☐ Belmont
15 ☐ James	35 ☐ James	54 ☐ Hohl	73 ☐ Taylor
16 ☐ Carr	36 ☐ Dailey	55 ☐ Stanford	74 ☐ Wisdom
17 ☐ John	37 ☐ Stanford	56 ☐ Wallace	75 ☐ John
18 ☐ Hamilton	38 ☐ John	57 ☐ Thornton	76 ☐ Ripy
19 ☐ Shaw	39 ☐ Milan	58 ☐ Douglass	77 ☐ Bergen
20 ☐ Musgrave	40 ☐ Converse	59 ☐ Roberts	78 ☐ Gladstone

$2.25 each

79 ☐ Hastings	87 ☐ Dixon	95 ☐ Doyle	103 ☐ Taylor
80 ☐ Douglass	88 ☐ Saxon	96 ☐ Baxter	104 ☐ Wallace
81 ☐ Thornton	89 ☐ Meriwether	97 ☐ Shaw	105 ☐ Sinclair
82 ☐ McKenna	90 ☐ Justin	98 ☐ Hurley	106 ☐ John
83 ☐ Major	91 ☐ Stanford	99 ☐ Dixon	107 ☐ Ross
84 ☐ Stephens	92 ☐ Hamilton	100 ☐ Roberts	108 ☐ Stephens
85 ☐ Beckman	93 ☐ Lacey	101 ☐ Bergen	109 ☐ Beckman
86 ☐ Halston	94 ☐ Barrie	102 ☐ Wallace	110 ☐ Browning

Silhouette Special Edition

$2.25 each

111 ☐ Thorne	133 ☐ Douglass	155 ☐ Lacey	177 ☐ Howard
112 ☐ Belmont	134 ☐ Ripy	156 ☐ Hastings	178 ☐ Bishop
113 ☐ Camp	135 ☐ Seger	157 ☐ Taylor	179 ☐ Meriwether
114 ☐ Ripy	136 ☐ Scott	158 ☐ Charles	180 ☐ Jackson
115 ☐ Halston	137 ☐ Parker	159 ☐ Camp	181 ☐ Browning
116 ☐ Roberts	138 ☐ Thornton	160 ☐ Wisdom	182 ☐ Thornton
117 ☐ Converse	139 ☐ Halston	161 ☐ Stanford	183 ☐ Sinclair
118 ☐ Jackson	140 ☐ Sinclair	162 ☐ Roberts	184 ☐ Daniels
119 ☐ Langan	141 ☐ Saxon	163 ☐ Halston	185 ☐ Gordon
120 ☐ Dixon	142 ☐ Bergen	164 ☐ Ripy	186 ☐ Scott
121 ☐ Shaw	143 ☐ Bright	165 ☐ Lee	187 ☐ Stanford
122 ☐ Walker	144 ☐ Meriwether	166 ☐ John	188 ☐ Lacey
123 ☐ Douglass	145 ☐ Wallace	167 ☐ Hurley	189 ☐ Ripy
124 ☐ Mikels	146 ☐ Thornton	168 ☐ Thornton	190 ☐ Wisdom
125 ☐ Cates	147 ☐ Dalton	169 ☐ Beckman	191 ☐ Hardy
126 ☐ Wildman	148 ☐ Gordon	170 ☐ Paige	192 ☐ Taylor
127 ☐ Taylor	149 ☐ Claire	171 ☐ Gray	193 ☐ John
128 ☐ Macomber	150 ☐ Dailey	172 ☐ Hamilton	194 ☐ Jackson
129 ☐ Rowe	151 ☐ Shaw	173 ☐ Belmont	195 ☐ Griffin
130 ☐ Carr	152 ☐ Adams	174 ☐ Dixon	196 ☐ Cates
131 ☐ Lee	153 ☐ Sinclair	175 ☐ Roberts	197 ☐ Lind
132 ☐ Dailey	154 ☐ Malek	176 ☐ Walker	198 ☐ Bishop

SILHOUETTE SPECIAL EDITION, Department SE/2
1230 Avenue of the Americas
New York, NY 10020

Please send me the books I have checked above. I am enclosing $_____
(please add 75¢ to cover postage and handling. NYS and NYC residents please
add appropriate sales tax). Send check or money order—no cash or C.O.D.'s
please. Allow six weeks for delivery.

NAME _____

ADDRESS _____

CITY _____ STATE/ZIP _____

Silhouette Special Edition